'A richly detailed work of investigative crime writing perfect for fans of procedurals and spy fiction alike' – *LitHub*, on *The Coldest Warrior*

'Vivid and sympathetic… a worthwhile thriller and a valuable exposé' – *Kirkus Reviews*, on *The Coldest Warrior*

'Chilling… more than an entertaining and well-crafted thriller; Vidich asks questions that remain relevant today' – **Jefferson Flanders, author of *The First Trumpet* trilogy, on *The Coldest Warrior***

'Vidich spins a tale of moral and psychological complexity, recalling Graham Greene… rich, rewarding' – *Booklist*, on *The Good Assassin*

'Cold War spy fiction in the grand tradition - neatly plotted betrayals in that shadow world where no one can be trusted and agents are haunted by their own moral compromises' – **Joseph Kanon, bestselling author of *Istanbul Passage* and *The Good German*, on *An Honorable Man***

'A cool, knowing, and quietly devastating thriller that vaults Paul Vidich into the ranks of such thinking-man's spy novelists as Joseph Kanon and Alan Furst' – **Stephen Schiff, writer and executive producer of acclaimed television drama *The Americans*, on *An Honorable Man***

'*An Honorable Man* is that rare beast: a good, old-fashioned spy novel. But like the best of its kind, it understands that the genre is about something more: betrayal, paranoia, unease, and sacrifice. For a book about the Cold War, it left me with a warm, satisfied glow' – **John Connolly, #1 internationally bestselling author of *A Song of Shadows***

THE
MATCHMAKER

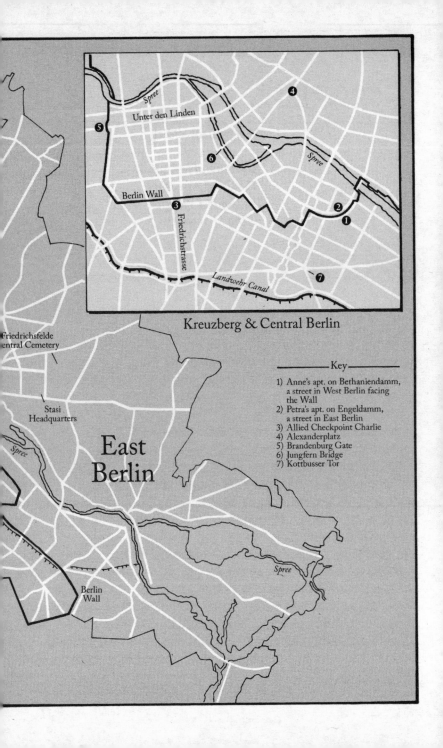

Kreuzberg & Central Berlin

Friedrichsfelde
Central Cemetery

Stasi
Headquarters

East
Berlin

Spree

Spree

Spree

Berlin
Wall

Unter den Linden

Spree

Berlin Wall

Friedrichstrasse

Landwehr Canal

Key

1) Anne's apt. on Bethaniendamm,
a street in West Berlin facing
the Wall
2) Petra's apt. on Engeldamm,
a street in East Berlin
3) Allied Checkpoint Charlie
4) Alexanderplatz
5) Brandenburg Gate
6) Jungfern Bridge
7) Kottbusser Tor

Also by Paul Vidich

THE
MATCHMAKER

A SPY IN BERLIN

PAUL VIDICH

NO EXIT PRESS

First published in 2022 by No Exit Press,
an imprint of Oldcastle Books Ltd,
Harpenden, UK

noexit.co.uk
@noexitpress

ISBN
978-0-85730-449-0 (Paperback)
978-0-85730-450-6 (Ebook)

2 4 6 8 10 9 7 5 3 1

Typeset in 11 on 13pt Minion Pro
by Avocet Typeset, Bideford, Devon, EX39 2BP

Printed and bound in Great Britain by CPI Group (UK) Ltd, Croydon, CR0 4YY

For my mother,
Virginia Vidich

There's no future
No future
No future for you
　　　　　– 'God Save the Queen,'
　　　　　　the Sex Pistols, 1977

PART I

1

KREUZBERG, WEST BERLIN

1989

PERIL CAME EARLY TO the apartment on Bethaniendamm, overtaking the changes that were sweeping through the streets and alleys of a divided Cold War Berlin.

Anne Simpson stood at the ironing board in her kitchen doing one of the chores that were a part of her morning routine, when she heard cries in the street. For a moment she thought it might be her husband. A premonition darkened her face, but she put it aside and held onto the idea that his tardiness was the oversight of a forgetful partner. She tried to concentrate on the blue jeans' stubborn wrinkle, but her mind was elsewhere, and hot iron grazed her wrist. A curse burst from her lips. At the sink, she ran cold water over the burn.

She always became restless waiting for her husband to return from one of his Central European business trips, but this time there was an added complication. They had argued terribly the night before he left and then he was gone at dawn. She had awakened feeling alone and resentful. It started with her suspicions about his work, but it became the disagreement that was a frequent part of their young marriage – she wanted a child and he said that it wasn't the right time.

As she was storing the ironing board the apartment's doorbell chimed. She glanced at the wall clock as if, by some unconscious association, knowing the time would better prepare her to confront him when he walked in. She vigorously wiped her hands on a dish towel.

The jeans were still warm when she slipped her legs into the pants, fingers fumbling with the zipper. On her way across the living room, she glanced in the beveled wall mirror, thinking that it was best to look cheerful. She shook her hair to give it body and shaped it. As an afterthought, she undid the blouse's top button, revealing the pearl necklace on her pale breasts. It had always been their agreement that when he returned from a long business trip, he rang the lobby buzzer – to warn her, he liked to joke, in case she'd taken a lover while he was away.

She glanced out the window to see if he'd stepped back and was waving. There was only tobacco haze from the Turkish café next door and a gaggle of children hanging on their mothers' *jilbabs*, pointing at a couple of guys with orange cockfighting hair and steel-studded leather jackets. The neighborhood had become just that. Streets bleeding into streets of the old Berlin now taken over by immigrants and young squatters. Store windows burst with boxed fruit shaded by overhanging balconies and everywhere rude political graffiti. It was a lively cosmopolitan city with a thriving punk music scene but always conscious that it was a walled-in enclave surrounded by Soviet armed forces.

Again, the chime.

'Coming!' She grabbed the yellow rose she had bought as a peace offering and pressed the buzzer twice to open the unreliable lobby door lock.

Leaning over the hall's railing, she looked down four flights into the dark stairwell. She listened for his enthusiastic run up the stairs, taking two at a time. There was only silence.

'Stefan?'

Behind her, the elevator suddenly opened and a man she didn't recognize stepped out.

'Anne Simpson?'

'Yes. Can I help you?'

'I'm James Cooper, American embassy. I've come about your husband. Is he here?'

'No.'

'We thought you might know where he is.'

She took Cooper in all at once. A man in his early forties with a grave face and an exaggerated expression of concern that he didn't try to mask with a polite smile. He removed his hat and held it solicitously in one hand, using the other to brush back hair that had fallen to his forehead.

'I'm sorry. Who are you?'

'Jim Cooper.' He presented a business card with two hands, nodding slightly. 'Consular officer.'

'He's not here. I'm expecting him.' She knew his type from her job – foreign service officers in tailored suits and Oxford wingtips who were equally good at seeming confident or naïve. They were always holding ad hoc meetings in the courtyard, talking in whispers and keeping the mystery of who they worked for.

Cooper's eyes were sympathetic and somber. 'We believe he may be missing.'

Missing? The word hung in the silence that followed. Without being aware of the sensation until it gripped her, she felt cold. *This was a mistake*, she thought. *He was looking for a different man, perhaps one with the same name.* Her mind grasped for reasons to doubt the claim. But one question led to another, the end of one becoming the beginning of the next and her thoughts became clouded.

'I don't understand.'

A neighbor's door suddenly opened, a pleasant-looking middle-aged man in a collarless shirt emerged, and upon seeing two people in the hallway, he quickly descended the stairs. In the open door, stood a startled young drag queen in pink slippers and a sheer peignoir under a kimono, which she abruptly closed. Dark eye shadow graced her face and her short black hair was slicked back. She cocked her head at Cooper and turned to Anne, speaking over the soft jazz coming through her door. 'Do you need help?'

'Can we go inside?' Cooper said.

Anne acknowledged her neighbor, 'I'm okay.'

Cooper entered the bright living room and stopped at the wall mirror, taking in the apartment's eclectic furnishings like a realtor evaluating a new listing. The original splendor of old Berlin remained in the elaborate ceiling plasterwork, parquet floors, and several graceful casement windows with views across the Wall into East Berlin. But the original Beaux Arts details suffered neglect. Repeated coats of paint obscured the craftsmanship and a naked light bulb was in a ceiling fixture designed for a chandelier. Parquet tiles had loosened in spots, or were missing. Sunlight coming through venetian blinds illuminated the black lacquered finish of a Steinway piano.

Anne looked at his card again. 'I don't understand. Missing? What does that mean?'

'We don't know where he is. We thought he might be here. My job is to help Americans who find themselves in trouble or in need of help to deal with local police matters.' Cooper removed his coat and laid it across his arm.

She thought hostilely that she hadn't invited him to stay.

'The Polizei found his wallet. I was told to come here before they arrive to be the first to inform you. And to speak with you. To see if he was here, or if you knew where he was. To help you through this.'

She stopped listening when she heard the word *wallet*. 'Found where?'

'Landwehr Canal.'

She was confused. 'He's been in Vienna.'

'They confirmed it's his.'

'I see. Which part of the canal?'

'The Polizei will know. They're searching the water.'

Her hand went to her forehead, dimly aware in the moment that she was short of breath, and then her heart started to race and a sudden lightheadedness overcame her. Without knowing it, she had backed up against the wall and was slowly sliding down to the floor. Her hand went to her mouth realizing all that she didn't know, knocking her glasses off.

'Mrs Simpson!' Cooper knelt at her side, retrieving the lenses.

She smiled. 'I'm okay. Thank you.' She went to stand, but her left knee buckled. He caught her arm and helped her to the sofa.

'Sit here.'

She looked at him. 'Is he dead?'

'He's missing. There is no reason to jump to conclusions.'

She nodded. He seemed nice enough, like a therapist paid to listen, and she thought his job must have trained him to provide comforting lies. Her mind had jumped to the worst thing, but she allowed herself to be open to his opinion. He explained again what he knew and bit by bit she stopped giving into fear. She projected optimism. She nodded at his reassuring composure and listened politely to what he had to say. Slowly, her urge to ask him to leave became gratitude that he'd come.

'The Polizei will have more information. They'll be here in an hour, maybe less.'

'I see.' She took a deep breath. 'Will you be staying until they arrive?'

'I can do that, yes. I have an idea what they'll ask. And what you should say.'

'What I should say?'

'What you know.'

She paused. 'I don't know anything.'

'Then that's what you'll tell them.'

She nodded. 'Can I offer you tea, coffee? There's fresh pastry.' She had bought it for Stefan, but now it would go to waste.

'Why don't you sit,' Cooper said. 'I can serve you. What would you like?'

He had done this before, she thought. His business card. His confidence. 'Tea would be fine.' She stood.

He motioned for her to sit. 'I'll make it.'

'You don't know where anything is.'

'I'll figure it out. Sugar? Cream?'

'Black, please.'

Cooper had disappeared into the kitchen and she suddenly felt very alone in the apartment. *Husband missing?* He was away for two weeks, but in that time she had never felt alone. He was away but would return. Now, aloneness came over her like a dark shadow. Waiting was torture. The mystery corrupted her reasoning. In spite of what she knew not to do, her mind filled with terrible thoughts.

Anne looked at the apartment door thinking that he would suddenly appear – lively, upbeat, offering foil-wrapped Viennese chocolate that he always brought as a peace offering. She imagined the exaggerated smile on his face. His jaunty step. His coat carelessly tossed on a chair. It's what had won her over – his optimism, his wit, his predictable routines. When he walked in, he would take her in his arms, kiss her, and smile. *Of course, I'm back. What's all this foolishness? I called last night, didn't I?*

There were no footsteps in the tiled hallway. No car honking in the street. No voice calling her name. Only the shrill sound of the whistling kettle.

Cooper returned with two teacups. She took hers with both hands and sipped, savoring the herbal fragrance. She hadn't been thirsty, but drinking tea was a ritual, and rituals helped her get through the day. He sat opposite, crossing his legs, and continued their conversation. She appreciated his effort to fill the time with chitchat about life in West Berlin – all the shallow details of idle conversation that took little effort to appreciate and made no demands on her attention. She listened indifferently to his remarks about the Turkish immigrants who'd moved into Kreuzberg. Inevitably, the conversation turned to the protests in East Berlin. They had only to look out her fourth-floor window to see the Wall that divided the city. The idle conversation made her feel more alone. She wanted to turn off the switch that kept him talking.

Lost in contemplation, Anne failed to hear his question. 'I'm sorry. What did you ask?'

'Where was he traveling from?'

'Vienna and Prague.' She couldn't remember if he'd gone back to Vienna or was coming straight home from Prague. 'He's a piano tuner. Orchestras hire him.'

'He travels a lot?'

'Pianos don't come to him.' Her glib reply cut off uncomfortable questions she wasn't prepared to answer.

'He's American, isn't he?'

She hesitated, uncertain. 'East German. My first husband was American.'

The phone rang. Cooper motioned for her to stay seated while he answered. She surprised herself by doing what he instructed, feeling even then that she was a pawn.

Anne moved to the window and stared in the direction that Stefan should have walked home from Kottbusser Tor, thinking: *Did he pass out in a bar? Did he miss his flight?*

Her eyes closed and her heart raced. All the little things that she had come to know about her husband, and resent, welled up – his forgetfulness, his lapses, his too-clever excuses, and the easy way he dismissed her concerns. She felt guilty for having those thoughts. She gazed out the window, looking at nothing. *How does a man go missing?*

Shock aside, worry at bay, she tried to think calmly. He had been traveling home from his weeklong job in Vienna. Prague was added. One week became two. Their call the night before had been a fine conversation. 'We'll talk when I get home,' he'd said. 'Make dinner reservations.' He'd said the name of their favorite restaurant. He had sounded hassled, but not any different from the many other times he had called while away, and as he always did, he ended the call by saying he missed her. Loved her. Then again, the mystery took over. Landwehr Canal was not on his way home from Tegel Airport.

'Anne?'

She turned and stared at Cooper.

'Do you mind if I call you Anne?'

A line being crossed. She pointed at the telephone. 'What aren't you telling me?'

'The police will know more. They'll answer your questions and I'm sure they'll have questions for you.' He looked at his watch. 'They'll be here soon.' He nodded at the muted television screen, where the network anchor interrupted his delivery to cut to a reporter giving an update on violent protests in Leipzig and across East Germany. 'There is a lot going on now. A lot of demands on their time, but I know this is important to them. Can I make lunch?'

Lunch? She looked at the wall clock. Stefan's plane landed at 8:45 a.m. It was now past two. The yellow rose lay on the credenza. Little irrelevant details clogged her thinking. *Lunch?* 'Sure, go ahead. You already know your way around the kitchen.'

She found herself thinking that it was surreal to be eating lunch with a stranger in her home. It felt like a bad dream. All she had to do was wake up.

Anne suddenly rushed to the television.

An ARD reporter stood in front of Landwehr Canal. She pointed toward an American patrol boat bobbing in the water by the cement plant where the canal entered the Spree. Stefan's photograph flashed on screen and then shrunk to a small picture-in-picture while the petite blond reporter described the search for the body of a missing East German.

Anne knelt close to the screen, hardly able to contain her shock. Her hands trembled as she watched news coverage shift to Polizei headquarters in West Berlin, where the ARD reporter thrust her microphone at a plainclothes policeman but he paid her no notice.

Cooper turned off the television. 'It's better not to listen to the news. Better to wait for the police. Reporters get their facts wrong. Speculation isn't helpful. I strongly suggest you wait for the BND.'

BND? It was part of her job to know the difference between the West German Federal Intelligence Service and the Federal Criminal Police, the BKA. *What would the BND want with him?*

2

POLIZEI

INSPECTOR ERICH PRAEGER, A tall man in late middle age with an erect military bearing, entered and stood in the middle of Anne's living room. Anne recognized him from the television as the man who ignored the ARD reporter's shouted questions. Praeger's flat expression hid whatever was on his mind.

He removed his green, tapered Tyrolean hat, revealing uniformly gray hair swept back on his forehead, giving prominence to his attentive eyes. He wore a brown suit jacket and a bow tie that was tightly knotted on a pale-yellow shirt. His overcoat was draped over one arm and his hat delicately dangled from two fingers. A shorter detective with a coarse appearance had arrived a few minutes earlier, and suddenly grew quiet in his presence.

'Frau Simpson?' Brusque politeness without the salute.

'Yes.' Anne wondered what he had done during the war. She offered to take his coat.

'We won't be long.' He presented his card with the embossed black eagle of the Bundesnachrichtendienst – the BND. Praeger turned to the man at his side. 'My colleague, Tomas Keller. BKA. A joint operation.'

At the coffee table, he passed over a *National Geographic*, open to a spread of red-eyed seabirds slick with oil from the

Exxon Valdez, and lifted a framed wedding photograph of bride and groom from a table. 'Is this him?'

'Yes.'

'The glass is cracked.' He nodded. 'A pity.'

'It fell two weeks ago. I haven't had time to replace it.'

'Where was the ceremony?'

'The Netherlands.'

Praeger arched an eye.

'We met in The Netherlands. Scheveningen.'

He set down the photograph, careful to place it exactly as he'd found it. Praeger asked a few more questions, covering ground that she'd gone over with Cooper. She repeated what she had said earlier, answers that she would repeat again and again in the next days. Anne saw a rigid man of few words who knew exactly what he wanted. When he spoke, he looked right at her as if he'd rehearsed his questions to reveal little about his thinking. When she answered, she had the uncomfortable feeling that he was looking into her mind.

He paused at a wall poster from an exhibit, *Art of Germany 1945–1985,* and moved toward the windows. 'And those?' Praeger pointed to high-power binoculars that sat on one sill.

'The rabbits.' Anne pointed beyond the Wall's razor wire fencing to the treeless death zone, where large rabbits lived freely without predators. 'My husband worried about them. The large ones set off the land mines.'

Praeger used the binoculars to look. When he was done, he placed the binoculars on the window sill. 'And you believed him?'

His sarcasm put her off and, in that moment, she started to dislike him.

Praeger moved to a desk that sat beside the bookshelves. 'May I?' He indicated the closed drawer.

Anne stepped forward, but Cooper's hand abruptly stopped her. Praeger poked in the drawer with his riding crop with the vague curiosity of a man not looking for anything in particular, but open to the possibility that he might find something of interest. He lifted a manila envelope and pushed aside papers, handwritten notes, pamphlets.

'What are these?' He presented a sheath of colored pencil sketches. Each drawing depicted five differently colored and shaped vases on a window sill. The arrangement of the vases changed in each drawing, and sometimes the shapes changed, but there were always five and they were always in a row on a window sill.

'He likes to draw. It's his hobby.'

'Bottles in a window? Anything else? Rabbits, perhaps?'

She hesitated. 'Sometimes flowers.'

'A wild imagination.' He dropped the sketches. 'Bottles in a window and flowers. Flowers in a bottle perhaps?'

'What are you looking for?'

Praeger took a vase with fluted neck from the window sill. 'A bottle like this?'

'What is this about?' she demanded, taking the vase. Frustration rose up in her. 'This is my home. Nobody has told me anything. What are you looking for?'

'Your husband. We need to speak with him. If you know where he is, you can save me some time.'

'I don't know where he is.'

'I didn't think so.' He looked at her. 'What can you tell me about yourself?'

'Is that necessary?' she said. She closed her eyes to calm herself, knowing that no good would come from being difficult. 'I work at the Joint Allied Refugee Operations Center at Clay Headquarters,' she said. 'I'm an interpreter. I debrief refugees from Poland, Hungary, and East Germany. I'm fluent in Russian and German. What else do you want to know?'

Praeger considered her question. 'Do you have a security clearance?'

'I do.'

'Did you report your marriage to the embassy?'

She wasn't aware of her loosening grip and the vase dropped, breaking.

'He'll clean it up.' Praeger sent his junior colleague to the kitchen. Praeger looked at Anne again. 'Did you?'

She knew the rules and had ignored them. It wasn't the embassy's business who she slept with. By the time the six-month grace period for reporting her relationship had expired, they were already married. It would have been easier to ignore the security requirement and leave her job before her violation was discovered. But she hadn't left.

'No, I didn't.'

'An oversight, I'm sure. It's easy to be careless about who you sleep with.'

She wanted to slap him. 'What do you want?'

'I have enough for now.'

Inspector Praeger abruptly pushed one arm and then the other through his bulky overcoat's sleeves. Without explanation, and in the same businesslike manner of his arrival, Praeger moved to the door, followed by his shorter BKA counterpart. But having come to the door, he turned.

'Frau Simpson, as a courtesy to us, please remain in Berlin.'

*

Later, when she thought about that day, Anne felt the events like a heavy weight on her chest that kept her from breathing, and she came to see how fate had caught up with her life. She had let three complete strangers into her apartment, but part of her had known for some time that one day men like them might show up. And when they did, bringing the news of his disappearance, her mind had fogged and her thoughts became disconnected, the specifics of the day, the names of the police, the details of the questions, even the date itself, were lost in that part of her memory that endured trauma.

In the weeks that followed, she would engage in an act of memory contortion to remember the day he disappeared. The Leipzig protests became a memory marker. When she was asked when Stefan vanished, she recalled that the protests fell on Republic Day, the 40th anniversary of the GDR, and by that unconscious association she would answer, October 7. With that date, other blocked memories of her husband flowed, and a dark tenderness arose. Memories of their marriage came in waves of loss, regret, guilt, and anger. How unlikely their story. How hard they tried to be good partners to each other, and not be prisoners of their expectations of marriage. To know how to be a couple without forgetting how to be individuals. She believed they had found the happiness that was possible between a man and a woman of different backgrounds and different languages – an earned love. Reading stories out loud to each other in bed before sleeping. It was a thing they did that neither of them had done with another lover. She would listen to him read, enjoying his soft tenor voice, and she'd feel content. That was all she ever wanted.

And then he was gone. Disappeared. Vanished.

Perhaps that was why she blocked that day from memory, and remembered it only by association with the tragic events of 1989. His disappearance and the televised violence that brought down the GDR were joined.

Stefan had always been intimately mysterious, even when he was naked in bed next to her. She often tried to look into his mind to know his thoughts, but he had remained remote, even when he was present.

3

LANDWEHR CANAL

Waking, Anne saw a shimmering light on the ceiling, the morning sun reflecting on bathwater she'd forgotten to drain the night before. She raised her head, letting go of the pleasant dream that stirred in the last moments of sleep and looked to the other side of the bed. Then she remembered. There would be no morning kiss, no light touch of his fingers on the small of her back, no gentle caress of her cheek – none of the careless sensual pleasures of waking beside Stefan.

She sat up. Took a deep breath. Slowly and quietly, she climbed out of bed and padded across the floor and looked in the living room. Improbably, she thought that he might be there asleep on the sofa. The depth of her disappointment was measured by the enduring mystery. In spite of her loneliness, a part of her preferred being alone.

On the way out the door, late for work, the phone rang. She answered it, thinking it might be Stefan, but when she heard Cooper's voice, her hopeful tone hardened. He said that he would be there in ten minutes and would fill her in when he arrived.

'We're driving to the canal,' he said when she slid into the passenger seat. She wore a scarf and boots in preparation for the day's promise of snow. 'The police are there now. A witness came forward.'

Witness to what? Anne felt a cold trepidation.

They drove in silence, moving along the street that followed the Spree, and through the side streets she saw the watchtowers on the other side of the river. She knew the route. It was the street she jogged every morning.

'How are you holding up? How did you sleep?'

'Not well.'

She looked away. It had been worse than that. She had tossed restlessly in bed, as her mind tried to banish the distracting images invading her dreams. She had lain awake for a long time, and when she finally accepted that sleep wasn't going to come, she'd taken a long run in the predawn darkness. Berlin's silent fog abstracted the licks and points of the streetlights along her path that followed the ominous glow of East German watchtowers. Jogging had always been a reliable companion. It helped keep her mind focused. Exhaustion, sweat, and sucking breaths in the cold drove away her anxious thoughts, and helped her achieve something not quite like calm. It was a long run alone on empty streets. A dark moon, curling fog, and gutters collecting fallen leaves. Her mind focused on her pace and the rhythm of her strides, reaching longer to meet a curb. Jogging helped her settle the images that came to her mind's eye. One image, then another, like a flickering film montage of a forgotten past. The first kiss. Laughter in a bar. Lovemaking. With each memory, she took a longer stride and a deeper breath to dispel the images. Then exhausted, hands on her knees, bent over breathing and weeping.

'We'll make this short,' Cooper said.

'Good.'

'The BND believes your husband was involved in espionage.'

She stared at Cooper.

'We won't spend more time here than necessary. You'll want to answer their questions and get on with your life. Not get caught up in this thing.'

Cooper turned onto a side street that paralleled the canal

and drove toward the Spree. They passed a parking lot of idled long-haul trucks, some with containers, others just cabs. It was a grim industrial area with low factory buildings that did nothing to brighten her mood.

Anne felt helpless in the face of everything she didn't know. She was tired from lack of sleep, which brought on a strange unreality. As a child, she greeted her father's Quaker faith with skepticism, thinking his invocation of the Lord old fashioned, like a horse-drawn carriage, but, in that moment, she wished she had a God she could turn to.

Anne watched Cooper be waved through a chain-link gate held open by a West German policeman.

*

A giant limestone mound rose beside the rusted cement kiln and to one side there was temporary housing for immigrant labor, RVs parked in random order. The cement tower cast a long shadow on cracked pavement sprouting grass browned by the passing season. A rising sun had burned off the morning mist and the sky was bright, cold, and cloudless, and the promise of snow was gone.

Anne had grabbed her coat and boots on her way out of the apartment, but now, as she walked toward men huddled together at the far end of the lot, she wished she had taken her gloves. She shoved her hands in her pockets and walked beside Cooper, eyes taking in the abandoned heap of rusted machinery beyond the tall mountains of sand. Between the mounds, and running along the Spree's far bank, was the graffitied Wall topped with razor wire. Further along, and set back, a scrubbed concrete BT-11-type watchtower loomed. Cawing seagulls circled overhead and tree branches torn by the evening's storm in the Lusatian Highlands were swept along in the gray, murky river.

Anne saw East German border guards in the tower with binoculars looking at the mouth of the canal, where scuba divers hung from the side of an idling U.S.-flagged patrol boat. One diver fixed his mask, as did a second, and both dropped below the surface. Two other divers worked at the base of the canal's stone embankment, fixing a swimming pool–like ladder to help anyone lucky enough to swim across the Spree without being shot.

'Frau Simpson, thank you for coming.' Inspector Praeger stepped away from the men, greeting Anne with a brisk nod. His Tyrolean hat did nothing to warm his ears, which were blushed pink, but he did wear gloves, which again reminded Anne that hers were at home.

'Join us.' Praeger nodded toward a short man with wire rim glasses and a thick scarf that made it look like he had no neck. What Anne noticed first was his indeterminate age – he could be forty or sixty-five. His face had the unhealthy pallor of a man with cirrhosis or a man who was a frequent patron of a tanning salon. His eyebrows were trimmed and his toupee was one of those obvious hairpieces of rich brown hair that ended abruptly on the ears. She thought he looked made-up – a man so interested in looking young that he looked false. Later, she would tell Cooper that she was put off by him, thinking that a man so eager to alter his appearance couldn't possibly be trusted.

'A witness,' Praeger said. 'He saw it happen.'

'Saw what happen?'

'There was an altercation. An accident perhaps. We don't know everything. Maybe a robbery.'

'My husband? Here?'

'It would appear so.'

Appear so? 'Accident? Robbery? Altercation? They are very different.'

Praeger waved over the man with the toupee. 'He filed

a report yesterday, but it went to the BKA and was not at first linked to what we are investigating. We came here this morning and this man described what he saw. In the course of our examination of the area, we found something we'd like you to see.'

Praeger turned to the man who joined them. 'Dr Knappe, please repeat what you saw.'

Dr Knappe glanced at Anne, nodding, and took his instruction, speaking in German. 'I was standing there when my poodle found a dead pigeon, so I let her have a sniff and while I did, I happened to glance at the canal. It was early. Thick fog was in the fir trees. I could barely see the bank, but I come here often, so I knew it was there. It was the day of the pileup on the autobahn.'

'Repeat what you saw.'

'It's not what I saw. I could hardly see. It's what I heard. A man's voice. The cry of a man being threatened or attacked. I ran, thinking I could help, but when I came to the bank, there was no one. Then I saw him in the water, face down, motionless. He was floating just over there.' Dr Knappe pointed to the patrol boat.

'He didn't stumble or jump. I remember the cry. He was pushed. I am certain it was the cry of a man who had been struck, and then shoved into the water.'

'People cry out when they fall,' Praeger said.

'This was a scream. Fright, not surprise. How does a grown man fall into the canal? There was fog, but I could see the body well enough and he would have seen the edge. His wallet was over there.'

Inspector Praeger turned to Anne. 'We haven't found your husband's body yet.'

Dr Knappe's hand suddenly covered his mouth, embarrassed. 'Oh, my. Please accept my apology. I didn't mean to offend, speaking so irreverently. Had I known…'

Anne thought his exaggerated sympathy misplaced, like a wrong-sized overcoat he was trying on. She pondered Dr Knappe's reaction and it seemed as false as his toupee. Obvious, uncalled for, and easily put on. Perhaps for that reason, and in light of what happened next, she clung to the idea that Stefan was alive. Even in the face of Dr Knappe's eyewitness account, hope lived on with the vividness of a dream.

Praeger looked at Anne. His voice deepened. 'Was your husband involved in espionage for East Germany?'

'You don't have to answer that,' Cooper said.

She stared at Praeger. She laughed. 'Espionage?'

He pointed to the trucks. 'Air conditioners have been fitted with false panels to hide people when they cross the border.' Praeger's hand swept the lot. 'They are expected to pay when they get out. If they don't pay, well, there are consequences. Some are Stasi agents pretending to be refugees.'

Anne didn't know what to say. She wanted to reject the idea that Stefan was involved in some type of racket, but the stubborn mystery left her without the confidence to reject even the most outlandish accusation. She looked at Praeger. 'How do you know it was him?' She turned to Dr Knappe. 'Did you know him? Could you even recognize him?'

'We have his wallet.' Praeger said.

'Maybe it was stolen.'

'There is another thing.' Praeger took a black instrument case from Detective Keller and presented it to her. 'This was found there.' He pointed to undergrowth by the lot's edge where shrubs grew wildly. Praeger opened the case. 'Do you recognize this?'

She touched the mother-of-pearl inlay around the zither's sound box, letting her fingers confirm what her eyes knew. She wanted to speak, but words were the prisoners of her shock. More than money, more than his wallet, Stefan prized his instrument, and would never be without it.

'It was dropped or hidden in the shrubbery.'

Anne knelt at the spot where it had been found, lifting a handful of earth and let it sift through her fingers. Her mind tried to find a logic to all that she had been told – but everything was unexpected and unthinkable.

'Did your husband need money?'

She shook her head.

'Did he carry a lot of money?'

'No.'

'Were there people he wanted to help?' Praeger looked toward the Turkish laborers who sat outside the RVs. 'Any idea why he would come here?'

She turned to the rusted kiln beside the mountains of sand and limestone, and then her gaze turned to the Wall on the other side of the Spree. 'He's a piano tuner.' Her voice was incredulous. She stood abruptly, and brushed off her hands to remove the dirt. She turned to Praeger. 'I have no idea why he was here. None of this makes sense.'

Just then, an East German patrol boat turned sharply from the Spree and entered the canal, engines shrill, moving at full throttle. A stern-mounted heavy caliber machine gun was manned by a gunner in a helmet and a yellow life vest. The patrol boat bore down on the American divers bobbing in the water, swamping them. It made a sharp turn and sped to the embankment where divers were installing the ladder, coming dangerously close. Again, the boat made an abrupt turn and headed a second time for the American divers bobbing in the water.

Cooper walked right up to the Polizei. 'Fire at them,' he shouted. When the policeman didn't move, Cooper grabbed the man's automatic weapon and fired in the water in front of the speeding boat. Two shots went unheeded so he emptied the magazine in an angry burst on the boat's hull.

'Enough!' Praeger yanked the weapon from Cooper and

motioned frantically at the patrol boat gunner, who was aiming his large caliber weapon to return fire. '*Nicht mehr!*' he shouted. '*Nicht mehr!*'

Praeger turned to Cooper, furious. 'We don't need to start World War III.'

'This is the American sector. Those are American divers.'

Praeger moved close to Cooper. His face stern and indignant. 'Common sense knows no nationality, Mr Cooper.'

*

Anne was slumped on her sofa feeling overwhelmed. She had asked Cooper to drive her home because the thought of going to work depressed her. There was nothing normal about her life now and after twenty-four hours she knew she wouldn't get her life back anytime soon.

Cooper had accompanied her upstairs. She'd begun to think of him like an adviser, or ally against the West Germans. She'd been startled when he fired on the East German patrol boat, thinking that he had acted recklessly, but then in the car ride back she'd listened to his frustration. She appreciated his decisiveness. Everything in her world was indefinite and confusing. His simple defiant act impressed her.

Anne listened to him give his report to someone on the phone, heading off whatever diplomatic catastrophe might follow from the incident, and she closed her eyes. The moments of relative calm gave way to an indiscriminate anger. She knew she should be angry at someone, but it was hard to sustain anger against Stefan, not knowing if he was at fault, and the obvious target for her anger, the police, she knew was misplaced. She was mute and helpless in the face of this thing she couldn't understand. Her mind grasped for the missing critical fact, which she felt was teasing her at the periphery of her brain, that would solve the mystery.

Anne went to the window and peered through the binoculars at the empty, overgrown death zone. One large rabbit hopped across the minefield and she waited for the explosion, but it didn't come. How easy Stefan's explanation had been. *I worry about them.* So easy and so unlike him. Anne shifted the binoculars a degree and looked at the grim, soot-scarred apartment buildings across the Wall. How often had he looked in that direction?

Anne lifted the framed wedding picture, letting her fingers trace the crack in the glass. One memory triggered another. Their argument. His arm knocking the frame to the floor. She gazed at the happy couple in the photograph thinking about the evening she'd rushed home from work, distraught, and found him peering through the binoculars, making notes in his diary.

That afternoon, staffing crises and holiday absences had drawn her into an urgent interrogation with two U.S. Army special forces. When she had entered the windowless basement cell, she saw a shirtless man strapped into a wooden chair with electrodes on his calf and breast. He was a big man, with a barrel chest and thick neck, whose head was hanging down. He was breathing hard. Blood leaked from his nose and his lip was split, but he looked up with fierce eyes. Anne had turned to walk out, but was stopped by the shorter American interrogator, who rejected her protest that this was not her job. She was directed to stand while the other interrogator injected the prisoner's arm, making him grunt and violently resist his confining straps. In a moment, the prisoner's face was pale and he experienced sweating, tremors, and nausea.

When the drug settled his mood, the taller interrogator started his questioning, which Anne translated to the prisoner, repeating questions when the man didn't answer. The interrogation paused when the prisoner became sickly green, vomiting, but then he recovered and his demeanor calmed and he became compulsively talkative. She translated his rambling answers into English and knew he was an East German by his Saxon accent. He talked quickly, nonstop, and her simultaneous translation was necessarily inexact, and as it continued it became chaotic at times, the interrogators shouting questions in English while the prisoner was still speaking German. She did her best to manage the chaos, sometimes omitting parts of answers or questions because she wasn't able to keep up. She had come into the room knowing nothing about the case, but she learned the interrogators wanted specific answers about the source of classified information that had fallen into Stasi hands. Anne translated the prisoner's defiant refusals, letting his curses speak for themselves.

In the course of his unhelpful responses, he'd broken down, wheezing and mumbling, and almost as a plea for the torture to stop, he had uttered a word. *Klavierstimmer.* Her mind paused, but, in the way the mind protects itself against danger, she turned to the interrogators, repeating the accusation quickly, fusing two words so the prisoner's answer became *klavierspieler* – pianist. The prisoner went into convulsions, thrashing and he gasped repeatedly. A medic was called, but the prisoner's head had slumped to his chest – eyes open and unfocused. The medic couldn't revive the prisoner. Anne was dismissed and warned not to talk about the incident.

Anne had been trembling when she got home. Revulsion sickened her and the man's utterance haunted her. Stefan had been sympathetic, but he dismissed her suspicions when she repeated what the prisoner had said. Stefan had laughed, eyes rolling, looking at her as if she'd said something preposterous. Hands in the air. 'Are you kidding. Me? Stefan Koehler. There are a dozen West Berlin piano tuners who work in Vienna.' Anne had presented travel receipts and pointed to his binoculars and diary, asking what he had written. Then the argument began.

4

BND HEADQUARTERS

Anne assumed that someone had accused her, for one morning that week as she left for work, without having done anything differently, she was arrested. Polizei put her in the back of the patrol car, refusing to answer her questions and ignoring her pleas to speak with the embassy. She was taken to a crowded waiting room in BND headquarters without knowing why she'd been picked up. She was told to wait among the other West Berliners and her case would be dealt with shortly. Everyone was on edge, alternately glued to the televised news report of the tensions at the Wall, or huddled together whispering.

An hour passed. She could stand it no longer. Worry and restlessness came over her. Not immediately, but slowly, after another twenty minutes had passed, just as she seemed to be accommodating the wait, she gave into the urge to do something, anything. Cry. Scream. Walk out. She found a pay phone in the hallway and called the embassy, getting Cooper on the line after a long wait. 'Something terrible has happened. I was picked up as I left home. I'm here with distraught families. Can you help me?'

'Where are you?'

'BND. A waiting room,' she looked around. 'Third floor. By the elevators.'

Her day had started badly. She had been awakened at dawn by her neighbor, Chrystal, who pounded on her door wanting to share news from the all-night disco. When she opened the door, Chrystal was talking intently on the telephone, trailing the long cord behind. As an outsider to the city, Anne noticed things that West Berliners took for granted, and one of those oddities was the West Berlin flat rate, a subsidy from West Germany, that meant any call, no matter how long, had one price. West Berliners talked endlessly, staying on the line while cooking, while watching television, while looking out the window, or carrying on two conversations at once. Chrystal put off whoever she was talking to and announced that war was close at hand. Anne knew her neighbor could be dramatic, but as the morning progressed, she saw how the rumor spread neighbor-to-neighbor in a wildfire of speculation, every conversation going on at length, sharing gossip from someone who was in a position to know. Beneath the calm of her acquaintances, she heard dark humor and fear. Soviet armored divisions were massed on the outskirts of East Berlin. Recently opened borders with Hungary and Czechoslovakia were closed again, then reopened. Shootings in Leipzig. Erich Honecker forced out in a bloodless, Soviet-sanctioned coup d'état. Shoot-to-kill orders issued and then rescinded.

*

Anne stood at the waiting room's window. Behind her, people were nervous, but strangely calm, and those old enough to remember recalled the Berlin Airlift forty years before. Palpable fear had settled in. One distraught man asked a policeman for information on his mother who lived in the East. People waited on word about a loved one, or a friend, hoping that information coming from the BND's network of informants would explain why calls to East Berlin were blocked, or why they had been turned back from a border crossing. In that room, men comforted wives, and mothers coddled children. Worried faces were everywhere.

Outside, a siren wailed with startling closeness. Further along the street, Anne saw troops of the Allied joint occupation force. Military police in shiny helmets blocked streets to permit Bradley Fighting Vehicles and M1 tanks to make their way past startled West Berliners.

Anne heard the noise at the same time as the people in the street, who looked up. A pair of low-flying MIG fighters streaked across the blue sky leaving behind blossoming contrails as they circled the city's air corridor. The powerful thrusts of their engines rattled windows and urgent conversations in the room were silenced by the sonic booms.

Anne joined others crowded in front of a television. An ARD news anchor reported on the events of the past twenty-four hours. Everyone in the room leaned in, listening, hungry for news. The anchor wore the unruffled expression of newsmen everywhere, projecting authority and inspiring calm while describing terrible events.

'It isn't clear if the GDR's new willingness to permit demonstrations is a genuine softening of attitudes or is a respite while the weary, overstretched security police look for ways to snuff out the opposition.'

'Anne?'

She turned and saw Cooper at the door. His face was flushed from the obvious exertion of a man who had rushed across the city. 'They want you inside.'

'What took you so long?'

'There is a lot going on in the embassy.' He looked at her reassuringly. 'You weren't arrested. I spoke to Keller and he said it was a mistake. They were told to bring you here. That's all.'

She pointed to the television. 'What's happening?'

'The press has no idea what is coming.' He pulled her toward a door on the far side of room. 'Hospitals in East Berlin have stocked extra blood transfusions. Doctors are on 24-hour call. Those aren't preparations for a softening attitude. They are precautions for a massacre.' He looked calmly at Anne. 'We'll be fine. West Berlin will be safe. The ambassador has been in touch with Washington.'

Detective Keller held open a door for Anne and Cooper. 'We apologize you weren't informed about the interview. When you didn't arrive, we sent police to escort you.'

'No one told me anything.' Anne refused an offer to shake Keller's hand and pushed past him into the windowless conference room. A brace of limp flags stood at the far end of the room, placed on either side of a color portrait of the West German chancellor and a large conference table dominated the center. It had the sterility of conference rooms everywhere.

Anne watched Detective Keller take a seat opposite her, and he proceeded to place a notepad and pen on the table.

'I will be taking notes so there is an official record of your statement. Can we proceed?'

'Yes.'

'Your husband gave you a telephone number to call when he was out of town?'

'Yes.'

'Whose number was it?'

'I don't know.'

'Why would he give you a telephone number for when he was away?'

'I don't know.'

'Was he concerned about something?'

Keller motioned to a young woman who'd entered with a tray of cups, a pot of coffee, and delicate biscuits. Cooper poured himself a cup and offered to pour one for Anne, who shook her head. While the two men took biscuits, and added cream and sugar, she rested her head on the table, closing her eyes.

'Are we boring you?' Keller asked.

Anne sat up.

'This won't take long. A few more questions. I might repeat questions that you've already been asked, but as I said, we are recording these. Is that satisfactory?'

'Yes.'

'Where did you meet your husband?'

'In the Netherlands. Scheveningen.'

'When?'

'Two years ago. December. Christmas. Is that specific enough?'

Keller frowned. 'The North Sea in December is cold, wet, and not a very romantic spot. It's an irregular time to visit a summer seaside resort.'

'I was divorced.' Her eyes narrowed. 'It was a good place to be by myself.'

'How did you meet?'

'Why is that relevant?'

Cooper placed his hand on her arm. 'Just answer the question. You'll get out of here sooner.'

She saw no need to describe how it was a difficult time in her life. She thought it irrelevant that they hear how she was lonely and depressed after her first marriage failed. No matter how she tried to see it as a mutual decision, it was his choice to end the marriage, and she was left feeling cast off. Angry and abandoned. She put on a brave face of public indifference when friends asked what happened. It was easier to say that it had been their choice. She wanted to get away from their questions and exaggerated sympathy and be in a place where she could indulge solitude and take stock of her life. The two weeks on the North Sea in winter had been gray and bleak, which matched her mood. There were no lively, cavorting couples to remind

42

her of her unhappiness. Then, one day at the end of her two-week stay, Stefan had appeared in her life. He had an endless budget for restaurants – the few that were open – and taxis. It had been an adventure. He'd made her laugh. Anne wasn't ready to let that go, to let this man corrupt that time with his conspiracies.

'We were introduced,' she said. 'I forget who introduced us. It's not important.'

'You don't remember? A German, a Dutchman?'

'No. The concierge maybe.'

'Do you know anyone who would want to hurt him?'

'No.'

'Was he depressed?'

She turned to Cooper.

'I'm asking you, not him.'

'He's helping. He's with the embassy.'

'I'm interested in what you remember, not what he thinks I should know.'

'Go ahead,' Cooper said.

'Suicide?' Anne dismissed the idea. 'Out of the question. Unimaginable.'

'Why would anyone want to kill him?'

'He's missing,' she snapped. 'Have you found his body?' She sat back in her chair and glared. 'How much more of this?'

'When did you last speak with him?'

Anne's memory failed her for a moment. 'The night before the Leipzig protests.'

Suddenly, the door opened and Inspector Praeger appeared. Erect, composed, impeccably dressed. His appearance commanded the room's attention and Detective Keller was silent in his presence.

Finally, Anne thought, *a step up in the chain of command and a step toward a responsible conversation with someone in authority.* She sensed Praeger's calculating intelligence. When he stepped into the room, she saw another man standing behind, and he too entered. He was tall, like Praeger, but older, and he had the confident air of a man who belonged in the room. Without saying a word, or acknowledging her, he took a seat at the end of the table. Anne waited for him to be introduced, but no one did. She thought there was something in his appearance – his silver cufflinks, the vanity in his fashionably narrow tie – that hinted he was not a policeman and possibly, not German.

'Shall we continue?' Praeger said. He removed a file from a leather case he had placed on the table. He nodded at Cooper, smiled at Anne, and ignored Keller and the new man, who remained quiet for the balance of the interview. Praeger opened a line of questions about Stefan's work, his clients, the cities he visited, the money he earned, and the amount of time he was away. It was a rigorous pattern of observation, question, and confrontation. Anne did her best to understand what his intent was before she answered, but soon she came to think he already had his answers and that his questions were designed to test her truthfulness.

'Who were his friends?'

'Neighbors. Acquaintances. People.'

'Where did you live when you met?'

'A small studio in Mitte. I moved in with him.'

'Friendly with the leftists and the Turks, was he?'

She didn't dignify his question with an answer.

'You're quiet.' He looked at her. 'There are many kinds of silence. The silence of the dead. The silence of consent. And the silence of ignorance. Which type of silence should I ascribe to you?'

She said nothing.

Praeger opened the manila folder and flipped pages of a document with his finger, stopping when he found what he wanted. 'Your husband traveled seven times in September?'

'I don't remember how many. A lot. Seven? Maybe.'

'Vienna on September 3rd. Prague a week later. Bonn and Warsaw September 15th and 16th. East Berlin four times in the month.'

'Yes.'

'Many trips in a short time?'

'Pianos go out of tune quickly.'

'Do they? I don't play the piano. I know there are different types: Steinways, Yamahas, Bösendorfers. Do they all go out of tune so quickly?'

'Call the orchestras. They'll confirm his work.'

'My colleague is calling.'

Anne saw Praeger take a handwritten document. The penmanship was small, cramped, and precise, almost as if it was a secret writing. 'Hotel Imperial one night. Bristol Hotel one night. Grand Mark one week. Excelsior Hotel three nights.' Praeger looked up. 'He has good taste in wine and books. Now, I see he has a taste for five-star hotels.'

'They pay his expenses.'

'He must be a very good piano tuner. Do you travel with him?'

'Once.'

'Where?'

'I don't remember.' Her eyes were fierce. 'Why are you asking these questions? You are making me feel like I'm hiding something, that somehow, inexplicably, I have answers that I don't have. There is another type of silence. The silence of confusion. Why are you asking these questions?' Anne leaned forward, exasperated. 'He didn't come home four days ago. That's all I know.'

Anne stood, but felt Cooper's hand restrain her. She threw it off. 'I don't need to answer these questions. I am an American citizen. I work for JAROC.'

Praeger motioned for her to sit. 'This is difficult for you. I need to gather all the information I can to move this investigation forward.' Praeger cut off Keller, who was about to speak. 'Until your husband's body is found, he is officially listed as missing. We have to consider the possibility that this case is a homicide. We would be irresponsible not to. Do you understand? I am asking these questions because we need to establish a motive. Who gained if your husband died?'

Anne heard a kind of apology in Praeger's explanation.

'We want the same thing,' he added. Praeger removed large black-and-white photographs from the folder and arranged them like playing cards, one row of six, then a second row, squaring each so they were aligned and facing Anne. One by one, Praeger pushed a photograph toward Anne and repeated his questions. *Do you know this man? Have you seen this man? Did this man associate with your husband?*

Two photographs were police mug shots of men with numbers on cards hanging from their necks. Tough men with bulbous noses and the insolent expressions of felons. The rest were photographs taken from a distance with a telephoto lens. Men in a crowd, or at a café with a woman, or at a pay phone. Some were in profile, all were grainy, none were women.

She looked from one to the next, pausing briefly on each to confirm her judgment. She didn't know any of them. The last photograph was taken with a telephoto lens. From the perspective, she thought it had been taken from across the street, or from a building, the subject unaware he was being photographed. A trim older man in a narrow-brim, Soviet-style fedora, crossing the street, head slightly turned glancing back, as if aware he was being watched. His hat shadowed his face and the grainy composition made it hard to make out his features, except for his surprise, caught by the surveillance camera.

She handed it back. 'No.'

The unintroduced man at the end of the table leaned forward and spoke for the first time. 'Can I see it?' He stared at the photograph for a long time without any expression whatsoever, and then he pushed it back toward Anne.

'You're sure?' he said.

American, she thought. She was uncertain she should answer a question from a man she didn't know. She turned to Praeger. 'I've never seen any of these men.'

Praeger presented a similar photograph to the one she'd just examined. She compared the two. Both were taken with a telephoto lens from a great distance and had a flattened, foreshortened perspective. Both were of men in late middle age, wearing a fedora, caught in a moment without knowing they were being photographed. In the second photograph, the man was stepping into a Chaika limousine, head turned slightly in the moment the camera's shutter opened. His eyes were alert to a commotion somewhere beyond the borders of the photograph. His face was also shadowed, hardly recognizable in profile. Grim, grainy, faceless. She compared one to the other.

'We think they are the same man,' Praeger said. Praeger slipped a police artist's pencil sketch toward Anne. 'This may help. It is a composite, a likeness, but maybe not a good likeness. Have you seen him?'

She compared the sketch to the photographs. The photographs were blow-ups, grainy, taken from a distance, frustrating in their vagueness. The sketch was a caricature, the exaggerated features of an older man, which could fit any number of older men, or no man.

'I can't tell. I doubt it. They are blurry. Who is he?'

'The Matchmaker. Your husband worked for him.'

Praeger swept his hand across the other photographs. 'And these men, we believe, worked for your husband.'

*

47

The interview ended. Cooper helped Anne into her raincoat, and the tall, well-dressed American at the end of the table walked out without saying a word. Anne was slipping her arm into her sleeve when he passed. Her urge to ask him why he was there was cut short by Cooper, who stepped between them. He helped her with her other sleeve and they moved to leave the conference room, but having come to the door, Cooper stopped.

'Give me a minute. I have an unrelated matter to discuss with Praeger. I'll find you in the hall.'

Cooper closed the door and turned to Inspector Praeger, who stepped away from Keller, so the two men were alone. Praeger's eyes were impatient. 'Well?'

'She an interpreter at JAROC,' Cooper said. 'I don't think she knows anything.'

'Do you believe her?'

'I do.'

'On what basis?'

'My gut.'

Praeger scoffed. 'A good act. I don't believe a word of it. How could she be so ignorant. So uncurious. Binoculars we found in the apartment, and her answer, "rabbits."' Praeger's expression disdained the idea. 'She is being dishonest. Maybe she is his accomplice. At the very least she is protecting him. I will have her arrested and we'll continue questioning her without the niceties of an interview.'

'No evidence implicates her.'

'He ran a network. He traveled under cover of jobs with orchestras. He coordinated drop points. Documents on Pershing missiles were handed off. He stayed in five-star hotels on a piano tuner's salary. He was the handler's handler, keeping the Matchmaker informed.'

Praeger's eyes narrowed and his jaw was set. 'She slept in his bed. Washed his clothes. Waited for him to return. Shared the intimacy of a married couple. Do you really believe she knew nothing? Suspected nothing?'

'She is an American citizen,' Cooper snapped. 'This is the American sector.'

'She is on German soil. This is a German counterintelligence matter.' Praeger slapped his file onto the table, punctuating the room's silence. 'Stefan Koehler was under surveillance for three months. We have travel itineraries, hotel invoices, suspected drop points. A week ago, we uncovered the registrant of a numbered Swiss bank account. Do you know what we found? Half a million marks in his name. How does a piano tuner get such a sum? We believe he was stealing from the GDR. He stole secrets from us and money from them.'

He considered Cooper for a moment, like a wary jackal pacing the perimeter of a camp fire. 'We planned to recruit him as a double agent, but someone else got to him first. His body will turn up soon enough.' Praeger stood perfectly still, his riding crop clutched in his fist. Then, like a sly cat, he smiled.

'She knows more than she lets on. Her lie. Keller told me. She was introduced to her future husband by someone whose name she couldn't remember. That is not a thing a person forgets.'

5

KEMPINSKI HOTEL

THAT NIGHT, ANNE SLID into a blue leather lounge chair
opposite Cooper in the Kempinski Hotel's bar. Dim wall
sconces reflected on brass fixtures and a wall of brightly lit
alcohol was illuminated behind the bartender, who poured
generous drinks. The room was filled with the cloying smell
of cigarettes and the coughing laughter of drinkers putting
aside urgent preoccupations from the day's headlines. Above
it all, the raucous din of American and British officers
engaging in flirtatious conversation with sullen German call
girls, who pretended interest in the small stage where Anne's
neighbor sat at a baby grand piano and entertained the
crowd with bawdy falsetto songs and off-color jokes. Marlene
Dietrich's *Blue Angel* publicity photograph was among the
gallery of celebrity photos on the wall, casting her pleasantly
sad smile on the room. Everywhere sparkling cocktails, sweet
murmurs of seduction, and a nostalgic spirit for the Berlin
from between the wars with its Strauss music and bohemian
charm.

Anne waited for the jolly waitress to drop a drink menu, and
she turned to Cooper, who told the waitress he wanted another
beer. He ordered one for her, too.

'What's this all about?' Anne said. 'What's going on?'

A stranger suddenly appeared, silent as a shadow, as though

he knew how to move through a restaurant without catching the waiter's eye. It surprised Anne.

Cooper made space for the man to join. He was tall, even as he bent to sit, and it was only when he'd settled into the banquette that she realized he was the man from the conference room. She looked intently at his face, veined hands, and graying hair still tinged with its original straw color, and she thought he was in his sixties. He had the full neck of a man whose age had crept up on his body, and she saw obvious vanity in his carefully knotted silk tie and bespoke Savile Row suit. She saw his expression soften when he lifted his face and looked at her with patient blue eyes.

'My colleague, Dick Winslow,' Cooper said. 'CIA.'

Anne turned to Cooper. 'What's going on?'

Winslow leaned forward, polite, but not obsequious, a man who carried his authority without having to show it. 'The BND believes your husband worked with a Stasi network that operates here and elsewhere in Europe.' Winslow let the implications of his news settle in and then he lowered his voice. 'We have evidence that supports their suspicion.'

'That's not possible,' Anne snapped, drawing attention from the neighboring table. 'You people are making things up.'

'Let me explain,' Cooper said. The waitress put two beers on the table. Cooper waved off the dinner menus. Suddenly, the bar grew loud as Anne's neighbor rose from the piano in her low-cut sequin gown and blew kisses at the rowdy GIs. 'I'm *the* Chrystal for those of you who don't know, and for those of you who do, I'm *your* Chrystal.'

Anne turned to Cooper and spoke over the loud clapping, 'He is my husband. Do you really think I wouldn't have suspected something?' Her face was stubbornly incredulous, masking the lie. She looked at Winslow. 'I don't know who you are. But I know a little about my husband. A Stasi spy? You have to be joking.' She laughed.

'Praeger believes you're hiding what you know,' Winslow said. 'He believes you helped him. He found half a million West marks in a numbered Swiss bank account. You're listed as the beneficiary. They want to arrest you.'

Anne started to speak, but stopped, not certain what to say. Stunned, confused, disbelieving, letting the news sink in.

'They have a good circumstantial case against you,' Cooper said. 'His trips. The bank account. The binoculars. Living together. Your job at JAROC.'

She stared. She brought her beer to her lips, but thought again, and placed it on the coaster, centering it carefully, thinking.

'This is all tragically unfortunate,' Winslow said.

'Oh yes, very unfortunate,' Anne said. 'But not tragic. He's not dead, at least you don't know that he's dead. I would call this more of a comedy of errors. Certainly, the two of you sitting across from me, have the comic faces of men who think you're being helpful. Well, you're not.'

'Come on, Anne!'

'No!' She fumed. She didn't say anything else for a long time. Her hands clenched and were knuckled white, and when she spoke her voice had the tightness of a violin. 'Stefan a spy? He's a piano tuner.' Even as she denied the accusation, she knew the truth. Their argument that day. Her suspicions. Old doubts were being clarified by a new perspective that came from seeing odd behavior through a new lens. She looked at Winslow like she would a doctor who'd just delivered a difficult diagnosis.

Winslow spoke calmly. 'We believe Stefan was sent to Scheveningen to find a way to get your attention. He was sent by a man we call the Matchmaker, who is head of counterintelligence in the *Staatssicherheit*, the GDR's ministry of state security. He has close ties to the KGB and Warsaw Pact intelligence agencies.'

Winslow leaned forward. 'The Matchmaker has a specialty.

He can pick women who will fall for one of his Romeos. You were Stefan's cover. The Matchmaker built a network of spies in West Germany who married women and carried out ordinary lives, all while collecting military intelligence on NATO's Pershing missile deployment plans, which your husband passed to the Stasi.'

Anne's hand trembled as she reached for her beer mug, thinking she wanted to smash it against Winslow's head. She was suddenly cold in the overheated bar. Numbness settled in, and with it, a feeling of violation.

'How was I chosen?'

'You speak German. You work at JAROC. You interpret for interrogations of civilian defectors and refugees from Warsaw Pact nations. Some of the information would be of interest to the Stasi. Did Stefan ever ask you about your work?'

She looked at Winslow. Indignant. 'Absolutely not.'

'They studied you,' he said. 'They would have known that you were divorced. A woman in her thirties with no children. They believed that you would respond to affection and attention.'

Her angered flared. 'You don't know me.'

'Anne!'

She pushed Cooper's hand away. 'You shouldn't presume who I am.'

'That goes without saying,' Winslow said. 'I'm here because Langley has gotten involved. I work for the director of central intelligence and Cooper works for Berlin's chief of station. It gives me no pleasure to say any of this, but we need to understand what happened – how it happened – so we can get to the Matchmaker. He is our interest. Not your husband.'

The conversation that followed surprised Anne, and the bits of information that Winslow shared made her curious, kept her from indulging her urge to leave. She heard his confidences like a confession, and who can resist the impulse be to let in on a secret? She crossed her arms and listened. The Matchmaker's name was Rudolf Kruger. Kruger was important to the CIA in a particularly important national security matter. The agency had lost a dozen covert assets in the Soviet Union and believed Kruger had information that would help address the matter.

As Winslow spoke, Anne recalled little inconsistencies about Stefan, things he had done that confused her, which she had dismissed, but now, when seen in a different light, took on a new meaning. His constant tardiness. Endless travel. How he dismissed her innocent suspicions with a kiss, or used a joke to cover up an awkward discovery. And there were phone calls that came when he was gone, which she answered, but there was no one on the other end. The list of things that she didn't understand, or overlooked, came to her now as a pattern of deceptions, culminating in the drugged prisoner's accusation. She saw the ruinous thread of incidents woven into a tapestry of deceit. She felt cold. Anne raised her eyes and saw that both men were looking at her.

'What?' she snapped and motioned to the waitress. 'Whiskey.'

When it arrived, she downed half the glass. She studied the amber liquor and then set the glass down. She felt the subversive effect of the knowledge drawing her into their orbit, and a part of her wished she could unhear what she had been told. The idea of returning to her apartment and seeing everything she'd shared with Stefan as a contaminated memory, kept her from leaving. As she listened to Winslow, Anne felt a desperate need to save herself.

She drank the balance of the whiskey slowly and listened reluctantly. Winslow explained how Kruger was smart about human relations. She heard in Winslow a vague admiration for his adversary's tactics.

'Kruger could blackmail as well as any of us, but he understood how to use the human need for affection to weave his web. It's nothing to feel good about, but you shouldn't take this personally. You were picked. It could have been anyone.

You weren't the first or the only one, but we want to make sure you are the last.'

Anne felt like she was hearing things being said about a different Anne Simpson, a woman of the same name, who shared her appearance, but it wasn't her. Part of her wanted to flee.

'Love silences doubt,' Winslow said. 'It blinds us. All of us. There is no shame in being a victim here. You trust a person you love and you ignore hints, clues, suspicions. The Matchmaker turned love into tradecraft. And when love ends, and it always does, you become expendable. Then, in place of love, there is fear. Fear will also silence you.' Winslow looked at Anne. 'You are probably feeling a little frightened now.'

Anne stared at Winslow with contempt.

'There is another emotion you might be feeling. Anger. I see it in your face. Anger at Kruger. At Stefan. You're probably angry at me. We'd like to use your anger to help us get to Kruger.'

Winslow motioned for another glass of water and saw that Anne's shot glass was empty. 'Another whiskey. A beer for my colleague.'

Winslow pulled a grainy black-and-white photograph from his attaché case and showed it to Anne. It was the telephoto shot they had shown in the interview, of a man of medium height in profile with a Soviet-style fedora, stepping into a Chaika limousine.

'I saw this.' She pushed it back. 'His face is blurry.'

'We believe this is Kruger – the Matchmaker. There are no known useful photographs of him. All we have are these grainy blow-ups. We know him as the man without a face. That poses a challenge. We want to get to him, but we don't know what he looks like.' Winslow paused. 'Did you ever meet Kruger, or see a photograph?'

Anne took back the grainy blow-up, studying the man's height and the shape of his shadowed face. 'Maybe.' She saw their excitement, and she felt the power of her ability to disappoint them. 'Stefan had a photograph in his desk. He usually locked it, but for some reason it was open. I looked inside and saw a man's photograph. It was odd. I thought for a moment that I had seen him somewhere, but I couldn't place him. Stefan came out of the shower and saw me looking.'

'Kruger?'

'He didn't use that name. He was upset I was in the drawer. I asked who the man was. Then, as he often did when I asked a question that he wanted to avoid, he joked. He said it was his crazy uncle. He used the same name. Matchmaker. I laughed. It was an odd description, not one you forget. That was the end of it.'

'Where is the photograph?'

'I don't know.'

'Is it in the desk?' Winslow asked.

Cooper intervened. 'Praeger looked. There was nothing.'

Winslow looked at Anne. 'Would you recognize Kruger if you saw him? It would be of great help.'

'Helpful to whom?' Her brow furrowed. 'You don't care about me, or him. You'll use me like he used me.'

Silence fell among them. Anne slumped in her chair and stared at the two men, ignoring the noise coming from the bar. All around them were cheering voices and fits of laughter in response to the cabaret performance. In the awkward pause among them, Winslow's pretense of civility vanished. He assumed the belligerent indifference of an intelligence officer confronted by an uncooperative witness.

'Did you report your marriage to Stefan to JAROC?'

She didn't answer.

'Poor judgment and a serious security violation.'

'Are you threatening me?'

'We're talking.'

Cooper intervened. 'She was lied to for God's sake.'

'That doesn't change the facts. Or, the consequences. You will be questioned. Your security clearance will be revoked. You will be dismissed. You may be arrested and serve prison time.'

Cooper stared fiercely at Winslow. 'That wasn't part of our deal.'

'Nor was her unhelpfulness.' Winslow turned to Anne, whose eyes were averted. His voice softened. 'It doesn't have to come to that. We need your cooperation.' Winslow's expression changed again – anger turned to sympathy, and like an experienced interrogator who knew how to work a reluctant prisoner, he was suddenly reasonable.

'Stefan most likely drowned. Murdered? We don't know. We have to assume he is dead. We want a little cooperation. We're not asking for much. We want you to act like he is alive – missing but alive.'

'Why?'

'Stefan is important to the Matchmaker. They can't afford for him to defect or be arrested. We want the Matchmaker to show his hand.'

'You're dangling me as bait?'

Winslow paused. 'Yes.'

She wanted to stand up and walk out, but she understood the disparity of power between them. Her voice remained calm even as her mind was a riot of thoughts. 'What do you want?'

'Did you have arrangements with Stefan? Ways you communicated when he traveled?'

'I don't understand.'

'Did you talk when he was away from Berlin?'

'He called me. I had a number in case of an emergency. Jim has it.'

Cooper turned to Winslow. 'An East Berlin exchange. Untraceable. No one answered.'

'There was one thing he asked me to do when he was gone.'

Anne drank the rest of her whiskey. The alcohol settled the trembling in her hand. 'I cut out classified ads in *Die Zeit* seeking a piano tuner who specialized in American Steinways. I saved them for him. He would call the telephone numbers listed in the ads. That was how he got his private clients.'

'Do you have the ads?'

'One from this week.'

'Where?'

'In the apartment.'

'Did you call it?'

'There was no answer.' Anne didn't like Winslow, but she had no reason to distrust him in the Kempinski Hotel. A part of her didn't accept his claim that Kruger was key to uncovering a traitor, knowing that it was dangerous to rely on freely offered confidential information, and JAROC's training had taught her to listen for obfuscations that lay beneath easy explanations. As she made her way home from the hotel, she struggled to understand Winslow's intentions.

PART II

6

ALONG KURFÜRSTENDAMM

WINSLOW STOOD IN THE crisp night air under the hotel's canopy and watched Cooper help Anne move past British and American officers toward the taxi stand. The wind had picked up and couples on the street drew together under the night's dark canopy. Boisterous laughter among the officers stopped when a Soviet colonel and a German prostitute walked past on Kurfürstendamm and then picked up again when they moved along, but for Winslow, the moment underscored his own somber mood. He pulled his tan gloves on, stretching his fingers deep into the leather, and stuffed the ends of his cashmere scarf into his coat. Winslow returned Cooper's quick wave and then watched the taxi, with the two of them, merge into traffic.

Winslow had inured his conscience to the lies he was required to tell for work, so he wasn't bothered that he'd misled Anne Simpson about the nature of his interest in Kruger. Cooper had warned him that the American woman might be reluctant to cooperate, and in the back of his mind he'd doubted Cooper's opinion, but the conversation in the bar confirmed that she would be a difficult case.

'Sonofabitch.' The curse slipped from his lips. There would be consequences. He could go only so far on his own to put the woman at risk. The agency's new rules limited his authority to act unilaterally and his options were not good. He could move forward on his own and beg mea culpa if his actions later came to light. Or, he could seek permission, risking that he would be denied, and then his only choice would be to go forward anyway. If caught, he'd need to explain himself. The outcomes were similar, but the appearance was different, and he had long ago learned that it was more dangerous to ask forgiveness than to seek permission. He might have broken the rule once, but he had risen in the agency, and it was now expedient to follow the rules, even if he resented them. The options weighed on him as he watched the taxi drive off.

Winslow was restless. It was too early to end the evening in the confinement of his hotel room. Even five-star hotels, which his pay grade afforded, had a lonely sameness, so he walked along Kurfürstendamm past the Victory Column until he saw the Brandenburg Gate's glowing halo. He'd been there as a young case officer when Jack Kennedy visited, he'd gone again when Reagan urged Gorbachev to tear down the Wall, and returned many times after that. Rome showcased the Caravaggios in Chiesa dei Francesi, Amsterdam had Rembrandt's *The Night Watch* in the Rijksmuseum, but Berlin's attraction was the brightly illuminated *Quadriga* on top of the Brandenburg Gate.

Walking gave him time to think. He knew there was no room for failure. Long ago he had made a grievous mistake. He hadn't understood how words had dominion over history. The official record of the Nosenko affair was written with the convenient omissions of colleagues who'd gone on to occupy the agency's top jobs and they showed little interest in exhuming the past. Their silence was a tyranny. No matter how many congratulatory pats on the back, or recognitions he received, the shadow of poor judgment cast by his unpopular view of the Nosenko affair twenty-two years before remained an unbleachable stain on his reputation. Until now. With her.

He thought of his options as he approached the Brandenburg Gate just beyond the Wall. It struck him that in this instance, with the weight of judgment on his side, there was a reasonable way to proceed.

He glanced at his watch. If it was 10:00 p.m. in Berlin it was 5:00 p.m. in Langley. He knew that the deputy director would have ended his day's schedule of meetings and he'd be at his desk reading morning cables just coming in from Hong Kong. In the taxi heading to his office in Clay Headquarters, Winslow rehearsed what he would say.

The MP at the compound's gate ignored the security badge Winslow presented and waved him through with a familiar greeting, 'Most people have left, but I'll call the guard and he'll let you in.'

Clay Headquarters' main entrance was dark, but there were lights in two second-floor offices. Nazi swastikas of the former Luftwaffe complex had been removed after the war, but ornamental eagles still projected from the austere stone cornices, and the compound still had the stark classical lines of empire.

Winslow made his way through his dark first-floor office and turned on his desk lamp, which illuminated the file he'd left out, and dim light filled the cavernous room. A stone fireplace anchored one end and, on the high ceiling, dark beams created a rectangular pattern. Empire lived on in the former office of Reichsmarschall Hermann Göring.

Winslow lifted the telephone handset with its secure connection to Langley, but then slowly placed it in its cradle. He reconsidered how he would phrase his request. Truth, he had come to learn in his career, was a dangerous impulse.

'It's Dick Winslow. Is George free?'

'It's late for you.'

'Past ten.' Winslow wasn't surprised by the question. Agency secretaries made it their business to know the little administrative details of the men they worked for.

'He's not free but he might be available for you. Let me ask.'

Winslow impatiently glanced at his wristwatch when time stretched out and he began to think that he was being made to wait. He had worked closely with George Mueller for several years, but despite that, or because of it, they were not close. They respected each other, but there was a distance between them that was the product of different backgrounds and different outlooks. Mueller was the Ivy League deep thinker who approached intelligence problems with the diligent patience of a scholar unbraiding the connected strands of a poem, pondering the allusiveness of the text. Winslow, a City College alum, was moved by impulses that emerged from the urgent demands to solve problems where the criterion for making a decision was not whether everything that needed to be known was known, but whether enough was known to act responsibly. They sat on opposite sides of caution. Winslow believed that too much caution prescribed delay and opportunity was lost. He embraced the imperfect world. Mueller believed that the urge to act quickly was the impulse of an impatient mind, and he clung to the belief that patience was the sign of genius. Too often fast action resulted in bad outcomes, and he cited agency failures. Their disagreements never ended in a stalemate – the boss's voice always prevailed, and that outcome echoed in Winslow's mind, lengthening the wait.

'Well,' Mueller said. 'What have you got?'

'She can get us to Kruger.'

'You're sure?'

'I'm sure that she is able to, but I'm not certain that she will cooperate.' Winslow paused. 'She has to feel that she is at risk. She won't come through for us if our threats aren't real. There is a lot at stake here.'

'What does she know?'

'Nothing about Nosenko or his involvement in the Kennedy

assassination. All I said is that Kruger is important to us.'

'The risks?'

Winslow knew the question was coming – it always did when he made a proposal. It was Mueller's predictable response to protect himself and the agency from embarrassment, in case he was hauled before Congress and confronted publicly with a failed operation. Winslow understood the need for the question, but he resented it. As the man on the front line who was expected to deliver results, the prospect of failure burned hotter than his boss's public culpability.

'We need her,' Winslow said.

'You knew Kruger. Drag up what you remember.'

Winslow felt his dislike for his boss rise up.

'We can't risk this becoming public,' Mueller said. 'There is no room for error for you or for me.'

The conversation ended when Mueller hung up.

Winslow moved to the large window that Göring had oriented for its view of the airfield where fighter aircraft landed and took off. Further off there was the glow of the city. So much hinged on her. How had it come to this? He knew that every operation had a moment when the unpredictable came up against the immovable, and it was at that point that failure too often resulted from caution.

At his desk, Winslow typed a memo to Mueller.

I knew Kruger years ago, but I don't know him. He has been a target for years and we have a unique opportunity to get him. His long career heading East Germany's counterintelligence operations has given him many touch points to Soviet intelligence, and in particular, he has a strong connection to the man with direct knowledge of Nosenko – Dmitri Krondashev, head of the KGB's First Chief Directorate. I believe that Kruger knows the circumstances of Nosenko's defection through Krondashev.

When Nosenko presented himself to me in Vienna in 1962, he claimed he had personally reviewed the case of Lee Harvey Oswald when he showed up in Moscow and offered himself to the KGB. The Warren Commission was supposed to have settled the question of Soviet involvement in Kennedy's assassination, but we had doubts and we still have doubts. The question of Soviet involvement is urgent – it has the potential to push the Cold War into nuclear war.

'Nosenko insisted that Oswald was a nut and not reliable for intelligence work. But when I interrogated him, I concluded that Nosenko was an agent of disinformation and not a bona fide defector. Kruger is the only man available to us who would know Nosenko's true intentions. Through Kruger's friendship with Krondashev we will get what we need. Kruger has been a target for years, so now, quite fortuitously, we have this woman, Anne Simpson, who is in a position to deliver him.

'You asked about the risks. They are real, but in my opinion, this is not the time to be squeamish about our tactics.'

Winslow removed the page from the typewriter and he corrected a misspelling with his pen. His word processor was an easier way to produce a draft, but a typed memo left no record on a hard drive.

Winslow looked up from the memo. So much time had passed since Nosenko had approached him in the lobby of his Vienna hotel. Old memories and old injuries swirled in his mind. His past caught up with him in that moment. There he was as a young boy on the Moscow River with his childhood friend, Rudi Kruger. Fifty years had passed. All the foreigners in Moscow had lived in one section of the city reserved for German emigrant intellectuals, American newspapermen, and Jewish communist playwrights. Stalin's purges had forced his father, a correspondent for the *Herald Tribune,* to return to New York, but Rudi Kruger's parents, German communists who'd fled Berlin to escape the Nazis, stayed. Winslow remembered the year well – a small group of young boys eager to share experiences in the foreign city, who took classes together, and recited poetry while canoeing on the Moscow River. They had the earnest aspirations of children hoping to make the world a better place, and they talked of dreams and the prospect of war. It all ended quite suddenly. Winslow's parents returned to New York, others left for London, but the Krugers stayed. Winslow later heard that Rudi Kruger returned to Berlin in 1945 with advance units of the Red Army tasked with setting up the Stasi.

Winslow put the page in the typewriter again. He added a final paragraph.

'Forty-nine years changes a man's face. I wouldn't know Kruger if he was put in a line of older men. I wouldn't recognize his childhood features on a sixty-two-year-old face. Time changes us too much. I wouldn't know his face to look at it, or his weight, his height, or the color of his hair. I wouldn't be able to recognize him. The BND's photographs are distant and blurry, but even if they were clear, I wouldn't be able to pick him out. That is why we need Anne Simpson. She has seen his face.'

Winslow removed the page and placed it in an envelope. He sealed it, signed the seal with his signature, and addressed it. 'Hand delivery. Eyes only. George Mueller.'

Encrypted cables were secure, but they were processed by men and women who might happen to read them before they landed on Mueller's desk. The typed paper would be read once and shredded.

7

BETHANIENDAMM

A FEW DAYS LATER

WHAT STARTED AS ANOTHER challenging day at work turned worse when Anne returned from Technical Services after her lunch break. Anne was approaching her office with an envelope containing the forged passport of a Hungarian defector, thinking about the man she'd seen watching her from the apartment across the street that morning, when someone yelled her name. By the tone, she knew something was not right. She saw her supervisor, a matronly civilian military employee who often scowled, standing in the hall with an army sergeant. He introduced himself as a security officer and said that he had questions for her. He asked if she would be kind enough to accompany him. There was nothing kind in his expression. She followed them to a windowless conference room in a restricted area of the building, where she sat across from a uniformed technician who operated a reel-to-reel tape recorder.

Questions came quickly. The sergeant was polite, but with each hesitant response, he grew more impatient, and his voice was harsher, more demanding and more threatening. She responded *yes* or *no*, or she couldn't recall, keeping her answers short until she knew what he wanted. The technician was instructed to play the tape. She recognized the East German prisoner's raspy voice and his snarling answers that became less angry as the drug calmed him. She heard his labored breathing and the American interrogator's shouted questions that she repeated in German. It was hard to decipher everything that was being asked or answered amid the curses and shouts.

'Replay it,' the security officer told the technician after they passed the portion of the tape where the prisoner could be heard saying *klavierstimmer*. 'Stop. Did you hear that?'

Anne heard her translation – pianist. The security officer asked how she made the mistake, mixing his Southern drawl with crude German, accusing her of intentionally mistranslating. Anne admitted the error, but denied that it was intentional. She explained that she had been pulled into the interrogation without warning and wasn't trained to handle what she encountered. The scene was chaotic and frightening. She looked at the prisoner's bloody face and listened to his gasping answers. Yes, she said, the word could be heard clearly on the tape, but it was impossible for them, standing there in the quiet conference room, to imagine how she had struggled to translate shouted questions and the dying man's gasping answers. Anne looked from her supervisor to the security officer, who stepped forward and roughly took her arm.

'Come with me,' he said.

Anne's supervisor blocked the man with her arm. 'It was a mistake,' she said sternly. She escorted Anne to her office and cautioned her not to discuss the episode with anyone. 'Take a few days off. I will handle him.'

*

Anne wasn't the sort of woman who sought help from others. It was in her nature to figure things out on her own. She wished she were a different type of person, the type who had friends in whom she could confide. But she wasn't. And her Quaker faith provided no answers. When she got home from work, she did what she always did when life was too much for her. She went for a long run.

Outside on the sidewalk, she was closing the front door when someone called out. Her auburn hair was pulled back in a ponytail and she wore a puffy vest over her track suit. Her gloved hand fumbled with the key on the lanyard that hung from her neck, and when she turned, she saw a short man in a trim suit standing beside a waiting taxi. JAROC employees were cautioned not to approach strangers, or let them approach her, so she began to jog. As she passed, the man came away from the taxi. She glanced at him and she knew she'd seen him before. Then he was in front of her, blocking her path.

'Frau Simpson? Do you remember me?'

Anne's expression was skeptical. 'From the canal?'

'Dr Knappe.' He bowed slightly from the waist.

Her previous encounter was still an unpleasant memory, but there was a pained look on his face and she hesitated before moving past.

'I knew your husband.'

She stared. 'How?'

'I treated him once for anxiety. I prescribed antidepressants. I should have known you were his wife. I made a mistake.'

'You don't need to apologize.'

'I didn't want to admit as much in front of the police. It's none of their business.'

Anne stood her ground when the man stepped forward, solicitous.

'The BND,' he said. 'Overpaid amateurs. Not like the Stasi. I know it is heretical to praise the other side, but if we don't acknowledge their talent, we become victims of our confidence.' He smiled. 'There is a joke. May I share it?'

Anne had made the mistake of listening to him.

'Why do the Stasi make such good taxi drivers?' He paused.

'Because you get in the taxi and they already know where you live.' Dr Knappe laughed. 'There is another.'

'One is enough. How can I help you?'

'Of course. Humor helps in these difficult times. Who knows what the Soviets will do?'

Dr Knappe put out his hand to shake hers, but she didn't respond. He stood for a moment doing nothing. She thought him strange, with his need to look younger than he was and his face a tawny pallor. His hand was white and his fingernails were neatly clipped and buffed. Everything about him seemed obsessively neat and clean. Anne had an impulse to rub dirt into his coat.

'I would have said more at the canal, but I was embarrassed. I thought I had insulted you. The tall officer in his Bavarian hat insisted that I was done and then there was the incident with the patrol boat. I had no opportunity to apologize. That's why I've come. I sympathize with how difficult this must be for you.'

She nodded. 'Thank you.' She zipped her vest, impatient.

'I feel better saying it.'

She started to move past, ignoring him.

'There's nothing I know that I didn't say at the canal.' His voice rose. Urgent. 'It was quick. I didn't say it at the time, but you should know. I believe it was a blow to the head and then he drowned in the river.'

Dr Knappe put his hand on her arm, but when she frowned, he withdrew.

'I suspect he felt no pain. Unconscious, he would have succumbed peacefully. A quiet, peaceful death. You can take comfort in that.'

A beat of silence. 'You're certain he was attacked?' she said.

'Quite certain. I heard his cry. And there was his wallet and zither.'

She looked at him. 'Why were you at the canal?'

'I make the walk for my dog. I'm a small investor in the

cement factory. They know me.' Dr Knappe stepped aside, letting her pass. 'Enjoy your run.'

The encounter ended as it began. Dr Knappe retreated to his waiting taxi, a pained expression on his face. As he stepped away, she felt him press a folded paper in her hand. The note was written in a physician's barely legible scrawl: *'He didn't suffer. He would have wanted you to know that.'* There was a telephone number.

*

Anne knew what to expect of the weather in the final week of October. The center of the Northern European plain had been flattened by glaciations, and weather rolled in slowly and stalled over the city for days at a time. With fall came a biting chill that kept Berliners stoically bundled up, and she too had dressed warmly for her run. She didn't plan a route and followed the path that she habitually took along the Spree, but distracted, she turned and came upon the graffitied Wall at the end of an alley, lurking like a fugitive. Images came in a flickering montage – Stefan's face, his frightened backward glances, the silence that followed two runners moving side by side. The images dimmed when she willed them away. A few minutes later, she jogged along a skirt of barren trees aware of familiar city sounds – cars honking, a woman's voice calling in distress. Then Stefan's voice in her ear whispering in the pleasant way he had, begging her to slow down, asking her to listen. She shut out his voice, concentrating on her stride.

She wiped perspiration from her forehead and calibrated her endurance against the distance that remained. Concentration freed her from distracting thoughts and a steady pace cleansed her mind of the altercation at work. They couldn't prove her lie. She relaxed into a pleasant oblivion and saw only the small world in front of her strides. How had she gotten to this place in her life? She looked for a future in her mind's eye but saw only darkness.

There came a moment when she found herself passing the cement factory's limestone mound and the parking lot of idled long-haul trucks. She approached the chain-link fence and stared across the Spree at the East German watchtower. Its searchlight moved over the murky water. The gulls were gone but the water kept its secret. She peered through the fence, looking through the mist for a floating body. She brooded over the mystery. A buoy's bell clanged in the swells of a passing patrol boat.

She took a shallow breath and felt the uncomfortable mystery rise up again. She wasn't a young woman anymore, but her suffering was still fresh. The glow of the tower's lamp burnished her cheeks with obstinate grief. In the moment, she wanted to believe that it was all a bad dream and all she had to do was wake up.

She opened her gloved hand to reread Dr Knappe's note, but a sudden gust of wind lifted it and carried it away, turning it around and around, and then sent it flying across the street into oncoming traffic. In that moment, her vision blurred and she felt the tug of uncertainty tempting her. Suddenly, she was in the middle of the street moving through traffic. Cars whipped by, swerving to avoid her, and one screeched to an abrupt stop, feet away, as she stooped for the note. The irate driver honked his horn twice and cursed her through his open window.

8

LATER THAT NIGHT

ANNE WAS BECOMING ACCUSTOMED to surprises, but she wasn't prepared for the scene that she encountered when she got off the elevator. Chrystal sat slumped against the hall's chipped plaster wall, her legs straight out, quietly weeping. Her wig lay in one corner and her face was bruised and bloody.

Anne was on her knees at her side, her voice urgent. 'What happened?'

Chrystal's whole body shuddered in one convulsive spasm and she looked up with pain and embarrassment. Anne saw a split lip and a purpled cheek. Tears mixed with eye shadow and streaked down her cheeks.

'Who did this?'

Chrystal breathed deeply and leaned her head back against the wall, but said nothing. She tried to smile, but winced when her lips parted. 'I must look like a mess.'

Anne put a hand on her cheek. 'You're fine. You don't have to tell me.'

Chrystal's eyes dropped to the floor. 'He took my purse.' She presented her wrist. 'And my watch. He hit me when I pushed him away. He didn't look suspicious when we met at Neues Ufer, but it's always the quiet ones you have to watch out for.' Chrystal stood up.

Anne's face was flush from the cold and her track suit was

dark with perspiration. They looked at each other and then, feeling a sort of communion, Chrystal leaned down to the string bag Anne carried and smelled the food she'd bought at the Turkish grocery.

'Chicken, garlic, cured ham, and I think a lemon. So, you didn't forget about dinner.'

'Dinner?'

'Yes, your dinner,' she said matter-of-factly, pointing at the string bag. 'You look surprised. Did you forget?'

Anne cocked her head, uncertain what Chrystal meant, not yet offended by her presumptuousness, but also surprised.

'Not dinner with me,' she said. 'I still have a show to do tonight. How bad do I look? Will lipstick and rouge do, or will I have to perform my Frankenstein shtick?'

Anne wasn't in the mood for humor, but Chrystal had a way of making her laugh and then, not wanting to laugh, she did.

'You are so more attractive when you laugh. You wear sadness like a nun's habit. It doesn't suit you and your visitors will be turned off.'

'What visitors?'

'First, there was a TV reporter from ARD. Very aggressive and pushy when I said I had no idea when you'd be home. "I'm not my neighbor's keeper," I said, which she took the wrong way, as if I'd intended an insult. She asked me to tell you that she wants to talk about Stefan. And then she asked what I knew and why the police were asking questions. She was insistent. I had to shut the door on her. She stood outside shouting questions.

'And then a man showed up for dinner. The front door must have been stuck open. He rushed up the stairs, huffing like a bull, out of breath. I thought he was Paul Revere without his horse.'

Anne stared. 'Who?'

'That embassy man.'

'Jim Cooper?'

'Yes. That's him. James Bond.'

Anne knew from her sarcasm that Chrystal's only lasting injury would be to her pride. 'What did he want?'

'What all men want.'

Anne grunted displeasure.

'You only had to look into his eyes to see a man with appetite. He came rushing up the stairs past me and my date. He had flowers and a bottle of wine. I told him you were out. He looked at me like I held a dagger, but then he stared at his watch and his eyes rolled in his head. He said, "All mistakes are bad, but some are worse than others."'

Chrystal smiled, but winced at the pain. 'Yes, that's what he said. All I could think of was George Bernard Shaw. The easiest way to sound witty, to avoid looking foolish, is to invoke the paradox.'

*

Anne was apologetic when Cooper got off the elevator. She drew her bathrobe tighter and stood in the doorway in bare feet. Her wet hair glistened and fell straight down as if each strand was weighted. She touched her hair self-consciously. 'I was in the shower. Come in.'

She took the bouquet of flowers he offered and added, chagrined, 'I forgot. I was jogging. It was a bad day at the office. I had a lot on my mind. I just need a moment to dress.'

'Did he tell you I came by earlier?'

'Chrystal prefers she. Yes, she told me. That's why I called.'

'Did I get the time wrong? Seven, right?'

'Yes. My mistake. Come in.' Her bathrobe opened when she reached for the bottle of wine and she quickly closed it, hiding her embarrassment. 'I'll dress. I'll only be a minute. Dinner is cooking. Come in.' She stepped aside to let him pass. Anne looked at the wine's vintage and the chateau. 'Did you pay for this or is it on expense account?'

'Out of my own pocket.'

They sat across from each other at the dinner table. She wore a comfortable cardigan and she had pulled her hair back so it fell behind her shoulders. She had prepared coq au vin with pearl onions, chicken breasts, thick-cut bacon, and carrots, which she served with saffron rice. The pleasant aroma and two glasses of wine turned their attention to dinner, with only a brief conversation about forgetfulness and a mention of the unfolding political crises in East Berlin. She was sipping her wine when she put down the glass and looked at him.

'Do you think he is dead?'

'Yes.'

'What makes you so certain?'

'The wallet. The witness. His zither. It fits a pattern. If he isn't dead, you would have heard something.' Cooper's expression was grave.

He's done this before, she thought.

'It's not what you want to believe, but the sooner you accept the fact, the easier it will be for you.'

She put her fork into a carrot, cutting it in halves, quarters, and eighths, and then looked up. 'What stage of grief am I in? Shock? Anger? Denial? Can you grieve for someone who betrayed you?'

She waited for him to answer, but saw that he didn't have one. 'An ARD reporter came by today asking questions about Stefan.' She saw Cooper's surprise.

'What did he want?'

'A woman. I wasn't home. She talked to Chrystal, but you can guess what she's interested in. It's the same thing I want – answers.'

'This can't get into the press. It would complicate matters.'

'What do you suggest?' She waited for him to answer, but she saw that he didn't have an answer, or if he did, he kept it to himself. Her eyes came back to Cooper. 'Stefan knew he was in danger.'

'How do you know?'

'I confronted him before he left for Vienna.'

Cooper set down his glass, alert.

'I had come home late. I found him looking at the Wall. He tried to deflect my questions, but then he said things were not going well. I assumed one of his clients was unhappy. Temperamental pianists blame the piano – or the piano tuner – for a poor performance. He talked of quitting.' She looked at him. 'I'm not sure how much I should say. I wasn't sure I should have invited you tonight.'

'Why not?'

She fingered a silver bracelet, a keepsake, turning it round and round. She met his eyes. 'I don't trust you.' A smile creased her cheeks. 'But I don't have anyone else to confide in.' She struggled to keep her torment from becoming obvious, but her glass shook in her trembling hand. She set it down. 'Today, I felt like I was going crazy.'

She looked at Cooper, trying to see into his mind. 'I don't know you. You showed up at my door and told me my husband was missing. You know more than you let on. You try to be pleasant. Are you being pleasant or are you using me? What do you want?'

'I'm here to help. Leave it at that.'

'Help who? Me? Winslow?'

'You can help us. It will work out better for you.'

She laughed. 'Can you promise that what I say stays between us?'

'I can't agree to that. I'd be lying if I did.'

Anne shook her head dismissively. 'That may be the first truthful thing you've said to me.' Anne looked at Cooper, trying to read his thoughts, but saw only his professional demeanor.

'God, this is hard,' she gasped. 'I hate this.' She took two deep breaths to settle her nerves and she poured herself more wine.

'Talking helps,' he said.

Now he's a priest, she thought. She began to speak, but hesitated, and then was silent. She looked into the dark scarlet of her wine, seeing herself in the reflection. She raised her eyes.

'I knew something was wrong.' Her voice was measured, but as she began to speak her confession came quickly in a rush of words. 'We rarely argued but we argued that night. I had come home late, upset, and I found Stefan with the binoculars at the window. I confronted him with the defector's claim of a Stasi agent working as a piano tuner. He laughed, dismissing it, calling it preposterous. I then presented him with inflated hotel receipts that I'd found. I asked what they were and why he was cheating his employers. He said that it was none of my business. I pressed him. He said he was falsifying invoices to save money for our move to London. I said I didn't want to leave Berlin. That's when he got angry. He said the money was for me in case something happened to him.'

Anne looked at Cooper. 'I wasn't sure how to react to his comment. Something might happen to him? At first, I thought it was a normal concern. He might step off a curb and be hit by a bus. I asked what he meant and I pushed him for an answer. He said he was in danger.'

'What type of danger?'

Anne shot forward. 'He brushed me off, as if he wanted to take back what he'd said. He kissed me, like he always did when he wanted to use affection to distract, but of course, I knew exactly what he was doing.' Anne paused. 'He made me promise that if anything happened to him, I would leave Berlin. He said it would be dangerous for me to stay in this apartment. Men would be watching.'

'Who?'

'He pointed to an apartment across the street. A man was in the window. I saw him again this morning.'

Anne turned off the living room light and moved to the casement window. She pulled back the closed blinds and peeked out. 'He's there now.'

She was joined by Cooper who stood behind her and looked across the street at the fourth-floor apartment. Below the moon, the apartment building opposite her window blazed black in the transparent shadow, but a radium wristwatch or a glinting buckle gave the man away. Anne's eyes adjusted, and in a moment, she saw a black figure silhouetted in the dark window. 'He's been there off and on,' she said, dropping the blinds.

Anne returned to the table and Cooper sat across from her. Anne lifted her wine, swirling the liquid slowly – thinking. 'I know Stefan lied when he said the money was to help us move to London. I confronted him. I said, "I'm your wife. Tell me what's happening." He was sitting where you are.' She raised an eyebrow and looked at Cooper. 'What do you know that you're not telling me?'

'I can have you moved to another apartment where they won't find you.'

'They? Who? The Stasi?'

'Probably.'

'I want to leave Berlin.'

'Winslow and Praeger won't agree. For now, you have to stay.'

They talked for another hour. Certainly, the wine helped relax her, and they opened a bottle of sweet Muscat when the burgundy was finished. Certainly, Cooper was a good listener. And certainly, she felt awkward sharing feelings for her dead husband with a stranger. But holding onto her silence was suffocating. The wine, the Muscat, and his patient concern slowly eroded her reticence. Her urge to share nagging thoughts became a confession.

'Meeting and marrying Stefan seemed like a dream,' she said. 'It was an adventure. He made me laugh.'

Anne went over the details of their first meeting, reliving it by retelling it, and in the process understanding it. 'Christmas was a bad time to be an American woman alone in Berlin. I had been divorced for two months and I needed to get away. There was a direct flight from Tegel to Rotterdam and the resort's location on the sea was enough. I had fond childhood memories of visiting grandparents by the ocean in Maine.'

Anne said restaurants were closed for the season, but that, too, attracted her. She walked barefoot on the sandy beaches in front of the boardwalk. Most of the grand Beaux Arts hotels were closed. The Ferris wheel at the end of the pier was shut down. It had been rainy and damp the first week, but not cold enough for snow. A biting, moist chill, a gray mist, then a pale winter sun. It rained most of the week and temperatures were never lower than 30 degrees and never higher than 45.

'Like my mood,' she said. 'Never enough sadness to cry, never enough joy to laugh. A quiet moody time for reflection. I chose the resort because it was easy to get to – a short cab ride from Rotterdam. The idea of spending New Year's among loud, partying drinkers did not appeal to me. I had the stamina to be by myself, so I booked a room with a sea view.'

Anne grimaced. 'I suppose I was the vulnerable person that the Matchmaker was looking for.'

Anne picked up the photograph of their wedding in a small Dutch church. A country priest performed a union between two lovers. She presented it to Cooper. 'I was happy. Perhaps he was, too. Happy because he got me to do what they wanted.'

Anne slumped in her chair. 'I accepted his story. He gave me a convenient explanation for being in Scheveningen in winter. Fog at Rotterdam had been thick. He'd missed his connecting flight and had a few days before the weather cleared for his onward flight to Hungary. We laughed, ate well, drank too much. At night we read to each other. From the beginning, books were a thing that we shared. The first night it was the *King James Bible*. There was one in the hotel room and I'd told him I was a Quaker, so he insisted. We read it for the beauty of the language. He was an atheist he said, but he enjoyed the poetry of the words. So, you can imagine, if you're in bed with a man and he says something like that, you believe him. You want to believe him. You're taken in.'

Anne paused. 'Every couple finds one thing to go back to when stress enters a relationship, and for us it was reading. In bed at night, he read to me. Shakespeare, Chekhov, Borges, le Carré.' She laughed self-consciously.

'Yes, spy novels.' She shook her head. 'A spy in bed with his so-called wife reading a spy novel. I can only imagine what he was thinking.'

Anne laughed quietly. 'He enjoyed the stories and the tradecraft.'

She wiped a tear with her knuckle and waved off Cooper's offer of a tissue.

'He had a good reading voice. I trusted his voice and he enjoyed reading out loud. It was a thing we did together. He said he had never done it with anyone else. I believed him. Was he lying? Possibly. It is also possible he wasn't. Can you understand that?'

Anne continued her account. Having shared one confession, it was easy for her to continue, and when one glass of Muscat became three, her urge to speak became a torrent of words.

'I didn't question the story. It was no more crazy than my own. He had a budget for taxis and a flagrant indifference for what things cost. And he was a musician. He could sing.

'Now, I see how those first days he was testing how easily I could be misled with a plausible lie. He wanted to know how far he could go without raising my suspicion.'

Anne considered a thought. 'I didn't want to believe it when

Winslow said it, but I now see what happened.' She'd had several days to reflect on the life they had shared. He said he loved her, and she had believed him. She thought about all the falsehoods, all the lies and yet, even knowing that, her heart ached. She wondered: 'Is it possible that happiness built on falsehoods is still happiness?'

'Did you ever suspect him?'

'No. Not then.'

'Nothing you saw troubled you?'

'It was a good life. You can live pretty well with half-truths. He was a kind husband. He traveled and when he was home, we were a normal couple. We did what every couple does. What do you want me to say? He was terrible? He wasn't.'

She looked away. 'I've thought about it. I haven't been able to stop thinking about it. I see how our meeting was an elaborate ruse.'

Anne described how she came to understand she had been taken in. 'I'm not stupid. I'm not naïve.'

It didn't come to her at first, but thinking about it while jogging, she made sense of it. The imbalance of their personalities worked to the Stasi's advantage. She was a quiet, introverted interpreter and he was a gregarious musician with easy charm who collected friends like a beachcomber collects shells, keeping a few, discarding most. Tall, good-looking, well read. He eased her social awkwardness and she was happy to become a part of his life, giving up a part of her own. He serenaded her with bawdy German folk songs on his zither, making her laugh until she begged him to stop. He bragged he didn't have to be good on the zither – just good enough. No one played the instrument anymore and for money he tuned pianos.

There was another power imbalance, she realized. The Matchmaker had studied her. Stefan knew things about her that he used against her and she knew nothing about him. The Stasi had marked her as a divorced, thirty-four-year-old woman without children looking at the horizon of her childbearing years. Gullible, vulnerable, eager for affection, looking for a man to make her a mother.

She looked at Cooper. 'God, how easy I made it for them.'

Then there was the imbalance of money. She had little and he seemed to have plenty. He could afford a large apartment. Piano tuning, he said, paid well enough and despite his complaint that there were never enough jobs, his generous expense account paid for restaurants, clothing, and five-star hotels. They enjoyed evenings at the theater, vacations, and slowly she'd been happy to give up her frugal life for his lifestyle. He bought off her curiosity with chocolate from Vienna, silk scarves from Milan, earrings from Venice.

'I didn't ask. I don't think I wanted to know.' She turned to Cooper. 'You asked if I ever suspected something. There was one thing. There had been a security alert at Clay Headquarters and we were sent home early. He had just returned from Cologne and was in the shower when I entered. I called out, but he didn't hear me. He'd left his attaché case open, which he never did, but it was there on this table.

'I found an envelope on top of his tools. It was addressed to him with a return address in East Berlin. The envelope was open. I found a photograph of a young boy inside. At dinner I asked him who it was. He was surprised and became upset. He scolded me for looking. He said the boy was a nephew and that was the end of it.'

Anne walked to the desk and removed a notepad. 'I copied the address.' She presented the paper to Cooper. 'Do you recognize this address?'

'No.'

'Do you know who the boy is?'

'No.'

'I don't believe you.'

'There are some things you shouldn't know.'

'There is nothing I shouldn't know. This is my life. I don't need you to protect me.'

Cooper hesitated. 'He has a son.'

Anne stood, covering her shoulders with a wrap she took from the back of a chair, and she intently fingered the silver bracelet on her wrist.

'His wife lives in East Berlin. That's her address.'

Anne turned. 'I'm not surprised. Would you have told me if I hadn't asked?'

'No.'

She was mildly annoyed. 'That's the second honest thing you've said.'

9

CLAY HEADQUARTERS

ANNE WASN'T SURPRISED WHEN Winslow summoned her to Clay Headquarters. The polite secretary said a car would be sent. The only thing that surprised her was that Jim Cooper wasn't the driver. She had come to think of him as her ally, possibly even a man she could trust. His predictable misrepresentations were oddly comforting, and she appreciated that he had been truthful twice. Twice honest was a refreshing change from two years in a dishonest marriage.

Anne presented her security badge to the military policeman at the main gate and the driver was waved through to the main building. Clay Headquarters' Nazi past always made the muscles on the back of her neck constrict, and she was aware of the perched stone eagles looking down as she passed through the main entrance. For a moment, the olive-green fatigues of the American MP became Waffen-SS slate-gray. Authority was all the same to her.

Anne didn't know what to expect from the meeting, so she decided to dress up, thinking it was going to be an evaluation interview and she should make a good impression. But, as the sedan arrived, she was suddenly frightened that she had dressed all wrong. She wasn't there to impress them. She removed her pearls and wiped off her scarlet lipstick with a tissue.

She followed a German secretary in high heels down a long

marble corridor, passing through a large carved wooden door that the woman held open. 'They're expecting you.'

Anne found herself in a cavernous room with a dark wood ceiling and a majestic stone fireplace that anchored one end. Wispy smoke from dying embers rose through the chimney and the room had the distinctive smell of burning wood, but the dying fire gave no heat to the large room, or to the four men who sat at a carved wooden conference table.

'Come in,' Winslow said, rising from his ladderback chair. 'Join us. Thank you for being on time. Traffic is terrible at this hour.'

Anne took Winslow's offered hand and they were stiffly courteous to each other. Winslow smiled a smile she didn't trust. He guided her to an empty chair and she glanced at Cooper, who had risen when she entered, but then sat quietly. Anne understood the pecking order. She expected Winslow and Cooper, but she was surprised by Praeger and Keller. Praeger rose stiffly and nodded slightly, while the shorter Keller hardly rose at all from his chair and then slumped down.

She sat across from the four men. The coffee cups on the table were empty, and a porcelain serving dish held pastry crumbs. Winslow pointed to the carafe. 'Coffee? We can have more pastry brought in.'

Anne shook her head. She looked at her interrogators, taking in their grim faces. They had the same drawn expressions, the same awkward reticence. She looked from one to the other and glanced at Cooper, who averted his eyes. *Something has been decided,* she thought.

'The Stasi are watching you,' Winslow said. 'They are hoping you'll lead them to your husband.'

'Stefan is dead,' she said.

'Yes, but apparently they think he is alive.'

Anne looked at Winslow, then at Praeger, who deferred to

the American, and she sensed Winslow's authority. 'How do you know?'

'It's our business to know these things.' Winslow walked toward the massive fireplace where a swastika carved into the stone had been left in place, rather than remove it and destroy the mantel's sculpted artistry. His steps echoed in the room and when he came to the fireplace, he leaned against it in studied disinterest. He suddenly turned. 'Perhaps he is alive. Perhaps he is dead. The facts, whatever they are, will emerge. What's important is that they *believe* he is alive. They want to find him and it appears that they think you can lead them to him.'

Winslow paced the room, his hands clasped behind his back, and approached Anne. 'Do you understand?'

'I called the ad twice,' she said. 'No one answered. I left a message. I did what I was asked.'

'Which address?' Praeger asked.

'The one I gave you.'

'Now you must go there and wait. If he doesn't come one day go back the next and wait at the same time. We need to question him.'

'I wasn't told to do that. You asked me to make a call. I did. My part is done.'

'Your part is done when we make an arrest.'

Anne shuddered. She thought she was done with what she'd been asked, and her interview was to be akin to an appearance before a parole board. She would be allowed to leave Berlin. Quiet filled her mind until the knobs in her head that controlled sound turned up, and she heard Praeger speaking harshly. His face was contorted with false charm and his thick lips explained there was a Stasi network to roll up, and one phone call was not enough.

Anne stood slowly, feeling faint. 'I can't do this.' Her voice was tentative and frightened. She turned toward the door, knowing the consequence of her decision to leave, and then heard her name called. She turned.

'There is a police car outside,' Praeger said. 'You can choose to be escorted to Spandau Prison, or you can sit here and listen to what we expect of you.'

'This is a joint operation,' Winslow said. 'They want your husband. I want Kruger.'

Anne stared at the four men with contempt. She saw their implacable expressions, and in that moment, she understood the full scope of her predicament. There was peril if she cooperated and peril if she did not. But, the consequences of refusing to help were immediate and the dangers of cooperating were further off.

'What do I get?'

Cooper lifted two typed documents for her to see. 'This is your exit visa. Here, a dismissal of criminal charges for mistranslating the prisoner's confession. It doesn't require a miracle. Just reasonable cooperation.'

She disliked them and distrusted them, but she couldn't ignore them. The realization came to her spitefully when she saw the eagerness in their faces. Now was the time to demand. She felt the confidence that came with the power to disappoint and the exhilaration that came from fear. She closed her eyes, imagining herself at the cliff edge of a deep quarry, a place she had gone as a child, and stepped forward to confront the danger.

'If I do this, I will need things,' she said. Her back straightened, her voice deepened. 'A forged passport in a name that will be easy to remember. And Krugerrands.' She threw out an amount.

She made her demands and felt herself stepping into the mind of the woman they wanted her to become – a recruit in their spy game. She had no idea what she would do with Krugerrands, but now was the time to ask, and she assumed that a use for the gold coins would become apparent when a need appeared. With each demand, she tested their willingness to go along. *God,* she thought. It felt good to watch Winslow and Praeger nod in agreement.

The meeting ended. Cooper was to be the errand boy for her things. Anne had stopped at the wooden door held open by the secretary, when she turned. She looked at Praeger.

'Have you found his body yet? Or, are you keeping that information from me?'

10

THAT NIGHT AND THE NEXT DAY

AFTER ANNE LEFT CLAY Headquarters, she went off to drink herself silly. She chose the Kempinski's bar. The smoky room off the main lobby beckoned because she knew it and she could find her way home. She was comforted by the bright laughter and the familiar gallery of celebrity photographs, and even the nimble fingering of the piano-entertainer was reassuring.

She took a bar stool and faced the wall of glittering liquor, catching the bartender's eye, giving her order. One whiskey came, and when she'd downed it quickly, another appeared, which she sipped, thinking about the men in the conference room. Self-important impresarios of an amateur production of espionage musical comedy. The whiskey warmed her and deepened her outrage.

She nodded at the stage. 'Is Chrystal here tonight?'

'Off tonight,' the bartender said. 'Tuesdays and Wednesdays.' He vigorously wiped a highball glass with his towel. 'Where's your guy?'

Anne frequently came to the bar in the company of Stefan, who had a job tuning the baby grand, and they'd been fans of Chrystal's cabaret act.

She shrugged. The witty answer she wanted to give, to avoid a serious conversation, didn't come to mind. She pointed at her half-empty shot glass. She wasn't sure why she'd come – a vague desire to not be alone in her apartment. A vague desire to be among people she didn't know, the comfort of having laughing people be a distracting soundtrack to her misery.

Anne knew she had stayed too long when she was the only woman at the bar, and a sullen man at the opposite end kept looking in her direction. She knew what he thought of her – a single woman drinking by herself – but she didn't feel enough contempt to tell him to fuck off.

She took the U-Bahn home and leaned her head against the carriage's window. Her thoughts wandered, but she kept coming back to what she understood from the conference room. There was only one way forward. No crying, no outrage, no self-pity would alter her predicament. Her innocence was unproven and unprovable, and there was no one to whom she could make her case. She couldn't walk away. And if she could, where would she go? The things she'd asked for. She laughed. What would she do with Krugerrands? She had remembered Stefan's jar of coins – now gone.

It was a 45-minute ride. Her mind went back to the moment in her hallway when Cooper stepped off the elevator and asked if she was Anne Simpson. It was three weeks since she'd said 'yes,' but it felt like three years. So much had happened. She looked out the darkened window and saw her reflection. A stranger's face. Her finger touched the contours of her flushed cheeks and her pale lips. *Who am I?*

The world before Cooper arrived had come to an end. She was now in a perilous new world with an uncertain future. Cooper's question – 'Anne Simpson?' – came to her again urgently, as if he'd just spoken. In her rational mind, she knew that nothing would be different if she had kept silent, but part of her wished she'd said nothing.

Vivid memories came to her, as if they weren't memories at all, but things she was reliving. The hotel bar with Stefan, their ride home on the U-Bahn, Stefan at her side, both of them silly with alcohol, laughing, kissing. She wanted that life back.

Late that night, she sat up in bed and looked at the other side, expecting to find Stefan asleep, with his pillow over his face. Fear gripped her. How could *this* happen? His deception, his death, the man in the window across the street, the danger she was in. What terrible things had she done in a past life to deserve *this*?

She wanted to cry, but she was too hungover.

*

In the morning, Anne swung her legs over the side of the bed, feeling disoriented. She had fallen asleep in her clothes. Cigarette smoke clung to her blouse. A button was missing.

She showered, holding her hair behind her head and letting warm water flow over her closed eyes. She let the stream massage her face, relax her mind. She thought about the men in the conference room – her demands. Passport and Krugerrands. What had she been thinking? Slowly, she allowed herself to think about what she had agreed to do.

She toweled her hair on her way to the living room and stood over the torn classified ad, staring at the West Berlin address. She stood in the living room, naked, and lifted the telephone. On the third ring, her call went through.

'Hallo?' Someone had picked up.

'Hallo,' she repeated.

There was static on the line and then she heard the line go dead. She dialed again and got a man's voice.

'I called before. My husband asked me to inquire about the job. He understands it is an American Steinway built in Queens in 1972. He can meet you.'

After giving a date, a time, and an address, she replaced the telephone in its cradle, stood, and looked out at the window across the street. Then she realized she was still naked and closed the venetian blinds.

Anne ate a breakfast of grapefruit and black coffee and set aside the classified ad. She had given the man the address Praeger provided and as she sipped her coffee, her eyes drifted to the East Berlin address she'd found among Stefan's things. She wondered about the woman who lived there. Distracted by her thoughts, she scooped a section of grapefruit and juice squirted onto the envelope. She wiped it with her cloth napkin. At one point, she consulted a city map, but finding the street only raised more questions. She held the mysterious address in her hand, radically aware of all the information that she didn't possess. Why on earth had she waited so long to look?

There was only one place Anne knew she had a reasonable chance of getting answers. When she left her apartment, she double-locked the front door and confirmed that she had the note with the East Berlin address and the telephone number Dr Knappe had given her.

'They'll spot you lickety-split dressed like that.'

Anne turned, startled, and saw Chrystal dressed in her kimono standing in the doorway. Her short black hair was slicked back and white pancake obscured the bruise on her cheek. 'You scared the shit out of me,' Anne said.

'Better me than them.'

'Who?'

'Two men outside in a car. They've been there an hour. They're not looking for me, I assure you, not the way I look. I have something for you.' Chrystal returned from her apartment with a pale-blue burqa that she placed over Anne and fixed the veil to leave only her eyes visible. Chrystal stepped back. 'I've been waiting for just the right occasion. It's perfect. Incognito,' she said. 'The Turkish shopkeeper might know what to look for, but the two Germans in the car won't have a clue.' Chrystal put on her own burqa and the two left together.

11

ALLIED CHECKPOINT CHARLIE

A IR CRACKED WITH THE cold. Anne's fingers suffered; she'd left her gloves in the apartment again. For a while the burqa had kept her warm, but she'd given it back to Chrystal a few blocks from home. What else had she forgotten?

Anne stood in the front of a long line that snaked back to the U.S. Army security hut that occupied a traffic island in the middle of Friedrichstrasse. A line of cars on her left waited to enter a large roofed area, where East German *Grenztruppen* used mirrors on long poles to look under cars, and, on a random basis, stuck a long rod into a gas tank, looking for a false compartment that could be used to smuggle people. Everywhere guards questioned drivers and others stood back, waiting to pounce. She watched the brusque movements of the East Germans, but military vehicles parked in the shadow of a side street caught her attention. She recognized the Soviet battalion marking on the Ural troop transport, and she also knew that the 7th Guards Division was supposed to be stationed in Dessau-Rosslau, 120 kilometers to the southwest. She stared. *What was it doing in Berlin?*

'Next.'

Anne stepped up to the Plexiglas window and slipped her passport in the slot toward the young border guard, who took her documents. He wore a high crown cap with black visor, forest-green epaulets, and a stern expression. He looked twice at her passport, and her military credentials, matching face to photo, comparing the likeness with the skeptical expression of immigration officers everywhere, looking for a reason to doubt the documents.

'Glasses.'

Anne removed her dark glasses.

'What business?'

She was prepared to tell the guard she was employed by the U.S. Army with business at the American consulate on Unter den Linden, but that wasn't necessary. Noise and shouts came from the line of cars. East German troops jumped from the rear of a military transport that pulled up. Urgent orders followed the shriek of a siren, and then the drama of a man plucked from a car waiting to pass to West Berlin. An uncertain moment filled the border crossing, and all eyes watched the poor man being dragged past snarling guard dogs to a livery van parked beside a Soviet T-62 tank.

The young guard returned Anne's passport, and waved her through, dismissing her, no longer interested in what she had to say. Her last stop was a bank kiosk, where she was required to exchange twenty-five West marks for the same number of East marks – inflated currency no one wanted.

*

Anne found herself at the corner of Krausenstrasse, standing in the shadow of Axel Springer's glass tower that cast its iconic presence across the divided city, a beacon of hope mocking East Berlin. The tower was her compass point on the unfamiliar street. East Berlin was a city she'd seen from her apartment window, but never visited. It felt both close and faraway, remote and familiar. She'd made a mental map, but landmarks were different in little ways, and she struggled to find her bearings.

Anne walked hesitantly, hoping to avoid the *Volkspolizei* deployed in pairs at intersections to disperse protesters.

To remain inconspicuous, Anne joined a bus stop queue and used her place in line to look around. High on a lamppost she spotted a video camera projecting from a swivel arm; in the gap between two buildings, she saw another; she suspected a third surveillance camera in the bull's eye of the target on the giant billboard that admonished East Berliners to be vigilant against NATO provocateurs. Surveillance everywhere, everyone being watched. She knew the best chance to go unnoticed was to fit in. When several people grew impatient waiting for the long-delayed bus, she followed a man and set out on foot, mumbling, 'I'm late. I can't wait any longer.'

The cold November afternoon fogged her breath and the meager sun was pale on the gray sky. The city Anne walked through was starkly different from her familiar, lively West Berlin, with its abundantly stocked shops and colorfully dressed pedestrians. In West Berlin, trees cut for firewood during the war had been replanted, but not in the East. Anne saw empty streets, muted colors, a grim sameness, and people who kept to themselves. Everywhere she turned there were vulgar apartment blocks next to dilapidated Beaux Arts buildings that had survived the bombing, their graceful facades still showing the shrapnel damage from street fighting in the final days of the war. Brown coal smoke hung in the sky and laid down a fine layer of soot. She saw a dulled humanity and a dispirited world. But occasionally, her eye caught a swatch of color – pink flowers in a planter on a high window, a schoolgirl's blue scarf, a teenager's flame-orange spiked hair.

Crossing the street, she hopped out of the way of an exhaust-spewing bus. Anne had come to a part of the city whose street signs had been removed to confuse outsiders, and she found herself on a large, mostly empty *platz*. Worried she was lost, Anne approached a middle-aged woman, asking for directions, but as she did, the woman saw Anne's red down jacket. The startled woman waved Anne off, taking refuge behind a brusque plea that she didn't speak English, even though Anne's question was asked in perfect German. Suddenly, there was yelling, and the woman glanced at the commotion. Plainclothes police confronted three teenagers who stood on a cement bench in front of the fountain. The two boys wore steel-studded leather jackets with safety pin epaulets, spiked hair, heavy boots, and defiant swaggers. The girl had a dog collar around her neck and her head was shaved so that only a short tuft hung down in front. They allowed themselves to be pulled off the bench, resisting with an indifferent attitude, but one pulled his elbow from the policeman's grip and began to yell. Another policeman took the punk teenager's arms, punching him twice in the head to subdue the kid. He dropped to the ground, going limp, and was dragged away screaming.

The woman drew close to Anne and pointed toward the U-Bahn station's entrance. 'One stop,' she said. She quickly gave Anne directions for what to do when she got off. And then she left, hurrying away.

*

Upon emerging from the underground station, Anne looked at the woman's directions that she had written down. She passed through a neighborhood heavily bombed in the war that was still a patchwork of empty lots among neglected architectural gems of the old Berlin. Window shades were closed, but then she saw one person peeking out at her, and then she noticed others.

Anne matched the address to apartment numbers on the street. She had learned Berlin's idiosyncratic system long ago. Numbers went up one side of the street and then continued in sequence back down, so #2 of such and such building was opposite #92. The confusing system, she thought, was the only thing the divided city shared.

The building Anne stood before had graceful casement windows, an elegant cornice at the fifth floor, and stone balconies. She approached the front door, trying to look inconspicuous by acting purposefully. Residents' names were listed on an aluminum panel. She confirmed the apartment number from the envelope. The name on the panel was unfamiliar.

'Can I help you?'

Anne was startled to find at her side a large woman in a snug overcoat and a conservative blouse buttoned to the neck. Her sculpted bouffant hairdo made her look tall.

'Who are you looking for?'

Anne hardly understood the rapidly spoken, guttural German from Saxony. Anne gave the surname from the directory. 'Herr Newmann.'

'You must be mistaken. There is no man in that apartment.'

'A woman then.'

'Petra Newmann.'

'Yes, that's her. I am conducting a survey.' Anne could see the woman knew it was a lie. *Petra*. A name. Anne felt the neighbor's eyes on her as she climbed the stairwell.

Apartment 5A was at the end of the hall. Anne took in everything at once. Rubber doormat, newspapers wrapped in twine, a soccer ball, and a boy's bicycle. A peephole in the green door and the number – a paste-on silver decal.

Suddenly, she felt an urgent desire to leave. It struck Anne that this was a terrible idea, but just then the door opened.

A boy stood before her, maybe fourteen years old. 'What do you want?'

Anne recognized him from the photograph. She saw the likeness – Stefan's dark hair, his lanky frame, the same wary, inquisitive eyes. In the photograph, he proudly wore a Young

98

Pioneer's uniform, but the boy in front of her had spiked hair, an AC/DC T-shirt, blue jeans held together with safety pins, and boots.

'Mom, it's for you.'

From inside the apartment. 'Who is it?'

'A woman.'

The boy's mother appeared at the door, wiping her hands vigorously on a cotton apron. 'Yes?'

Anne had rehearsed what she would say, but she wasn't prepared for this moment. She imagined a plain woman, or a woman who'd gained weight in middle age with the careless eating of someone who lived in a rationed economy. Nothing prepared her for the tall, attractive redhead who stood at the door. Under her apron she wore a forest-green blouse that matched her hazel eyes and a delicate silver necklace hung low where her top button was undone on freckled pale skin. Anne thought she was her age, or younger. Her arm was around her son's shoulder.

'Can I help you?'

Anne began to tremble.

The woman sent her son inside, out of the way, and closed the door, leaving the two of them alone in the hallway. She didn't smile at Anne, but she nodded, as if expecting her.

'I wondered when you would show up,' she said.

12

THE PIANO TUNER'S TWO WIVES

'Come in quickly,' Petra said. 'My neighbor will notice. She'll ask questions.'

Anne walked through a small vestibule crowded with athletic equipment, boots, and haphazardly arranged jackets and umbrellas of a household that wasn't expecting a visitor. There was an old building smell, like her own apartment, where the mustiness of age was embedded in the walls, ceiling, and floor. She entered a living room that was washed in late afternoon light. The furniture was modern and sterile – tans, olive greens, and soft pastels that were bleached of vibrant color. A globe chandelier hung from the ceiling, but it was missing one bulb. The walls were without art or photographs. The room had a pleasant feeling but little charm. Anne was directed to sit on a low, upholstered sofa that faced a boxy television cabinet with rabbit ears. An ancient vacuum tube radio sat prominently on an antique breakfront.

'Well,' Petra said. 'Here you are. Can I offer you drink? Tea or water?'

'Coffee.'

'There is no coffee. I don't drink coffee.'

'Tea then.'

Anne saw the boy through a half-open bedroom door, but when she smiled, he withdrew. A strange sense of dislocation came over Anne. Without any conscious effort on her part, she looked for evidence of Stefan's other life – his secret life. Or was his life in West Berlin his secret life? A few books stood on shelves like objets d'art, placed for show, and Anne rose to look. She removed one, then another, recognizing the canon of acceptable Socialist literature: Bertolt Brecht and Anna Seghers, which were mixed with the dull writings of party apparatchiks in the Writers Union. None of the books had the illicit joys of fiction, or the subversive tendencies of Nabokov and Borges, whose volumes sat on bookshelves in her Bethaniendamm apartment. So different, she thought. The apartments didn't represent the lifestyle of two halves of one man – they belonged, it seemed, to two different men. Her eyes settled on a framed family photograph sitting on the television.

'That,' Petra said, seeing Anne's interest as she set down the teacups, 'was our family vacation last summer.' Petra poured hot water from an electric kettle. 'How did you know to come here?'

'There was a letter with an address. I found the boy's photograph.'

'His name is Peter.'

'He looks like his father.'

'He is rebellious. He listens to the wrong music. His friends are older. They have been detained, questioned, and expelled from school. He insists on wearing his hair that way. One day he'll get in trouble just like Stefan got in trouble at Peter's age. They are alike.' Petra nodded at the photograph. 'You keep looking. Would you like to see it?'

'Yes, if you don't mind.'

'Mind? Why should I mind?'

Anne took the color photograph that Petra held out. Stefan wore red bathing briefs, his arm was around his son, who held his mother's hand. She wore a skimpy bikini. All of them were smiling for the camera. She recognized his briefs – a birthday gift from her. Behind them, the wide sandy beaches disappeared into a blue ocean of white caps, and on the beach topless women and naked men sunbathed.

'It was last August on the Baltic. Usedom Island. Our annual holiday.'

Anne stared at the photograph, fingers holding it tightly, and felt dizzy. *August?* she thought. It would have been during the time of his trip to Madrid for a difficult job with an unpredictable pianist. Three days became two weeks. He claimed his tan came from the Spanish sun.

She recognized Stefan's easy smile in the photograph, but his arm around his son's shoulder and his look of adoring affection were new. The picture opened up emotions in her, seeing him in his other life, startled by what she didn't know about him. Happy for him. Angry at him. Remembering their conversations about having a child together.

'He loved the boy, didn't he?' Anne said.

'He's his son. What father doesn't love his son. People fall in love, they marry, divorce. But a parent's love for a child is a fixed thing that never changes. Like the North Star.'

Anne stared at Petra. The choice of words. He had quoted Shakespeare to her, that love was an ever-fixed mark, explaining the reference to the North Star, and suddenly in her mind she heard Stefan say, 'You're the only one I've read to in bed.' Anne wanted to ask Petra if he'd read to her. She looked at the picture. The boy. Anne remembered their arguments about having a child. Too soon he'd said. Too difficult. Too complicated with his travel. Now, she knew why he'd resisted. She felt cheated.

Stefan had been gone almost a month. Anne felt his absence like a widening distance. Each new fact about him became another nail in the coffin of her past. She felt the first stirrings of acceptance. Those were the feelings that danced in her mind as she gazed at the photograph.

She handed it back to Petra. 'He's dead, you know.'

The impulse to hurt this woman – his other wife – came suddenly, without thinking. Innocent malice. She had rehearsed a different, kinder, way of delivering the news, but the photograph conspired against her urge to be sympathetic. Jealousy was not what she had expected to feel.

'I didn't know.' Petra's hand rose to her mouth, hiding her surprise. Her face blanched. She crossed the room and closed her son's door. Again, she sat opposite Anne.

'When?'

'The day of the Leipzig protests.' And then Anne remembered. 'October 7.'

'I'm not surprised.'

'Why not?'

Petra had lowered her head, but looked up. 'There was always that danger. What happened?'

'He drowned.'

'I'll need to bring him back. He has a family plot in Friedrichsfelde Central Cemetery with his parents.'

Anne felt an unexpected competition. Which of them had a better claim to his funeral? 'The body hasn't been found.'

'Was it violent? Peter will ask me and I will need to have answers.'

'There is an investigation. The circumstances are uncertain.' Anne watched Petra take in the news. 'I thought you should know.' Then, as they sat across from each other, Anne found the grace to give Petra comfort. She began to provide some of the details. Part of her felt deep empathy for this woman who had shared Stefan, and who felt his loss.

Petra stood. She took Anne in her arms, hugging her. 'Thank you.'

Anne initially resisted the embrace, uncomfortable with the affection of a rival, but gave into a mutual sympathy. Two women, different but similar. One brunette, one redhead, both tall, one olive-toned and the other pale and freckled. They had shared a husband. Two wives now two widows. Both victims of the Matchmaker with a shared past that Petra knew and Anne was discovering. They sat opposite each other and talked for an hour. Fear, jealousy, and apprehension were swept away by compassion and all the fragile emotions that come when looking into the mirror of death.

'You had your Stefan,' Petra said. 'I had mine. Which was the real Stefan? Perhaps they were both real.'

Petra looked at Anne. 'He was fond of you.'

Anne could only imagine why Stefan had told Petra about the details of his other wife. She wanted to ask, but instinct told her it was better not to know. Petra and Anne talked about their lives, their backgrounds – two strangers getting to know each other by sharing intimate life details. They discussed their childhoods, their family backgrounds, and how marriage brought each of them to Berlin. As they talked, they grew closer. They tried to create one past, filling in the other half of a husband's life.

Dark clouds had moved across the window when Petra said, 'You are me. We are the same. The same woman. Our stories are different, but our suffering is the same.'

Petra sat back, lost in contemplation.

'What's next for you?' Anne said.

Petra shrugged. 'He was gone most of the time. Now he's not coming back.' She nodded at the closed bedroom door. 'I need to think how I will share the news with my son. They were close.' She paused. 'Even when he was stopped by the Stasi because of his spiked hair.'

Anne stood to leave.

'Sit. There's time. The border doesn't close for hours. Don't you have other questions?'

Questions? Anne only had questions.

'Please stay with Peter for an hour. All of this will come out. It is better if he knows you, even if only a little, so he doesn't wonder about you. I was on my way to the store when you arrived. Stay with him while I finish the errand.'

*

Anne joined Peter on the roof of the apartment building, where ominous clouds threatened a storm and the wind had picked up. He moved quickly to show off his caged doves. Anne's eager interest in his hobby dissolved Peter's initial coolness and brightened his face. Slowly, bit by bit, the fourteen-year-old warmed to Anne. She listened to his explanation of the birds' abilities and instincts, and she saw that he was clever and smart. Being with him reminded Anne of how much she wanted a son. Even in their brief time together, she enjoyed his company and developed an affection for him.

'How do you know my father?' Peter asked, looking up at the threatening sky.

'We worked together.' It wasn't the truth, but it wasn't a lie.

'He likes his work,' Peter said. 'He promised that one day I would visit London with him.'

'Really?'

'Yes. I got my passport. We're going soon.' He hesitated, but then added, 'Let me show you.' He opened a padlocked door to a small rooftop shed. He pointed to a cassette recorder attached to a radio with wire antennas that wrapped the interior of the shed. 'I've recorded all the Sex Pistols' albums.'

Peter lifted a homemade electric guitar with sound box cut into hollow wood and electronics taken from other appliances. He slipped the strap over his shoulder and inserted the jack into a vacuum tube amplifier. He plucked the steel strings while his left hand slid over the frets, testing the pitch of each note and tweaked the guitar's pegs until he was satisfied the instrument was in tune. And then, suddenly, he launched into the loud, brash violent chords of an incendiary song, his fingers moving quickly over the frets with practiced precision. His eyes were closed, his head bobbed, and she heard him quietly sing the English lyrics. '*There is no future. No future for you...*' His right hand was fisted and his middle and ring fingers were fused in a congenital deformity. He saw her notice and he stopped suddenly. His hand dropped to his side, self-conscious, and then he returned the guitar to its stand. He smiled at Anne. 'My favorite song. "God Save The Queen."'

Peter was excited to tell his mother about the dove he'd released into the rain that returned to Anne's hand, but he didn't mention the guitar or the shed. Petra put down her shopping bag. Mother and son were talking rapidly to each other in the shorthand of a close family. They hurried to his room to continue the conversation. Anne overheard the boy say he liked the woman who worked with his father.

'He plays the guitar well,' Anne said when Petra returned.

'His father's talent.' She looked at Anne. 'So, you saw his fingers. He compensates. It's not a difficult operation but I don't trust the doctors at Charité. And there's no money. Wait here.' She returned to the kitchen with her shopping bag.

Alone, Anne moved to a window and glanced toward West Berlin. Beyond the raised cement scar that cleaved the sixty meters of death zone, she could see apartment houses along Bethaniendamm.

Her building was there in the middle of the curving street. She took in the short distance of the divide, but then her eyes settled on the colored glass vases that sat on Petra's window sill. She took one, then another, studying them. Five vases, five colors. She remembered Stefan's sketches.

'If I wanted to see him, I placed them in one order. If I had an urgent message, I placed them in a different order. We had a code. That's how we communicated.'

'And this arrangement?' Anne asked. 'What does it mean?'

Petra shrugged. 'Nothing. You can see your apartment

from here.' Petra was at Anne's side. 'It's there just before the Church.' Petra handed her the binoculars that sat on the sill.

Anne saw the red tile mansard roof, and dropping her line of sight a few degrees, she saw her apartment windows – venetian blinds down, slats open. Had she left them that way? She adjusted focus and looked into the living room. Storm clouds darkened the day, but dim afternoon light spilled onto the floor, illuminating the rug.

Anne was about to turn away when she saw a movement in the room. Someone was in her apartment. She turned sharply and faced Petra.

'What?'

'A man is in my apartment.'

Petra dismissed her concern. 'The Stasi will be removing anything that implicates Stefan. They'll also try and make you think you're crazy. They'll rearrange the pictures on the wall. Change the time on your clocks. You'll look at the wall and think, "that's not how the picture was hung." It's their harassment. They'll want to protect his network. They'll want to intimidate you. Silence you.'

Anne looked at Petra. 'They don't know he's dead.'

'You don't know what they know.'

'I haven't told anyone else.'

'If you know, others suspect. They're smart.' Petra's face became grave. 'When I saw him last, he thought he had been found out. He didn't know who.' Petra looked at Anne. 'He thought you were suspicious.'

God, Anne thought. Who was this woman who Stefan trusted enough to share his deepest suspicions? 'I stopped believing his excuses.'

Suddenly, a loud knock at the door. Then a pounding. Both women were startled.

'Stasi?' Anne said.

Petra pointed Anne to the bedroom. 'Wait there.'

Anne hid behind the closed door, certain that her anxious thoughts could be heard in the other room. Consciously slowing her breathing, she tried to control the fear that settled into her whole being. She closed her eyes and listened for voices, but the words were indistinct. Across the darkened room she saw Petra's queen-size bed. She banished images of Petra's legs wrapped around Stefan, making love.

'Anne, come out.'

Anne emerged from the bedroom and found Petra speaking to the stout woman with the sculpted bouffant hairdo.

'Oh, it's you again,' the woman said.

'This is Carlota, my neighbor,' Petra said. Then to Carlota. 'The other woman.'

'Hmmm.' Carlota looked Anne up and down like a discerning shopper evaluating a cut of meat. 'What took you so long. You must be the world's most uncurious wife.'

Petra nudged Carlota. 'Shhhh.'

Carlota glanced at the boy's bedroom. 'Have you met the boy? He is no longer a child. He's an adolescent filled with doubt. Always listening to music that sounds like a pig being slaughtered. When his adolescence ends, so will his doubt.'

Anne listened to the woman express loud, dangerous opinions about the GDR. She openly mocked living in East Berlin. 'We need to pretend we live in a Socialist utopia free of capitalist greed, free of unemployment, free of consumer goods, free of privacy.'

Having started her tirade, Carlota went on at length. 'The man you saw outside sweeps the sidewalk all day. His job isn't a job, but he always looks busy. He pretends to work and they pretend to pay him. He's a meatloaf with mush for brains. Everything he says is a silly maxim: Sooner or later you die; A good divorce can improve a bad marriage; You learn something new every day. All nonsense.'

Carlota, who hadn't given any reason for her visit, was

suddenly gone, leaving without explaining why she had come.

Anne turned to Petra. 'She should keep her mouth shut. She'll get in trouble with the Stasi talking like that.'

Petra waved her hand dismissively. 'It's a clever act. She is the Stasi. Our neighborhood informer. *Inoffizielle mitarbeiter.* Your visit will be reported. She's probably making the call now.'

13

THE MATCHMAKER

THE LIGHTNING WAS DISTANT and dramatic, bright flashes illuminating a dark, stormy sky, bathing the somber street in pools of glistening silver. Buildings reflected the illumination and successive strobe-like flashes lit up men running in the street. A figure disappeared and then was there when the next brilliant bolt carved the sky.

Nothing was predictable, Anne thought, as she walked quickly toward the U-Bahn station to make her way to the border crossing before it closed. The weather. His other wife. She went to meet Petra to satisfy her curiosity and unload her anger. Instead she came away feeling sisterly toward Petra. It wasn't a feeling that she expected, but she didn't resist it. When they hugged upon parting, she felt warmth toward the woman she had wanted to dislike. Nothing was as it seemed.

As she ran to the station's cover, the unpredictable happened. Intermittent rain hit her face, and a deluge at the end of the street marched toward her in a fury of wind and thunder. The street became a riot of men and women without umbrellas seeking cover in doorways.

Anne ran, holding her coat closed, eyes focused on the clutch of people huddled under the cover of the station. A terrible torrent was approaching. Anne stepped out of a doorway, preparing to dash across the street, when she heard a man call her name. The urgent tone and its close proximity caught her attention. The man stood a few yards away, looking right at her. He stood without coat or umbrella and stared. This man recognized her – a stranger knew who she was. Having gotten her attention, the man stepped forward.

'Frau Simpson.'

She was impatient to get away. 'Yes.'

'Come with me.' He pointed toward a black Chaika limousine parked across the street.

'I am an American citizen.' She displayed her passport. 'I'm late.'

'Of course. Come with me.'

'What is this about?'

'A formality. Follow me.'

Everything in Anne's being understood she should resist his instruction. She glanced around, looking for a way to escape, but there was only the approaching downpour and the somber faces of defeated souls staring indifferently. *Formality?* The word repeated itself in her skeptical imagination. She allowed herself to be guided to the parked limousine. He opened the front passenger door and she slid in. Just as the man sat in the driver's seat, the deluge struck. Drenching rain hit the windshield, blurring the view, and thunderous pounding on the roof produced severe claustrophobia in Anne. She went to open her door.

'We won't be long,' the man said. He had a thick neck that bulged around an overtight necktie, and his flat nose gave him the appearance of an old boxer. Having started the car, he pulled into the street peering through the blinding rain.

She became aware of a man in the back seat. He wheezed like a smoker short of breath. 'We'll get you to the border before it closes. Don't worry. And if you ride with me you won't get wet.'

Anne turned to see who spoke, but the driver's hand shot out, preventing her from looking back.

'Better to keep your eyes forward,' the wheezing man said.

Anne couldn't place the voice – polite but firm, and she heard guttural consonants from a different part of Germany. A Northern accent. From a remote German town, she thought. An old German accent.

'I understand that you've met his son. You surprised me. Perhaps you were surprised that he has a son.'

The man talked to her as if they were familiar, as if he knew her. 'Do you understand?'

She nodded. She tried to imagine the face that belonged to the voice.

'Don't worry. You're safe. But you are right to be concerned for the boy. He is already rebellious, not wearing normal clothes. No one wants to see him hurt.'

'What do you want?'

'We want the same thing. The boy shouldn't suffer.'

'Why would he suffer?'

'A boy suffers when he listens to forbidden music. He is bored in school and cuts classes. He has a bad temper and gets into fights.'

Anne heard the man flick a lighter and she smelled his cigarette.

'We got your phone message. I thought it made sense to meet tonight while you're in East Berlin. It's more convenient for me. Where is he?'

'Who?'

The man coughed. 'Stefan.'

'He's dead.'

'That's what you'd like me to believe. Have they found his body?'

Anne stared ahead into the rain.

'The dead have a way of showing up. It is only the living who hide.'

Let him talk, she thought.

'I guess you know that he worked for me. My best Romeo.'

Anne heard his cold sarcasm and felt dread. She wanted to turn around and confirm his face, but the urge passed. In her mind's eye, she saw the blurry photograph of the man's profile caught in the telephoto lens, which dissolved into the formal graduation photograph of the young, unsmiling future head of State Security's counterintelligence. Anne listened to him, a smoker, tight chest, talking in measured breaths. He explained that Stefan was a good officer, perhaps his best.

'Corruption changes even good men,' he said. 'He forgot the Socialist ideals that make us equal in the eyes of the State. He acquired a taste for material things. I didn't see it at first, but then I discovered that he'd developed a taste for bourgeois life – a professional bourgeois, with his taste for hotels, clothes, food.' The man coughed. When he spoke, his voice was full of disdain. 'I don't like people who think of themselves as professional this or that. It's fine if you're a professional singer, artist, or engineer, but I don't like professional Jews, professional homosexuals, professional feminists, or what he became. I don't like people who abdicate their individual identity to became part of some precious group, beating their breasts, proud to be this or that. It is a fraud. Oh, we have homosexuals and ambitious women, but they don't go around saying, "Look at me."'

'He developed a taste for wine and fashionable suits. He said it was expected of him by the artists he associated with. For some time, I believed him. Or perhaps, I wanted to believe him.'

The man's voice lowered. 'His theft is an unforgivable crime. His mistake was not knowing when to stop. Too many large invoices. We traced large sums to a Zurich bank. The account is waiting for someone with authorization codes to claim it.'

'He means nothing to me,' Anne said.

'These arrangements hurt women like you, but it is a cost of our Cold War.' The man exhaled. 'Boys like Peter get hurt, too, but he doesn't have to suffer. He can have his own life and grow up to make his own way. You can give him that chance.'

'I have nothing to give. I am an interpreter.'

'You have more than you think. Stefan liked you.'

She scoffed.

'He set up the bank account. You are the beneficiary. I have every reason to believe that he will contact you. When he does, you'll let us know.'

'He's dead.'

'You don't want the boy to suffer.'

She closed her eyes and the sound of the pounding rain on the roof was an unbearable drumbeat. 'What do you want?'

The man reached forward and dropped a note in her lap. 'Call this number when he contacts you. Know that we are watching.'

Anne recognized a West Berlin exchange. She crumpled the note and tossed it into the back seat. 'Wipe your ass with it.'

Anne felt the driver's hand on her arm, and she heard the man in the back wheeze in anger. 'You don't want the boy hurt.'

'Was it easy to ruin my life?' she snapped.

There was a beat of silence. 'You're still a young woman.' He uncrumpled the note and handed it to her. 'It will come out better for everyone if you do this.'

*

Anne stepped out of the Chaika limousine into the rain. The car was stopped at the candy-striped barrier on the East Berlin side of Allied Checkpoint Charlie. Brilliant arc lamps revealed rain hitting the pavement and overflowing into gutters. The harsh light made an uncomfortable stage and she looked toward the U.S. Army security hut for shelter.

Before she dashed across the security zone, she turned to look back. An arc lamp illuminated the limousine and she caught sight of the man in the back seat. An older gentleman's face. The face of a rational man, a thinker, a man who wore his struggles behind a grim mask. It was the face she'd seen in the photograph. The same Soviet-style fedora. Calm eyes and a cigarette in his mouth. The Matchmaker.

East German border guards waved her through. She tightened her collar and ran quickly through the puddling rain, hearing only the din of the downpour. A U.S. Army military policeman with a white stripe on his green helmet waved her toward the brightly lit hut. She presented her passport, which he dismissed gruffly.

'The border is closed. You have to go back.'

Water soaked Anne's hair and ran down her face. His indifference, coming as she held out her passport, became active hostility when she pushed it toward him again, saying, 'I am an American citizen. I work at JAROC.'

'The border is closed. It opens tomorrow morning.'

Anne felt a presence at her side and then she saw Cooper. She never thought she'd be glad to see his face, but she felt relief and gratitude when he presented his security badge to the MP.

'I'll take her,' he said. 'Call the embassy if you need to. They'll verify my credentials.'

While the MP dialed a black rotary telephone, Cooper turned to Anne. 'Get what you wanted?'

Anne was surprised by Cooper's intervention and by his question.

'Go ahead,' the MP said, handing back Anne's passport.

Cooper took the passport before Anne could grasp it. 'I'll keep this for now.' He led her by the arm to his parked embassy car, opening the passenger door. He ran through the rain to the driver's side, getting soaked.

'What were you doing in East Berlin?' he asked, closing his door.

'I don't need your permission.'

'Who was in the limousine?'

'The Matchmaker.' Palpable surprise. She met his skeptical eyes. 'I'm certain it was him.'

'What did he want?'

'He's accusing Stefan of treason.' Anne repeated the Matchmaker's accusations about inflated invoices, expense account fraud, and the numbered bank account, holding back only a description of the man. 'Do I believe the accusations? Yes. Stefan enjoyed living well and he wanted to move to London. They are threatening the boy. I won't be responsible for that.'

'What does that mean?'

She turned to him. 'What do you think it means?' Anne grabbed Cooper's arm. 'When they discover that Stefan is dead, the boy and the mother will be arrested.'

'It's not our business.'

'It's my business,' she said flatly. 'The boy is fourteen. He shouldn't have to suffer.' There was a beat of silence. She looked at Cooper. 'I want you to get them West German passports.'

Cooper drove through the rain-swept street. Silence settled between them.

'What are you going to say, "it's not authorized?"' Her sarcasm came sharply.

'Don't go there.'

'Where is that?'

Cooper hit the steering wheel with his palm. 'I can't do it. I just can't.'

*

Anne invited Cooper up to her apartment. She poured herself a whiskey and looked at him like he was an old friend about whom she was having second thoughts. She offered him a glass and he joined her. They stood at the window and looked out toward East Berlin. Winds had swept away the storm and the sky was a canopy of stars. She handed him the binoculars and pointed to Petra's apartment.

'Look at the vases in the window. That is how they communicated. The building with the two chimneys.'

'There's nothing to see.'

'Fourth floor window on the right. The vases in the window. They had a code. The arrangement of the vases, the different colors, meant something. Danger. Meet up. Like his drawings.'

'Did you suspect him?'

'Suspect?' She said the word carelessly. 'I was surprised by his morbid fascination with the rabbits. I wondered about that.' She pondered Cooper's question. It was the second time he had asked. 'At some point you have to trust your husband. Otherwise why are you together?'

She finished her whiskey and suggested they go to the roof. They climbed one flight of stairs and emerged from a bulkhead onto the peaked roof. The rain had stopped. Winds had blown away the cloud cover and left a night sky with a pincushion of stars.

Anne had thrown a sweater over her shoulders, but otherwise endured the November chill. Not cold enough to snow, but too cold to be outside without an overcoat. They stood on a narrow walkway that ran along the peaked roof's ridge between opposing chimneys. Stars above winked. The drenching storm had dampened protesters' bonfires, and wispy smoke rose straight up from smoldering wood across the city. Above all that, the television tower at Alexanderplatz blinked blue like a giant Christmas ornament. Laughter of protesters carried across the clear night air and mixed with songs of protest.

Both halves of Berlin lay before them, joined under the vast celestial canopy. West Berlin was bright with the cacophony of nightlife, streets were rivers of moving cars, and somewhere a distant siren responded to an emergency. Its sister city was a darker, quieter place. Rude new buildings and crouching older homes looked sad in their darkness. Roads were ghostly. The dim glow of ten thousand candles rose from Pariser Platz by the Brandenburg Gate.

Anne stood next to Cooper. He'd put his coat on her shoulders, and she'd wrapped her arms around her chest to stay warm, but still she shivered. He wore only his shirt, but was obstinately stoic in the cold.

'I think he's alive,' she said, meeting his startled eyes.

She pointed across the brightly lit death zone to the rows of dim apartment buildings that followed the curving Engeldamm. Petra's window was lit and the venetian blinds were open. She handed Cooper the binoculars.

'The order of the vases has changed again. She is signaling him.' She paused. 'No body. The Matchmaker's claim. Too many coincidences.'

14

CLAY HEADQUARTERS

EARLY NOVEMBER

THE AMATEUR HAS ONE advantage over the professional. Free of experience that can make an investigator overly cautious, the amateur can move forward recklessly. The clever adversary will anticipate the predicable actions of the professional, but for the same reason the amateur's bold choices go unanticipated and enjoy the advantage of surprise.

Winslow and Praeger believed that Stefan was dead. It suited their purposes to believe he was dead. And because it was in their interest to operate on that assumption, they never fundamentally considered that he might be alive.

No one took Anne seriously when she first made her claim, but the confirming evidence came from Dr Knappe's sudden disappearance. He hadn't answered his telephone after she made repeated efforts to reach him. A rapid search of the cement factory, where he was a minor investor, turned up that he hadn't been seen for several days. The convincing bit came when it was discovered that his medical license was a forgery. Dr Knappe, the sole witness to the incident at the canal, was missing, and his testimony was rendered unreliable.

Anne was in Winslow's office in Clay Headquarters feeling vindicated. The four men opposite her felt a sense of quasi-victory with the news – even as it abruptly quashed their carefully formulated plans. Having better information was always welcome and would result in a new approach – and a better plan.

This conclusion came from Winslow. He said it at the end of a longer summary. He rose from the conference table after hearing from Anne, and paced the room, hands behind his back, head bowed slightly, and began expounding upon the new facts. Winslow was a careful thinker who didn't resist controversial facts that upset conventional wisdom, but he could also be quick to embrace expedient alternatives to stubborn problems.

Anne didn't know what to make of his casual thinking out loud. She watched him pace, trying to understand him, and where he was going with his suggestions. She had felt uncomfortable in the room during her first visit – intimidated by the four men with their deep rivalries and haunted by Nazi ghosts – but now having their attention gave her confidence.

'So!' Winslow had stopped in the center of the room. He stared at Anne. 'All his precautions for what purpose? His missing body. The wallet. A false witness. If he wanted to escape, he could have done so. Why didn't he just take his money and head for Argentina or Istanbul? He didn't have to create this fiction. So why did he? The boy? You say it's about the boy?'

'Yes.'

Winslow pondered. 'So, you would have us believe that he knew he was taking a risk, but if he could convince the Stasi – and us – that he was dead he had a chance of getting his son and his wife out of East Germany.'

Anne looked across the conference table. 'Gestapo chief Heinrich Müller was never captured or confirmed dead. He's still missing. Stefan would know that and he'd use it, replicate it.'

Praeger stood. He walked to the massive stone fireplace and suddenly turned to her. 'Has he recruited you for his game?'

Cooper laughed.

Anne felt Praeger's eyes on her, studying her, as if he were trying to look inside her mind. 'If I said no, would you believe me?'

Winslow put his hand on Praeger's shoulder, but the German ignored the gesture. He leaned on the wooden conference table and looked directly at Anne and around the table. 'Can I summarize what we know?'

Praeger waited for an objection, but got none. 'This started as a missing persons investigation. It became a murder investigation. Now it's a manhunt.' He looked at Anne. 'You can understand how, as the person who lived with him, who decided to make an unauthorized trip to East Berlin to visit his wife, you are a person of interest to us.'

Praeger pulled a manila envelope from his leather portfolio. He removed several black-and-white photographs that he pushed toward Anne. 'Look at these men. Have you seen them?'

Anne pushed them back. 'I don't need to look. Have the faces changed?'

'Humor us,' Praeger said.

Anne looked at Cooper, who nodded to do as requested. 'Can I have my passport back?'

Cooper slid it across the table.

Anne remembered each photograph. A few mug shots. Photographs taken with a telephoto lens. Blurred faces that were hard to make out. She paused on one grainy photograph and studied the older man. There was a similarity in the jawline, and the vanity of a man who hadn't gained weight with age. She pushed it back.

'I know the hat. He was wearing it in the car. He is a smoker with asthma. I haven't seen any of the others.'

Winslow studied the photograph, but the blurred image didn't give up reasonable details of identity. 'Rudolf Kruger,' he said, as if to say the name was to confirm the identity of the person in the photograph.

'What about these?' Praeger presented Anne with color

photographs of Stefan Koehler. One photograph showed him in the Vienna train station in the company of a blond woman. Another in Madrid with a dark-haired woman at a café. There were photographs of him in Beirut, Lisbon, Bonn. In some he was close to his companion, whispering. Other photographs captured a kiss.

Anne flipped them away. 'He worked for the Stasi. He lied to me. What am I supposed to say? He had girlfriends.'

Praeger's eyes were skeptical. 'This is a man who loved his son?'

Anne stared at Praeger across the table with fierce eyes. When she stood, she glanced at defiantly at Cooper and Winslow. She shoved one arm into the sleeve of her raincoat, and then the other, cinching the belt at her waist.

'I don't need this.' She marched to the door, but stopped before leaving and turned suddenly. 'I'll be at home if you want to arrest me.'

*

Anne trudged up the wooden stairs to her apartment, feeling the weight of their collective indifference and the new burden of Berlin life. Walking through the underpass at the Berlin Zoo Station by a Beate Uhse sex shop, looking past the prostitutes and panhandlers, she had seen a man following her. He was half a block back in a ski cap and leather jacket when she passed punks drinking at Kottbusser Tor, and he was a lurking presence outside the U-Bahn station. She usually took the stairs two at a time to stay fit when she hadn't gone for a morning jog, but that evening she climbed slowly, delaying her return.

She no longer thought of the apartment as hers – it was Stefan's apartment. She'd moved in with him. It was hers only through the fraud of their shattered marriage. Now, his ghost laid claim to the place.

Anne entered without turning on the light and dropped her handbag to the floor. She stood in the dark. She didn't want to be reminded of him by the apartment and his things. She had an impulse to walk out and leave Berlin, disappearing the way that he had disappeared. Gone. Vanished. No trace. She would start over in a city that she'd never visited: Vancouver, or Singapore, or Buenos Aires. Anonymous among strangers.

Anne held her passport. Inside her handbag was her address book, wallet, and the Krugerrands. How easy it would be. She had done it before. Run off. That's how she came to Berlin. How much money would she need to start over? The Krugerrands would buy a plane ticket, but that wouldn't be enough. Suddenly, she opened the drawer where she'd seen Stefan hide private papers, and searched the jumble of envelopes for bank statements, handwritten notes, anything where he might hide a paper with the details of the Swiss bank account. It wasn't there. From the depths of her disappointment came despair and then an urge to be rid of him.

She angrily emptied Stefan's desk into a large plastic garbage bag. First, she swept the top of the desk, and then she dumped out each drawer. His tailored two-piece suits hung in the closet. She tore them from the hangers and stuffed them into a garbage bag and then she threw away his starched shirts, Ferragamo ties, sweaters, and his large collections of Italian loafers. She removed socks and underwear from the dresser's top drawer and came upon an open box of lubricated rubbers, which she dropped into the bag. As she purged the apartment, she found the cracked wedding picture. She got rid of it, too.

'What are you doing?'

Anne was dumping the garbage bags in the hallway when Chrystal's door opened. Anne saw her neighbor's startled expression at the huge pile.

'Housecleaning.'

Chrystal held a silk necktie that she'd retrieved from one

bag. 'I'll keep this if you don't mind. I need these for my day job. Let me know if I can be of help. So much stuff. I can't imagine what would happen if I moved.'

It took Anne two hours to efface Stefan from the apartment. She rid it of his possessions but it was harder to erase him from memory. He was in her mind; jogging beside her along the canal when she tossed out his running shoes; he was there when she swept his toiletries into the garbage bag; there, too, when she threw out his collection of Eric Ambler novels, indignantly ripping pages. He was there, like an uninvited guest, when she piled the bags in the hallway. *Good riddance,* she thought.

She bagged his things and set them outside her door, but getting rid of his physical presence didn't remove him from her thoughts. He was at the kitchen door chatting with her when she searched the refrigerator for a beer. He stood by while she watched television, reminding her that she was drinking too much. She threw her glass at him – the ghost of him – and it shattered on the wall.

Anne slipped into a cold bath. She shivered as the frigid water surrounded her and the chill took her breath away. She slipped down so the water came up to her chin. Slowly, she gave in to the numbing cold. It was a thing that she did as a teenager when she wanted to block out her parents' furious arguments.

Cold purged fear and anxiety and opened up an empty mental space where she could clarify where she was in her life. She closed her eyes and heard her mother's quiet sobbing. How frightening it had been to see a grown woman weep, defeated, like that. Anne felt the cold making her warm, losing sensation, and a quiet peacefulness brought down a dark curtain on her thoughts.

Her eyes snapped open. She sat up, violently coughing water from her throat, and breathed deeply. Her skin was pale blue and her fingers wrinkled like a newborn's.

Anne stepped out of the bath and got into bed naked,

wrapping herself in the covers until her terrible shivering stopped. Warmth came peacefully under the blankets, relaxing her. She pulled the pillow over her face, blocking out the street light, and felt comforting darkness.

A thought came to her. A way out. She considered the idea, tested it against its many dangers, but it slowly took hold. She knew what she would do.

15

BACK TO EAST BERLIN

NOVEMBER 8

WINSLOW STOOD AT THE open window of the old Berlin building that looked down on Checkpoint Charlie's U.S. Army security hut. It was not yet 9:00 a.m. He adjusted the focus of his M19 army binoculars to sharpen the image

'There she is.'

Seventy-five yards away a woman was stepping into the queue of people waiting to pass through East German border control.

He cleaned the lenses that had fogged from cold air coming through the window, and he looked again at Anne presenting her papers. She wore a scarf on her head, dark glasses, and tan raincoat.

'How can you be sure?' Praeger asked.

'The coat. And she's predictable.' Winslow looked at Praeger. 'That's why returning her passport was the right thing.'

They watched Anne move to the head of the queue, trying to look inconspicuous, but in doing so, appearing nervous.

Praeger grunted. Proven wrong, he was silent. He saw Anne in her raincoat. The line was mostly foreign businessmen and a few tourists, and the vehicle lane had old Volkswagens and Trabants waiting their turn. Everything was being checked.

'Is she alone?'

'Cooper is there. He already passed through.'

'I thought she was going first.'

'If she's stopped, we abort. He'll keep out of sight. She won't know he's there unless things go wrong.'

'Something always goes wrong,' Praeger said.

Winslow didn't answer. He handed Praeger the olive-green 7x binoculars and took the cup of coffee held by an orderly. Cold air sweeping in the open window drew steam off the hot drink, which Winslow sipped, looking at the heavily armed forces on opposite sides of the checkpoint. The 39th Special Forces Detachment observation post operated in the shadows of the Cold War's front line; a secret garrison known only to a privileged few in Clay Headquarters and their Soviet counterparts in a corresponding command post a few blocks away. Two advance outposts peering at each other, watching for early signs of hostile action. Visible to each other, but invisible to German civilians on the streets below. Soldiers of Special Forces Berlin kept surveillance of the Soviet enemy with the vigilant preparedness of frontline soldiers everywhere. They had flak jackets, assault rifles, and the grim expressions of men who knew they would be the first casualties of war.

'She has their forged passports,' Praeger said. 'She'll lead us to him, if he's alive.'

'You still think he's dead?' Winslow didn't hide his disdain.

'We'll see.' Praeger added, 'She doesn't know we found the JAROC forger she used.'

Winslow looked away. 'Don't underestimate her. She'll do what she thinks we won't expect.'

'Whose side is she on?'

'Her own.'

The beat of silence ended when Praeger said, 'I got a call from George Mueller, deputy director, CIA. I assume you know him.'

Winslow slowly turned, taking in the news that Praeger had spoken to his boss. 'What did he want?'

'He asked for an update. Why didn't he ask you? Or maybe he did and he was confirming the truth of what you told him.'

The two men stared at each other. Praeger smiled. 'He said I should keep an eye on you.'

A telephone rang somewhere in the large room. A corporal in a Kevlar helmet and body armor approached Winslow.

'There is a problem, sir.'

'What?'

'We heard from our contact in the consular office near Unter den Linden. East German soldiers have surrounded the building and are not letting anyone in or out.'

'Why?'

'They don't know. They heard the border will close today. No one will be able to cross back to West Berlin.'

'Problem?' Praeger asked.

Winslow knew that every plan carried risks, but the only bad plan was the one that didn't anticipate failure. 'The border won't stay closed forever,' Winslow said. 'Cooper's been in East Berlin before. He'll know what to do. If she's in trouble, he'll intervene. When the family crosses, we'll be there to close the trap.'

Suddenly, the boom of a low-flying airplane rattled windows and drew all eyes to the sky. A pair of Soviet MIGs carved an arc across the gray sky and then disappeared over the city. In the silence that followed, a distant rumbling could be heard, and then it became obvious to all that the ground vibrated with the approach of heavy vehicles. Anxious cries rose from the street, and when Winslow stepped to the window he saw East Germans watching lumbering Soviet tanks.

Winslow glassed the streets with the binoculars. He couldn't see Anne any longer, but he knew she must be among the crowd lined up watching the armored convoy.

'She's not there,' Praeger said.

'She's there. You don't know where to look.'

'This won't work,' Praeger said. 'The idea. A Pied Piper with false documents and a family following behind, waiting for Kruger to pounce. She's not clever enough.'

Winslow lowered the binoculars. 'She's done this before. She is confident. Maybe too confident.'

'An amateur.'

'Yes, an amateur,' Winslow turned. 'If you had your way, we'd still be looking for his body in the canal.'

The shrill ringing of an alarm brought the large room to a nervous standstill. Helmeted men had the anxious expressions of soldiers ready to face the unexpected. A yell somewhere and then Winslow joined several men who swept across the room to peer out windows on the adjacent street. Sandbags hid the black muzzles of .30 caliber machine guns.

'There!' a voice shouted.

Winslow leaned forward to look out the window. His gray hair lifted in the breeze and the chill stung his cheeks. The MIGs had made a wide arc over West Berlin airspace, crossing the invisible boundary in an obvious provocation. But it wasn't the presence of the MIGs that drew his attention.

A loud, raucous crowd gathered at the end of the narrow street. Beyond that, swelling into an open platz, there were shouting East Berliners. They passed near the twelve-foot-high concrete Wall topped with barbed wire. They were a motley crowd, full of the faces of discontent: people in blue jeans and denim jackets; others in red ski parkas and running shoes; professionals in hats and business suits; parents with children on their shoulders. Loud voices yelled. Drums were a booming rhythm that accompanied a steady chant of, 'We are people! We are not rowdies! We are people!' One man broke from the crowd and proceeded to spray paint the slogan on the Wall. Yelling protesters egged him on, a chanting chorus.

Then Winslow saw the source of the rumbling. An armored vehicle with a water canon appeared from around a corner, facing the marchers. East German *Volkspolizei* with truncheons, gas masks, and plastic shields advanced on the crowd.

'This changes things.'

Winslow turned to Praeger. 'Cooper will call it off if he needs to.'

'Some plan.'

'Go to hell,' Winslow said.

16

ALIVE

That afternoon, Stefan Koehler was alone in his Engeldamm apartment following the unfolding events on television with no flattering delusion that the changes afoot would mean an end to his troubles. He was a marked man. In every alternative he imagined, Stefan came to the conclusion that he was condemned to the guillotine in the GDR's National Execution Facility. He fully understood that his escape was the only way forward and the raucous upheaval in the streets was at best a temporary respite from the regime's manhunt.

Nevertheless, when his beloved son entered the apartment with Petra, it was easy to ignore the dangers of what he had set in motion. It had been his decision, but she had agreed, and their son understood the perils of staying. It was better to risk escape in the tunnel under the Wall than to suffer the type of separation that would come if his rebellious son was detained. There was urgency in his thoughts, too; a turbulent desire to take advantage of the demonstrations to make their escape.

In that moment, he accepted his son's embrace, but he looked at Petra standing in the doorway and saw only caution on her face.

'Was Dr Knappe there?' Stefan held his son affectionately, mussing his hair playfully.

Petra was motionless in the doorway. She met his eyes

without answering. When he became confused by her silence, she stepped to the side, revealing the person standing behind her in the hallway.

Anne Simpson stepped forward. She faced the family gathered in a tight knot. Her face was calm, but also resolute, a woman who moved cautiously into an uncertain moment.

'No one saw me,' she said. 'They are all watching the latest news of the protests on their televisions.' Anne bore her sudden appearance with dignity, nodding at Petra. 'She didn't know that I was waiting in the stairwell. She was as surprised as you are.'

Anne saw Stefan with his arm around his son's shoulder. She recognized the bond of father and son that she first saw in the beach photograph, and in the moment of their reunion there was no mistaking the boy's attachment and the father's concern. It was a bittersweet thing to see, and it reminded her of what she wanted for herself. But none of that was in her conscious mind. She stood before them aware of being watched.

'Why are you here?' Stefan asked.

'You need to ask?'

Petra quickly invited Anne in, and pulled Stefan to one side. Anne removed her scarf, but kept on her raincoat and remained standing by the television. They faced each other, awkwardness hung in the air. She stared at Stefan, taking him in all at once, the dead man come to life. He wore the handsome leather jacket she bought him on their second wedding anniversary.

Anne nodded. 'You have no idea the excitement your disappearance caused and how much interest there is in your miraculous resurrection.'

Stefan laughed nervously. He hit a cigarette pack on his arm, popping two, and offered her one. 'I've quit,' she said, accepting one anyway. He drew on his cigarette compulsively and blew smoke from the corner of his mouth, but his eyes stayed on her like a wary fugitive.

'What do you want?'

She opened her handbag and produced two forged West German passports. 'These will help them cross the border. Passports with new names.' She watched him examine the documents, flipping the pages, studying the ink, and names. He handed them back.

'I have my own way.'

'And risk them?'

Stefan drew deeply on the cigarette and kept his eye on her, judging her. 'My plan is a good plan.' He waved at the documents, dismissing them. 'Who made these? The CIA? Who is on the other side waiting?'

'They'll be safe. It was a favor. I had them made.'

'I'll be arrested.'

'You'll be alive.'

'I am prepared to take my chances.'

Tension filled the silence that followed. Without being asked, but in the spirit of hospitality to lighten the mood, Petra said that she would make tea. She forced a smile, looking from one to the other. 'I think we all need something to warm up with. To mark this occasion. Who would have thought we'd all meet?' Petra looked at Anne. 'I want to hear what you have to say.'

Two wives, no longer widows, sharing the same concern. It was a somber moment among them, and then Petra was gone to the kitchen with her son.

Anne faced Stefan across the coffee table without Petra to adjudicate their reunion. Her knee was folded over her leg, bouncing slightly, and she gazed at him. She had questions that she wanted to ask, but she wasn't certain she would believe his answers. His first lie had become a world of lies and she wasn't certain how she would know if he was being truthful. His compounding lies had become an ungainly artifice, drawing attention to itself, but she had been blind to it.

'You were good at remembering your own lies,' she said. 'I was taken in.'

He nervously drew on his cigarette and then stood, pacing the room. In a moment, he sat again and looked at his feet. She waited for him to look up.

'You owe me an answer.'

'What do you want me to say? I'm sorry? Of course, I am. I didn't choose you. They did.' He muttered something she couldn't hear. He pulled nervously on his cigarette.

She hated him, but she had once loved him. Those conflicting feelings left her uncertain whether to accost him or embrace him. She met his eyes and, for a moment, she thought he would unburden himself.

'Here.' Petra had suddenly entered from the kitchen. She set down the electric kettle and arranged the teacups she'd brought on a tray. 'Did I interrupt? Should I leave?'

'Stay,' he said.

The two women exchanged a quick glance and Petra poured the hot tea while the silence among them hung on. 'Chamomile is calming, and we need calm.'

She was returning to the kitchen when suddenly the muted television was alive with pictures of street demonstrations across the GDR. Petra turned up the volume and everyone in the room listened to the newscaster. Hated General Secretary Honecker was out, replaced by a new man. Ominous pictures of a human tide entering Alexanderplatz filled the screen. The small personal drama in the living room was overshadowed by the excited emotions on the demonstrators' yelling faces, which tested the amassed Stasi's fickle tolerance for protests. The two halves of the divided family witnessed history in the making, aware that neighborhood reservists had been called up to active duty. Television cameras looked past the vast crowd with candles toward heavily armed riot police on the side streets, waiting to strike.

Sipping tea, they anxiously watched to see if the attack would start.

'What will happen?' Petra asked. 'Will it be worse than 1953?' They had all heard the stories of the Soviet Union's brutal suppression of the workers' uprising. Cudgels swung indiscriminately at women and children and the frightening chaos in the streets when Soviet tanks rolled into a crowd, crushing students.

'We are leaving tomorrow night,' Stefan said. He set down his cup. 'The Stasi will be concerned with the protests. We will go unnoticed.'

'They are closing the border.'

Stefan shrugged. 'There are other ways.' He looked at the documents. 'These will be helpful when we're on the other side.'

'How will you cross?'

Stefan judged her. 'Better that you don't know. Your ignorance can't betray us.'

'Stop!' Petra set down her cup. 'She is here to help.' Petra looked at Anne. 'There is a tunnel. You will come with us. It will be safer for us, and you, if you join us.'

'Did they send you?' Stefan demanded.

'No one knows I'm here.'

Stefan crushed his cigarette in the ashtray, grinding it slowly, and then he looked at her. 'You don't know what they know.' Stefan went to the window and drew aside the blinds. He looked down into the street where the buildings curved along Engeldamm. He motioned to Anne.

'Look.' Stefan pointed to a man leaning against a lamppost, self-conscious with his newspaper open. 'He's been there for thirty minutes reading the same page. He followed you.'

Anne was shocked to see Cooper, but then she came to see how lucky it was that Cooper was outside and not some stranger. She knew him well enough to be confident in how to proceed, but she also understood how she'd been deceived. Knowing that Cooper had followed her was a turning point.

'He will be a problem,' Anne said. She looked at Stefan.

'When I leave, I will take him with me. The documents will be helpful when you get across.'

'You'll help us?' Peter asked.

Anne smiled. 'Of course. Is the tunnel safe?'

'Safer than staying,' Stefan said. 'He's watching the apartment. How long before others arrive?'

'We're leaving tomorrow night,' Petra said. 'Dr Knappe has arranged it.'

Anne paused. Now she understood. The eager witness with his false charm, he'd been a part of it all along. She handed Stefan the passports. 'Take them.'

Petra studied the new names and the picture of her son, dressed in his Pioneer's uniform before he'd spiked his hair. 'Who made these?'

'Someone I trust at JAROC.'

Stefan shook his head. 'They'll see these and know who they're looking for.'

'They don't want you,' Anne said. 'They want the Matchmaker.'

Stefan considered her comment and then laughed dismissively. 'Rudolf Kruger is like a dead man to them. We talk about the dead to remember them and keep them in our thoughts. The more people talk, the more that is said about the dead, particularly by people who are good with words, the further away from life the dead person becomes – he becomes a hologram. An invention of their fears and paranoias to whom they attribute all sorts of unlikely accomplishments. They can have Kruger if they can find him.'

'And you?' Anne asked.

'I'm not dead yet.' Stefan mussed his son's hair. 'I'm alive. I prefer it that way. We can do this ourselves.'

Petra put her arm on Anne's shoulder, comforting her, and turned to Stefan. 'Why are you stubborn?'

'You don't need my help.' Anne moved to the door.

'We do.' Petra's hand on Anne's arm stopped her. '*I*

need your help. *My son* needs your help.'

Anne saw the plea in Petra's eyes. In that moment, Anne was moved by her rival's concern. Her red hair, hazel eyes, her dignity, and her plea. Anne could only imagine what Petra's life had been like in those two years – her fears, the deprivation, her son's rebelliousness; she wondered if the tall confident woman asking for help had felt the terror of jealousy.

Anne turned to Stefan. 'And you?'

Anne recognized his stubborn German pride and there, too, behind his smug assurance, the remoteness that had always been between them. The person who'd been so close, but also so faraway. Even now she didn't know him.

'We accept,' Petra said. 'We leave tomorrow. I will dress like I'm going to work. Peter will have his backpack as he does every day when he goes to school. Everything normal.'

Petra nodded at Stefan. 'He will leave after us. You will drive with him – a couple together won't attract attention. The Stasi are looking for a single man. Together you will be safer. We will all meet at the address.'

'Whose car?'

'Dr Knappe parked across the street. Stefan has the keys.'

Stefan pushed aside the venetian blind and looked down at the pale-green Trabant parked near Cooper. 'Tomorrow there will be another protest,' Stefan said. 'We will drive in the opposite direction. If we are stopped, we will say we're going to Charité hospital.'

'The address?'

'When we are in the car.'

Anne said goodbye and moved to the apartment door. Upon stepping into the hallway, she heard her name called and she turned.

'You should be careful,' Stefan said.

'What do you expect,' she said. 'And what about your neighbor?'

'No one has seen her.'

17

JUST OFF INSELSTRASSE

ANNE KNEW THAT THE best way to hide her surprise was to appear indifferent, and so she approached Jim Cooper from the opposite side of the street, wearing a headscarf and white-framed sunglasses. She walked right up to him, startling him. She thought he was a comic figure standing by himself, trying to appear inconspicuous. November's dusk had brought a light snow and an early winter. Flakes drifted, moving one way then another on the quiet street.

'I expected you,' she said, touching his coat in a familiar way to put him at ease. 'I guess you had no trouble finding the address.'

Cooper was visibly startled. 'Full of surprises, aren't you? We need to get away from here.'

The two of them fell into step together, two people who had been strangers moments before, now a couple like couples everywhere, walking, casually engaged in conversation.

Cooper touched her elbow. 'Keep walking.' He urged her along. 'You were being watched,' he said.

'Really? I didn't know.'

'Don't look back. Keep walking.'

They had gone several blocks when Cooper glanced back, but spoke to her. 'We'll walk to the next corner, turn left quickly, and we'll run. You'll follow me. We'll head for the first block on the right. There is a place to hide. Keep walking.'

Anne happened to glance back and she confirmed there were two suspicious men a few blocks behind. She looked at Cooper to judge what he knew, what he had surmised, and what she should withhold. 'They followed you, not me,' she said.

Cooper pushed her forward. 'Turn now. Run.'

Two weeks of shortening days brought a cold front that moved with vigor, but it hadn't discouraged East Berliners who joined the daily demonstrations. Men and women in wool coats leaned into the light wind and blowing snow, holding hand-painted placards. Cooper and Anne moved past one tightly knotted group when he gave his order. Anne followed him, with a jogger's stride.

Ahead, by a small square, where the street divided into a V, a tense crowd was excitedly alive. Two opposing groups faced each other. Three beaten and bleeding protesters were sheltered in the arms of their sympathetic comrades. The person worst hurt was being carried to an ambulance parked on a side street. The crowd behind opened up to let the injured woman pass, calling out concern, and then directed their rage at the other group.

Three riot policemen whose cudgels had inflicted the injuries were now confronted by the taunting crowd. They wore the false confidence of frightened police retreating slowly. Fear in their eyes as the crowd shouted, 'Shame on you.' The helmeted police were young men, too, likely schoolmates of the injured demonstrators they had been ordered to beat.

Wailing police sirens could be heard in the distance, which gave brief pause to the teenagers who held cobblestones they'd ripped from the street. They advanced on the three policemen like a wolf pack circling prey. People everywhere were a loose moving sea of humanity, shifting from one danger only to escape bloodied, and reassemble to engage another phalanx of shield-bearing riot police.

'This way,' Cooper said.

He sprinted around the corner into a narrow street, and as he had promised, there was another street on the right, which he turned onto, grabbing her hand. He slammed into a shallow recessed door in the second building and Anne followed. They took quick sucking breaths and tried to make themselves invisible. The perimeter of a streetlight ended at the bottom of the building's steps. Urgent voices of the pursuing Stasi got louder, but then grew faint as their footsteps disappeared down the dark street.

'The border is closed,' Cooper whispered. 'We're stuck here. You have to come with me.'

'You have no authority here.'

'It's not about authority. It's common sense. I know a place where we can spend the night.'

Anne heard the violent clashes a few blocks away, but over the noise of sirens she could also hear singing. Soprano voices carried in the cold air like a defiant choir using song to battle the police.

'I've stayed here before,' he said. 'The streets aren't safe.'

The hotel was an inconspicuous, older five-story building that once held grand apartments, and could still pass for a place where East Berliners returned after work, except for a red neon sign in the ground floor window that read simply: Hotel. A plump young woman with dimples and blond curls stood behind the small lobby's registration desk. She looked away from the television when Cooper entered.

'Hallo.'

While Cooper approached the desk, Anne moved to the fireplace, where blue natural gas radiated heat around concrete logs, and extended her hands toward the warmth. She watched the delicate flames, but her ears were tuned to the conversation at the desk. She recognized a Polish accent in the girl's low German.

'Room for one night,' Cooper said.

'There are no rooms for foreigners.'

Anne stepped up to the desk, presenting her false East German identity papers. She looked at the clerk and spoke in a perfect Hamburg accent. 'You are the foreigner here, my dear, not me. Just one room for me and my husband. Otherwise we spend the night in jail. I'm sure you can accommodate two travelers stranded because of the demonstrations.' She indicated the noise on the street. 'We brought medicines for relatives.'

Anne kept talking, inventing a housebound, sick aunt. She saw that the clerk's compassion deepened with the story that Anne told and then the girl relented, out of sympathy and social deference. Anne signed the register for both of them.

The hotel room on the fourth floor was closet-sized and cold. The creaking door barely cleared a double bed that was crammed between the wall and a dresser. There was enough furniture to fill a room twice the size. Two side tables, the dresser with mirror, a spongy chair, and the double bed were stuffed together.

Anne stood just inside, taking it all in, and felt a sudden acute social claustrophobia. This was where they would spend the night. Anne tested the spring in the mattress and then sat against the wooden headboard, legs straight out. 'Here we are.'

Cooper took the overstuffed chair. 'Better here than in the street.'

She stared at him, a tall man whose long legs shot forward from the chair, who looked strangely ill at ease.

Sometimes Anne felt like she had lived her whole life in one month. At other times it seemed like just hours since Cooper had stepped off the elevator and asked if she was Anne Simpson. The feeling had come to her before, and she felt it again together in the strange hotel room. The dislocation of the violence in the street, the city, the cold night. She felt no connection to anything in her life. She could be in any hotel room in any city with any man.

'Was he surprised to see you?'

'Surprised, yes. But maybe also relieved. He seemed less clever. Smaller. The emperor without his clothes. Do you know what I mean?'

'How did you feel?'

'I felt for his son. And his wife. They are the ones who will be hurt.'

'And you?'

She shrugged. She looked at Cooper to understand his reason for asking. 'Anger. Denial. Acceptance. All the stages of grief balled up together.' She tried to laugh. 'His son loves him.'

'Every kid loves their parents.'

'Did you?'

'Sure.'

She turned away. 'Not every child gets the parents they deserve.'

Anne's hands were at her side and she leaned back against the headboard, closing her eyes to cut off the conversation. She didn't want their discussion to become about her. She was aware of the obvious – they were together in a cramped hotel room with one bed.

When she opened her eyes, she saw him looking at her. She was fond of him in an unexpected way – his forthrightness, his decency, and the intelligence that went along with the work that required him to hold two opposing thoughts in his head at the same time. It made him complex and unpredictable. She was drawn to him but she was also wary of him.

They had met earlier in her life, and later in his, and the imbalance of age made the easy intimacy between equals difficult. No good would come from crossing the line. She was drawn to him but not in the way some younger women find comfort and stability in older men. His attraction was his cynicism and the way he was trained to be fully skeptical of the world. He would never become attached and he would never surprise her with sloppy affection.

Cooper left in search of food that could pass for dinner, but he returned less than ten minutes later empty-handed. 'There is no kitchen. The restaurant across the street is closed.' He held up a bottle of wine. 'This is supper.'

Cooper produced two paper cups from the bathroom, which he filled, and raised his. 'What to toast?'

'Nothing.'

'Nothing!' He raised his cup. 'Nothing will come of nothing.' He drank his, poured himself another, and raised his cup again. 'To nothing.' He leaned against the dresser and contemplated her on the bed.

'Are you disappointed in him?'

'Stefan?' She threw back her wine as if it were whiskey. 'Yes, of course, I'm disappointed. Two years of my life I lived ignoring the clues. Pretending. He was doing what he was paid to do. I allowed myself to ignore what I should have seen. I'm disappointed in myself.' Her expression became provocative. 'What haven't you told me?'

'I followed you here.'

'I know that.'

'I get along with Winslow because I have to.'

'I know that, too.' She saw his surprise. 'The way you talk to him. Chummy if you need to be. The whole of your cynical self gives you away. I could never do what you do.'

'What do you think I do?'

'Lie for a living.'

He laughed. 'We all lie. I lie, you lie. You're good at it. The difference is that I get paid to lie.'

'That's a cheap excuse for a bullshit philosophy. You're lying to yourself if you believe that crap. The people you work for say that to justify what they do, as if saying "we all lie," makes it okay.'

He shrugged, unamused.

Anne suddenly disliked him. 'You're a smug, not very funny – what? Intelligence officer? Spy? What do you guys call

143

yourselves?' She slumped against the headboard. *God, this is hard,* she thought. She was quiet for a long moment. Her cup was almost empty and she sipped it dry. She wished it was whiskey.

Anne looked at Cooper. 'Maybe I didn't want to know what Stefan did. His absences, his clever excuses. I knew something was wrong, but I didn't want to lose what I had.' She looked at him. 'Have you ever been married?'

'Once. It didn't work out.'

'What happened?'

'It's not a thing I like to talk about.'

'You think this is easy for me?'

Cooper nodded. 'I worked too hard, shared too little. She was also to blame. I found out about her affair by accident. We tried to repair the marriage but we were too far apart. It became obvious the marriage was over. We were sad, but relieved. It turned out we were better at being sad than happy.'

Anne watched him, thinking that he was being half truthful. She smiled at Cooper. 'Where would you like to sleep?'

'Here in the chair.'

'It's a double bed. You can stay on your side. Pillows between us. Our own Berlin Wall.'

He laughed. 'I'll take the Western side.'

*

Anne shivered in the cold shower's first meager flow, but she lingered to let the small electric water heater kick in. Her face turned up to receive the soothing warmth and her fingers plugged her ears. Hot water finally came steadily. It had crossed her mind to let Cooper sleep with her. Water flowing over her breasts stirred desire, but the thought of sex left her uncomfortable. It would come later, perhaps. Not tonight.

When she stepped out of the bathroom, she wore a towel wrapped around her middle. He had fallen asleep on his side of the bed in his clothes, back to the pillows. She was glad he was asleep.

*

Anne lay in bed listening to his quiet breathing. When she was certain that he was asleep, she removed the pillow wall and lay beside him. She wanted the comfort of companionship without the complications of intimacy. She surrendered to her need for physical contact. Her head lay against his shoulder and she felt his warmth and his steady breathing, but there was another thing that she sensed.

Sitting up, she looked down at his face feeling the restlessness of his sleep. When she kissed his forehead, she felt warm beads of perspiration on his skin. She felt him struggle with adversaries in the wild dominion of his dreams. She gently placed her hand on his damp forehead and said a prayer to comfort him, and to ask forgiveness for what she would do. Then she lay down beside him, drawing close. Excited by danger.

*

Morning sun peeked through the room's small window. Pale light strengthened as the dawn hour passed and gave way to the first bright rays of sunlight that struck Cooper's sleeping face. He covered his head with a pillow, but then sat straight up, as if coming out of a dream, suddenly remembering where he was. He saw that he was fully clothed. When he turned to the other side of the bed, he realized Anne was gone.

He found her note on the dresser. She had written James on the folded paper in her cramped cursive script, which put him off for a moment. He had been Jim to her except when he first came off the elevator, and felt a need to be formal.

Cooper knew the note wouldn't be good news. Notes were

for awkward goodbyes and troubling confessions. Setting it aside, he splashed water on his face in the bathroom and used soap on his fingers to brush his teeth. He was sitting on the edge of the bed when he opened the note.

I didn't want to wake you. I'll make my own way back.

Christ, he thought. He tried to imagine how much forethought she'd put into her flight. Certainly, she had planned it. His job would be more difficult now. Knowing that he'd come for her, she would avoid the places he was likely to look.

Cooper lifted the room's telephone and asked for an outside line from the lobby clerk. He was surprised when the West Berlin number he dialed rang. He was certain the telephone circuits would have been cut.

'It's me,' he said, when he recognized Winslow's voice. He didn't use his name. There was no reason to further excite the curiosity of Stasi operators who would have intercepted the call being routed to West Berlin.

'It's early. Where are you?'

'Still here.'

'And our friend?'

'Nothing yet.'

'And the girl?'

Cooper stared at the empty bed. 'With me.' He knew that he would pay for his lie later, but there was no easy way to explain all that he knew without jeopardizing his own safety. The audience for the lie were the Stasi listening to the call.

'Watch her.'

When Cooper hung up, he looked around the room for anything that she might have left. He tore the note and flushed it down the toilet. He had ten minutes before the Stasi arrived to question the desk clerk.

18

THE WALL
NOVEMBER 9

To PASS THE TIME while she waited for the family to emerge from the apartment on Engeldamm, Anne stared at the Wall just beyond the parked Trabant. Following cracks on the concrete surface kept her mind off all that could go wrong. She mapped the meandering veins and found herself exploring the estuaries that moved through the spray-painted slogans, looking for escapes from the labyrinth, and then to challenge herself, she made a guessing game of how a crack's depth related to its length. There was nothing else to look at, except curious passersby, who glanced at her, and who she tried to ignore.

Petra was the first to emerge from the apartment building's lobby, briskly stepping into the morning chill with her handbag. She passed the old man bent over his broom, sweeping a stretch of sidewalk. She nodded at him, but hurried along; she had no patience for his chitchat today.

Peter came next. He stormed out of the door with the urgency of a schoolboy late for class. His wore his triangular blue Pioneer's scarf, a white shirt under an overcoat, and a garrison cap that covered his mohawk. He gripped the straps of his heavy backpack to keep it from bouncing as he ran down the sidewalk.

Stefan emerged last. His hat was pulled over his forehead, his collar turned up, and he moved with the obvious nervousness of a man not wanting to draw attention, and, in doing so, drew attention. Anne was surprised by his unsophisticated clumsiness, particularly for a man who'd slipped across borders, but then she saw the placard under his arm, and she knew he was obviously putting on a good show of a protester headed to a demonstration.

He approached the Trabant and tossed the car keys to Anne. 'You'll drive.' He took the passenger seat, and when Anne was behind the wheel she turned to him.

'Which way?'

'Toward the church. Drive slowly.'

Anne pulled up to a stop sign at the end of the block, and in that moment, she happened to look left. Carlota stood on the sidewalk carrying a suitcase, and she leaned forward to look past Anne into the car.

'She's seen you,' Anne said.

'Drive. Keep driving. She's a crab. She doesn't move straight toward anything. We'll be at the tunnel before she decides what to ask for in return for reporting me.'

'Straight?' she said.

He gave the address.

'I don't know Brunnenstrasse.'

'Why would you? We have time. Peter and Petra are moving on foot. We will park a few blocks away and wait. There will be a lot of waiting.' He turned to Anne. 'How much did you tell him about me?'

Anne gripped the steering wheel, aware that they were alone. She stared ahead, angry. 'He knows what I know, which is nothing.'

'I wanted to warn you, but things were already dangerous.' He looked at her. 'Life was intolerable for Petra. The Stasi started with their games. When she was at work, they entered the apartment. They left the radio on, put moldy food in the refrigerator, deposited gifts in the toilet. They wanted her to know they'd been there. Then they gave Peter an incorrect medical diagnosis – saying he needed to be quarantined because of measles. I had planned to leave eventually, but their suspicions were accumulating, and time was running out.'

Anne was speeding, staring straight ahead. 'Was I just a prop?' Her voice was matter-of-fact, but her knuckles were white in a tight grip.

'Are you asking how you were chosen?'

'I'd like to know that, too.'

'You came to Kruger's attention. I don't know how. There are several East German women in the embassy and one of them may have suggested you. He never told me how he picked you, but it's logical. American. Divorced. Unhappy. In Kruger's mind that made you a good candidate. You fit his profile. I saw your file. All the things you told me about yourself I already knew.'

Anne couldn't believe she was having this conversation. It was as if she were discussing some other Anne Simpson, some other woman with the same name.

Anne swerved into the left lane to pass a tram that was slowing to stop. As she did, a panel truck pulled out and she braked violently to avoid a collision. 'Shit.'

'Calm down,' he said. 'There's time.'

Anne proceeded past the panel truck, whose indignant driver had his hand out the window, cursing. 'What else?' she asked.

'I was told to find a way to approach you. I flew to Rotterdam with your photograph.'

'Which one?' The meaningless detail seemed suddenly important.

'Your embassy ID photograph.'

Anne grunted. She never liked it. She'd been told to smile and when the shutter snapped, she'd felt like an imposter.

'It wasn't hard to find you. I had the photo and your name. You were the only American woman in the resort. Easy to spot. Kruger had figured it out. The cover story, the theft, my zither performance.'

Anne remembered those moments. A teenager had grabbed her purse and run off. Stefan saw it happen and caught the boy, returning her purse. 'All a ruse?'

'I gave him twenty guilders. I told him I needed an excuse to become a hero. He bought the story because it was basically true. I saw you, I saw the boy, and I had Kruger's suggestion.'

Anne stared ahead, struggling with her memory of Stefan's approach, holding her purse. She heard him equivocate and change his story, saying the boy had been one of them. 'How could Kruger know the trick would work? How could he know that I wouldn't just thank you and go on my way?' Anne turned to Stefan, eyes fierce. 'How could he know that I would fall in love?'

Anne wanted to unspeak the word, but it was gone from her lips, and tears in her eyes opened a wound. She had loved him. She didn't love him now, but that didn't deny the fact that at one time, not long ago, she had been drawn to him with the whole of her being.

'How could he have known?'

'Not all of his romances were successful. Not all of the matchups worked out. This one did.'

She wanted to hit him.

'I needed to make it work,' he said. 'Something I never told you. For me, it was a chance out of that world. I planned my escape from the beginning.'

Stefan pointed out the windshield. 'VoPo. Slow down.' He added, 'He chose you because you were pretty, had a good job, and were just divorced. You were an American woman in her thirties, living in West Berlin. The only thing that mattered was that our marriage provide cover for my travel to Vienna,

150

Prague, and Bonn to handle their agents. They used me and then I used them.'

'You were good at it.'

'What does that mean?'

Anne pounded the steering wheel with her fist. 'I slept in your bed for two years. You owe me an answer. Was I your whore? Is that what I'm supposed to think? You lied to me. You laughed with me. We made love. Was it all a made-up act that I couldn't see?'

'Don't.'

'Don't what? Pretend I had no feelings for you? How can I do that? I would rather have those feelings knowing they were part of a cynical scheme than to deny myself the memory. Yes, I loved you. Now I don't. You are no better than they are. You're one of them. You've done a horrible thing.'

'What the hell do you know,' Stefan shouted. 'At least you survived. This is a game for Kruger. You and I are expendable. I am terrible and he is evil. You think the Americans are better? The CIA has a claim on morality?' Stefan threw his hands up in incredulous disgust. 'Winslow? Cooper? They're the same as Kruger.'

Without any conscious effort on her part, Anne had begun to speed again.

'Slow down,' he said. His voice calmed. 'I was trained for this. To lie, deceive, steal. It's wrong, but whose God is judging us? The men at the top don't care about you or me. They are happy to count measurable victories with shattered lives.'

'You're wrong,' Anne shouted. 'That is a hopeless world. How could you do what you're doing now if you believed that?'

'I don't believe in anything. I don't believe in the GDR, the Party, Socialism. Christianity. For me, for my generation, children are our only hope.'

Anne was driving past a group of peaceful demonstrators walking in the opposite direction, heading toward a crowd gathering in Alexanderplatz, a somber crowd, couples hand in hand, and fathers with children on their shoulders.

'They have hope,' Stefan said. 'I just have my son. He was going to be detained. He is the one thing I will give my life to protect. And you,' he said. 'You, too, survived.'

Anne stopped the car to let protesters pass. 'What does that mean?'

'Oh, Anne!' he cried. 'You have no idea.'

'Tell me.'

'You found the photograph. I tried to deflect your questions, but I knew something had changed. I was required to report your suspicions. Kruger ordered me to get rid of you.'

'What does that mean?'

Stefan turned away, avoiding her. His face lost color.

'Kill me?'

He faced her. 'It was a stupid idea. They were smart about you, but ignorant about me. The idea that I had no feelings for you. That I could put a pillow over your head while you slept. He gave me forged documents to prove I was in Vienna the night you were to die. It was a good alibi. You'd be found two days later when I returned. An investigation would find the apartment had been burglarized. Turks in the neighborhood would be blamed. A dead wife. A robbery gone bad. He had it all worked out.'

Stefan sank back in his seat and was quiet. Then he motioned for her to stop. 'Pull over. We're here.'

Dr Knappe emerged from the crowd and was at the car's window.

Anne stared straight ahead. Her face was drained of color and her mouth slightly open in stunned disbelief.

'I couldn't do it,' Stefan softly. 'I had been planning my disappearance for months, but everything moved up. I couldn't warn you.' He looked at her. 'That's why I disappeared.'

Dr Knappe knocked on the closed window. 'Hurry,' he said.

19

BRANDENBURG GATE
THAT NIGHT

THERE IS A MOMENT on a November dusk when the dying sun hovers motionless over Berlin's rooftops. Deep shadows come alive in the gloaming as the wary populace waits for streetlights to come on one by one.

It had been a long day of waiting. Peter had led them to a Lutheran church, where the young rector greeted him by name, and they joined a motley group of protesters, rebellious youth, and liberal congregants who passed out drinks and sandwiches. It was a small, cozy scene. A band rehearsed in the basement. Bored kids were drinking and smoking cigarettes. They wore punk outfits – metal studs on leather jackets held together with safety pins, spiked hair, torn jeans, and ear piercings. Two teenage girls lip-synced the lyrics of the album they passed between them, and then their voices joined in, '*Shit and boredom have no borders, everyone is taking orders.*' The album cover was soft-core porn – three topless band members covered in mud, eyes wide, tongues out, like sexy savages. The family kept busy doing the little things that help pass the time. Petra knitted a sweater for her son, but the others lacked the concentration to be productive, and they alternated between going out to bring back a newspaper and sharing overheard gossip. In that way, they passed the hours. But then it was time.

They left the church individually and rejoined as a tight group. They walked in shadows, moving from one recessed doorway to the next, waiting until *Volkspolizei* patrols passed. Dr Knappe gave them duplicate keys to 7 Schönholzer Strasse and instructed them which apartment they could enter to find the trapdoor that led into the old tunnel. Twenty-seven years was a long time for the popular imagination to forget the old escape route, but the Stasi's thorough record-keeping assured that the street number would not be forgotten.

'From the trapdoor we will lower ourselves to the tunnel. It goes under two streets and comes out in a basement beyond the Wall.' Stefan looked calmly at the group. 'It is large enough for one at a time. Petra will go first, then you. I go last,' he said, putting his hand on his son's shoulder. He looked at Anne. 'Stay here. When we are safely in the apartment, I will signal from the street.' He lifted his flashlight. 'One flash and you come. Two flashes and get away as fast as possible.'

'I don't like this.'

'It is safer than trying to cross the border with your forgeries.' Stefan looked out the dark alley toward Schönholzer Strasse two blocks away. There were a few parked cars, and a three-legged dog moved in the shadows. In the distance, they heard the songs and chants of protesters.

'Now,' he said, and the family slipped into the street.

Anne watched the three of them move quickly in the darkness beyond the perimeter of streetlights, avoiding surveillance cameras. She looked for signs the VoPo were waiting to pounce, but the family made it safely onto the sidewalk and then turned onto Schönholzer Strasse. She didn't let the restraint placed on her awaken serious fears. She knew Stefan was trained for this and she knew he would protect his family with his life. But a premonition darkened her face when she saw them disappear around the corner. She began to count the seconds, and then seconds became a minute, and one minute became ten. She clutched her hand and without thinking, she began to move into the street to get a better view.

Suddenly, the family was racing toward her on the empty street. Peter came first wide-eyed with fear, followed by Petra, and Stefan came last, glancing over his shoulder. When they slammed into the alley's darkness, Anne saw Stefan's disbelief.

'Someone betrayed me,' he said, gasping for breath. Again, he had the face of a man who held the fate of his family in his hands. He met Anne's eyes.

'Stasi were parked at the address. They knew.'

There was a moment of stunned silence. They understood that it was unthinkable to return to the apartment on Engeldamm. A deepening dread settled on the small group. Whatever brief hopes had been ignited in their minds were now extinguished by the night's sober reality.

Anne wasn't ready to let the evening end in failure. *You don't concede that easily*, she thought. *You play the game and hope the other side makes a mistake.* She thought about the high school hundred-yard dash competition that she'd won because the lead runner had fallen. There was no shame in winning that way.

By some concomitant association of thought and sight, she noticed that her shoelace was untied. As she bent over, she heard protesters give a rousing cheer. The sound was so vivid, so real, that it took her breath away in that moment. She had the very real feeling that she was sprinting the final yards to the tape. Crowd sounds filled her ears and sweat poured down her face, her father's voice somewhere in her mind urged her on.

Premonitions are strange things. So is fear, and so are impulses. And the three combined into one for Anne at that moment. She finished tying her shoe and she looked up, following the sound of excited voices. She stood, perplexed by their tone. Alive, urgent, and jubilant. The voices echoed between the buildings and through the empty street, but no one could be seen.

Anne stepped into the street, seeking provenance for the voices. She stood still, ears alert, listening. An ominous din was approaching, and over it boisterous shouts and the rhythmic rumble of marching feet.

'There,' said Peter.

They all turned to the far end of the street, where it intersected a boulevard. An army of demonstrators on foot moved like a confident rabble ignoring a gathering enemy. Men and women and children bundled against the cold, some shouting, and from time to time a fist was raised high in the air, which encouraged others, and then a whole section of the mob raised a fist in unison, chanting, '*Die Mauer muss weg!*' The Wall must go!

A pink Trabant moved slowly in the thick sea of marchers, tooting its horn occasionally, not to open a path, but in the spirit of jubilant noisemaking. Candles held by the crowd made the moving mass look like a river of phosphorescence. Somewhere, a solitary soprano voice rose above the din, hushing the crowd. Her voice was clear and bright in the cold air and her emotional singing of 'Auferstanden aus Ruinen' moved others. Soon marchers joined in singing the national anthem.

Anne ran to the edge of the crowd and stopped a young woman in ski headband. 'What's happened?' she asked.

'The Wall's opening. The radio announcement came from Schabowski himself. We are marching to the Brandenburg Gate.'

'When?' Anne asked.

'It's opening starting now.'

Anne turned to the family, who'd joined her. They were stunned and skeptical. The sea of swelling energy and of anxious upheaval of wave upon wave of people, whose hope was yet unfathomed and whose force was being felt, moved like a river in the night. Anne and the family joined the hopeful sea of swaying shapes with faces brightened by the expectation of change.

A shrill cry. A lone voice in the crowd pealed danger. Its tone was urgent and then everyone heard the ominous rumbling of heavy vehicles. Fear didn't come like a lightning bolt, striking suddenly and without warning. Fear came slowly, working its way gradually against the understandable instinct for caution, until another voice somewhere in the crowd shouted, 'Tanks!'

Anne heard the terrible growling engines and felt the earth beneath her shudder from the slow-moving treads. Singing stopped and marchers broke up and fled. The street emptied in front of the approaching Soviet T-62 tanks, and then, surprising even the most frightened, the rumbling stopped. A young woman with a single white rose stood in the tank's path. She was joined by a teenager in a jogging suit who tossed rose petals at the tank commander in his turret. The teenager was lifted on someone's shoulders and he placed his flower in the mouth of the tank's barrel. Other protesters emerged from side streets when they saw that the tanks were halted. A tense standoff ensued between friendly protesters and cautious Soviet soldiers.

Protesters swept forward, heartened by the shocking sight of a single girl with a flower blocking the Soviet tank. Waves of men, women, and children poured from behind cars and alleys and moved peacefully through the streets, alive with expectations. Seeing the march carry on, Anne and the family joined the crowd running in the street.

The gloomy Brandenburg Gate was marooned in the middle of no-man's-land and illuminated by swan-head arc lamps that flooded an empty Pariser Platz. East German armored vehicles lined up to one side of the vast square. Beyond a harmless barrier of potted foliage there was the inner barrier of chain-link fencing, and beyond that, one hundred yards away, stood the Berlin Wall that curved around the neoclassical monument. The Brandenburg Gate loomed over the divided city.

Anne knelt just inside the first wall, behind the plants, and looked toward the monument. GDR politicians kept Pariser Platz free of the anti-tank barriers and watchtowers that ran along most of the Wall, but the presence of armored cars and vigilant snipers deterred East Germans who would try their luck. She crouched beside Petra and on her other side Stefan and the boy joined her looking for a path to freedom. Brilliant light from the arc lamps spilled through the tall stone arches.

All around them, wary demonstrators milled by the chain-link fence, like prison inmates looking at freedom. Anxious faces suddenly were hopeful, too, while others were frightened and solemn. Rumors spread along the thick mass of people who faced off against the East German border guards who stood inside the security zone, each ten feet from the other. The Wall was opening, or had opened, at Bornholmer Bridge, but each rumor had a counter-rumor and facts were casualties of the evening's chaos. There were only the armed border guards and tension. Nothing in the moment suggested that the hope on the faces of the crowd would be realized that night.

A cry went up. Anne turned. 'There.' One longhaired teenager was over the inner wall and ran hard across the empty platz. His first effort to scale the Wall failed, but then he was joined by another young man, who lifted him on his shoulders, and the teenager's hands reached the curved cap on the top. He pulled hard and then he was up. He had summited. He was bathed in light from the Western side, where a large raucous crowd greeted him. He was momentarily dazed, frozen in ecstatic disbelief. He looked from his perch like a mountain climber claiming victory upon reaching a difficult peak.

'He'll be shot,' Petra said.

They all waited for the rifle's muzzle flash and the hollow sound of the high velocity sniper's bullet. It didn't come. Anne watched the well-spaced border guards stand nervously in front of the swelling crowd. She turned again to the single man on top of the wall, who, feeling confident in his accomplishment, did a little jig. He waved frantically for others to join him. Two men, inspired by his success, left the crowd and raced across the empty patch of earth, ignoring the yelling border guards.

Anne felt a tug on her arm. Petra pulled her along toward a group of middle-aged men who worked furiously to widen a hole they had cut in the fence. When it was wide enough, one man slipped through and he was followed by two more. They headed toward a gap in the line of border guards, who began to close ranks.

Anne saw Stefan look at her and Petra, assessing their willingness to brave a run.

'This isn't safe,' Petra said, embracing her son tightly. 'Any minute they will start shooting.'

A cheer went up. Provoked by the teenager performing his jig, a mobile television platform rose on the western side of the Wall. Video cameras broadcast the unfolding drama to viewers across the city. Powerful television arc lamps misted vapor from their heat and illuminated the three men who ran across Pariser Platz. One by one they arrived at the wall and arms reached down to help them up. One border guard raised his rifle and took aim, but hearing a shouted order, lowered his weapon.

'We must go now.' Stefan pointed further along Unter den Linden's wide boulevard where a black Chaika limousine and a linen service panel truck approached the concrete barriers. Anne turned when she heard Stefan's urgent command and stared at the familiar limousine that was now stopped a short distance away. Floodlights struck the car's windows, illuminating the interior, and she saw Rudolf Kruger's face staring at her. The arc lamp's beam swept across the car and Kruger's hand rose to shield his eyes.

Six men in ski masks jumped from the rear of the panel truck. They were followed by a stout woman in a fox *shapka*, who stepped forward with a haughty expression and vigilant eyes, eager to prove her worth. Carlota looked at the crowd gathered at the fence, studying faces with a prosecutor's calm eye.

'There they are,' Carlota cried. She became agitated and gestured at the family.

'We have to move,' Stefan said. 'Let's go.' He widened the fence's gap so his wife and son could pass and then he slipped through. Once on the other side, Stefan held his impatient son back from running toward the Wall. He turned to Anne. 'Stay if you like. Don't think your American passport will protect you from their fists.'

Anne hesitated. She glanced back and, in that moment, she stood apart from the family, and she knew she was not one of them. She saw Petra's pleading face, yet she hesitated. There was no time for all of them to reach the wall safely.

Suddenly, Peter dashed toward the death zone. 'Wait,' Petra called out, distraught. She hesitated, then followed her son, and immediately Stefan left the safety of the fence and ran after them.

'Halt! Halt!'

The six men rapidly approached and again Anne heard the order to halt. She didn't have to see who'd spoken to understand the danger. Then, her name was called. The guttural voice, the wheezing breath.

Kruger had come out of the limousine wearing his hat, and pointed at her. The others were already running toward the Wall and it was only Anne who held back. The others had left, but were not yet safe. There was another fifty yards before they reached helping hands at the Wall.

'Come,' Stefan yelled back at Anne.

'Don't,' Kruger called out. 'You'll be shot.'

Anne calibrated the danger in increments of mortal risk. She rarely thought about the moment she would die. It always seemed faraway, in another lifetime, a sort of dream experience.

She thought death would come for her in a quiet way, like a curtain falling while she slept. But now, the possibility of dying, and dying violently, was in front of her, taunting her.

'You'll be treated well,' Kruger said. 'We'll arrange an exchange. You for him.'

Anne stepped forward, hands raised high over her head in surrender, but as she walked, she kept her eyes on Kruger. She saw the dark shapes of men advancing from one side. Anne had no idea what she was going to do, but she embraced the uncertainty like an old friend who'd made an unexpected visit. How often had she been given an opportunity to do a good deed? It was a far better thing to forgive Stefan than to hold onto the bitter poison of resentment. He had refused to kill her and she felt the debt.

Loud yells from the Wall encouraged the fleeing family, and Anne measured the seconds until they reached safety. Hands over her head, she walked toward Kruger, counting down the time. She was aware of the first men who approached. The threat was clear in their masked faces and clenched fists. In her dreams, danger always presented itself as faceless evil.

Now, she thought. *It's time*. Anne spun around, ducking through the hole in the fence. Her runner's mind calibrated the distance and she focused on the finish line at the Wall. Her first driving strides took her beyond the line of dispersing border guards and she hit her sprinter's speed, keeping pace to cross the distance without slowing. Her arms moved at her side and she was again on a track competing against herself. Encouraging voices on the Wall were a ringing chorus. She was in her small world, ignoring the rooftop snipers. Her strides came with the calculated rhythm of a runner who knew how to conserve energy for the last wrenching sprint. Deep sucking breaths filled her lungs and she blinked to clear blurring sweat from her vision, focusing on the looming Wall.

At that moment, Anne sensed a change in the danger and

began to run faster. She shut out frantically shouted orders and the hysterical wail of a nearby siren, shaping her mind to the approaching Wall and the hands lowered to pluck her from danger.

The sniper's first bullet hit the concrete with a dull smack, sending cement fragments into the air. The second shot struck her forearm and she shuddered, knocking her off her stride, but momentum kept her going forward. Her hand grasped the crimson flowing from the wound and she became numb from shock.

A rope had been lowered from the Wall, but she couldn't grasp it, hands slippery with blood. Arms reached down to help her up, but shock set in, and she seemed to wander, confused. Anne looked up into the concerned faces. She raised her wounded arm and shook her head.

Stefan leaped to the ground and was at her side. He lifted her up onto his shoulders and into the helping hands of men on top of the Wall. They gripped her under her shoulders and brought her to the top.

Stefan had let go of her foot when the first masked men arrived. One struck Stefan's shoulder with the butt end of his Kalashnikov, sending him to his knees. The second Stasi officer kicked him in the gut, causing him to curl up, hands covering his head to protect against their blows.

Cries of protest came from the crowd on the Wall and appalled faces looked for help from an absent authority.

Kruger approached Stefan. His Soviet-style fedora was pulled down on his forehead, hiding his face in shadow, and he looked at his former officer, bleeding from his mouth and ear.

'The Wall is coming down, but not for you.'

Kruger motioned for Stefan to be taken to the panel truck waiting across the security zone and then he looked at the two distraught women on the wall, whose eyes filled with anguished tears.

'He will get what he is due. No more, no less. You can take comfort in that.'

There were jubilant shouts and excited cries coming from the crowd, dispelling twenty-eight years of division. A rocket lofted into the night and exploded in a shower of incandescent sparkles over Pariser Platz. Another exploded and soon the sky was a brilliant display of fireworks. East Berliners streamed through the chain-link fence and became a festive crowd at the loathed Wall, hands raised to be lifted up from their misery. Hammers and chisels began the work of tearing down the Wall. Strangers hugged, sharing love and joy. Everywhere an exuberant crowd celebrated, unaware of the single exception to the night's triumph.

Young people on top of the Wall danced jubilantly under the sky of colorful starbursts and waved at the television platform, where NBC broadcast the fall of the Wall live to a stunned worldwide audience. Joy was everywhere except on Anne's and Petra's grim faces as they watched Stefan's limp body being lifted into the rear of the linen service panel truck.

PART III

20

HOHENSCHÖNHAUSEN PRISON
DECEMBER

ONE NEVER KNOWS WHEN the winds of change may blow. East Berlin awakened from a long restless slumber feeling the first spirit of freedom, and with it came angry voices. Calls for justice pealed from church pulpits and fed the hunger of persecuted citizens to set right four decades of repression. Calls for retribution against the responsible politicians and the system of surveillance that detained citizens without explanation or took them from their homes in the middle of the night were loud and strident. Vengeance and retribution are swift, they said, and it was only justice that required time. They were met with the opposite convictions of the Old Guard speaking on state television, who proclaimed that collective responsibility required people to be tolerant. Berlin, they said, was not the Paris of 1789. Deposed party chairman Honecker was not King Louis XVI. There was no purpose in marching party apparatchiks before an angry mob in Alexanderplatz who would come to watch blood spill when the blade came down.

In the days and weeks that followed the toppling of the Berlin Wall, a fresh spirit of forgiveness triumphed over angry calls for revenge. No good would come from unleashing vengeance of coworker against coworker, neighbor against neighbor, brother against brother. Respect was civilization's remedy against the poison of intolerance.

*

There was a long period in which there was no word on the fate of Stefan Koehler. He had disappeared into the chaos that ensued following the fall of the Wall, but this time there was no official urgency to find him. The loss of one man was insignificant in the historical moment that was redefining the lives of eight million people. There were sightings of a linen service truck at Stasi Headquarters, but when Petra inquired, she was met with indifference. Calls to the morgue provided no information. Stefan had vanished in October, and then reappeared like a man risen from the dead, only to suddenly disappear again in November.

Anne was with Petra in her apartment when a linen service panel truck delivered Stefan's pine coffin. Two prison guards carried it into the living room. The taller, older man held the coffin's rear, and a short, stocky assistant carried the front, and asked Petra where she wanted it placed, saying they had orders to deliver his remains. He explained that mortuary workers had walked off the job and no bodies were being accepted. Cemetery workers had also been furloughed. All funerals were delayed. 'No one told the dead,' the older man joked.

Petra had gotten short notice. After three weeks of desperate calls and institutional silence, a call had come the day before. He'd been found in his prison cell. He'd taken his own life. Petra demanded to see the body so she could prove her suspicion that he'd been tortured and murdered. The body would provide the incriminating evidence.

Anne was unable to dissuade Petra from clawing open the coffin's lid. Anger vibrated in Petra's voice, waving off Anne's plea. Anger and indignation kept her from reason. There was only incomprehensible disbelief that her husband had been returned to her in a pine coffin delivered to her living room.

The claw end of the hammer pulled the nails, producing a

great aching screech of steel being extracted from unyielding wood. The first two nails were the hardest to remove, but then the leverage of the lid helped and suddenly the top was off.

Anne and Petra saw a cardboard box inside, and inside the box, they found a sealed plastic bag with cremains. Next to the box there was a black-and-white photograph of Stefan's beaten face – eyes closed, face out of shape. The face of a dead man.

Petra looked at it stoically. The living drawn to the dead. She handed it to Anne.

She took a deep gasping breath, struggling to contain her bitter grief. The two women embraced, but neither cried.

Before leaving, the older prison guard handed Petra an envelope. Inside, Petra found an invoice for the cremation. She looked at the sum and thought it a cruel joke. The two women stood over the coffin unable to find words to express their feelings. Each understood that Stefan was young in years, but old in the treasonous acts that led to the forfeit of his life. Petra pulled her son close in an emotional embrace.

Later that week, she and Anne made their way to Hohenschönhausen Prison on the city's outskirts. Anne angrily confronted the prison warden, who stiffly apologized for the invoice. He said it was a mistake, a mix-up. The state would cover the charges for the natural gas used in the oven.

'And his death?' Petra demanded. They stood opposite the warden in his office. He was a precise, tense, middle-aged man who seemed uncomfortable with his new obligation to tolerate insults and demands.

'Suicide,' he said.

'I want to see his cell.'

'It's not permitted.'

Petra presented an official document stamped by a new authority that had opened investigations into the deaths of

Stasi prisoners. The warden examined the document and handed it back.

'I will have you escorted.'

*

'He was murdered,' Petra said loudly to Anne. They walked behind a guard down a long lime-green corridor fresh with the astringent smell of cleaning products.

'You could see it in the warden's face,' Petra said. 'His callous look.'

Cell doors along the corridor were wide open and the political prisoners who'd been recent guests were all gone. Cells were quiet and empty. Their echoing footsteps on the concrete floor were the only sounds. Anne glanced in one cell as they passed. The prisoner was gone, but the evidence of torture remained: wall shackles, metal mattress, and the hint of human stench.

'Here,' the guard said. He had stopped at an open door.

Cell number 203. Anne noted the detail, which like other seemingly innocuous details, stuck in her mind. She would later write the cell number down. It wasn't significant, but it was where he had died, and she thought it respectful to hold onto something specific. It helped her think of his death as less lonely.

The door was heavy iron with a small opening for food to pass through. There was a small, grated window near the ceiling. Light entered but the window was too high for a prisoner to look out, even if tiptoeing. Vertical iron bars covered the window's opening. 'He was found hanging with his belt around his neck.' The guard pointed to the iron bars.

Anne tried to imagine Stefan, face beaten, being able to hang himself. She imagined one end of the belt in his hands, the other end wrapped around his neck, as he leaped up. In the moment he was at the apex of his jump, he'd have to knot the belt on the bars. Anne listened to the guard describe how Stefan had been found.

'The miraculous accomplishment of a contortionist.' Petra spat her words at the guard.

Anne saw faint writing bleed through the freshly whitewashed plaster wall. Stefan, or some other prisoner, had written on the wall. The blue letters bled through but were blurred and indistinct.

'We don't even know this was his cell,' Petra said when they were leaving. 'We don't know anything. We'll never know.'

*

Rudolf Kruger's disappearance took Winslow and Cooper by surprise, but the magnitude of the unfolding changes made his disappearance a minor incident in the aftermath of the collapse of the GDR. Where once the Stasi had been feared, they were now absent, some living quietly, harboring their resentments, and others denying their past. Sightings of the vanished former head of Stasi counterintelligence were peddled by other former Stasi agents looking for a reward or a favor. Rumors were everywhere. Escaped to Moscow, hiding in a cellar, or living openly but unrecognized. Old stories of Nazis who'd escaped in the final days of the Third Reich were brought up as if, by example, they proved the truth of the rumor that he'd fled to Argentina or made his way to Lisbon, where he had a son.

21

JUNGFERN BRIDGE

WINSLOW STOOD TO ONE side of the cluster of men gathered at the bridge railing. The river's banks had frozen during the New Year's Eve cold, but dark water moved slowly in the middle of the canal, making its way toward the city center. Winslow watched two men at the railing wave instructions to a scuba diver who had popped to the surface. Excited yells and one man pointed toward a shadowy object beneath the surface, 'There, there.'

A bloated object rose to the surface face down in the water. It was the second corpse that week, and seeing one didn't make it any easier to see the second. The dead had always had an uncomfortable claim on Winslow's sensibility; they were a distasteful part of the job – finding them, identifying them, and when necessary, making them. Winslow stood alone, away from the group, taking in the operation without being part of it. He preferred to remain unseen, unnoticed, and unphotographed, a man invisible to the world even as he influenced it. His need for secrecy matched well with who he was. He lived modestly in a quiet Virginia suburb among neighbors who had no idea who his employer was, and every August he vacationed in a clapboard home on the Maine shore. His half-mile of coastline kept him out of sight of neighbors and gave him the seclusion he craved. When he needed human contact, he drove to the nearby fishing village and had dinner in the bar restaurant among the locals, whom he had befriended. They were friendly, happy to share local stories. No one knew what he did when he wasn't out in his yard repairing his old whaler, and no one cared. He was left alone.

His month off every year gave him time to think about his life, and he took comfort in going about his day without actively putting himself at risk, or responding to a crisis that put other men at risk. The job had begun to wear on him and he looked forward to his retirement on the Maine coast. His parents were in the local cemetery, as was his wife. Something had changed in him when she passed. Her laughter had been the bright spirit in their marriage and when cancer silenced it, something in him had died. The hollow in his chest filled with regrets.

Winslow watched the corpse being maneuvered to the river bank. He turned to Anne, who had moved closer to look and now stood at his side.

'Early this morning someone fell or jumped. Or was pushed.' Winslow added, 'If it's Kruger, I need you to identify him.'

The diver held a rusted iron cleat that protruded from the stone embankment and his free hand pulled a rope that was attached to the corpse. Three tugs and the corpse came closer to the bank. The police officer in charge of the recovery held a long pole that he used to guide it to the bank. In the process, the body turned over and the face turned up. Blood leaked from the mouth and spread in a widening stain on a soiled shirt.

'Well?' Winslow asked.

'It's too far away,' Anne said. The corpse being maneuvered to shore was pulled by the diver hand over hand. Current from the rain a few days before eddied around the bloated body making the rope taut. Anne stepped down the stone embankment to the water's edge.

'Well?' Winslow repeated.

Anne forced herself to look. The face was puffed up with a sickening pallor and oddly misshapen from hours in the water. She turned away and shook her head. 'The nose is flatter, the jaw is different, and there's no hair.'

'You're sure?'

'It's Petra's neighbor, a woman named Carlota, the neighborhood informer. She looks different with a shaved head.' Anne looked at Praeger and Cooper, who separated from the cluster of men, and joined the little group, and she stared at Winslow. 'It's a waste of time summoning me every time a body is found. Kruger's not dead any more than Stefan was dead when he first disappeared.' Winslow, like the rest of the agency, had been caught unprepared by the collapse of the GDR. Plans were upended and the void left by the Soviets' retreat left East Berlin an unpoliced zone with citizens startled by their freedoms. Winslow saw how some former Stasi denied their past while others disappeared. Sightings of Kruger were reported, but Winslow dismissed most as unreliable. The orthodox way to disappear was to become an unrecognizable corpse, or to simply be gone without a trace. But Stefan had done that and Winslow knew that Kruger wouldn't go that route. The unclever spy, like a bad general, makes the mistake of fighting the new war with tactics from the last war. If Kruger was going to disappear, he wouldn't become a body lifted from the canal. But there was the chance that someone with a grudge had gotten to Kruger, and Winslow couldn't rule that out.

'You are probably right, but I can't risk that you're wrong.'

Praeger shook his head. 'Kruger sees us running around looking at every corpse while he makes his way to Moscow. Or Lisbon. He knows what he's doing.'

Winslow had heard all the wild speculation, but he dismissed most of it because he knew that a man in hiding, frightened for his life, would be cautious before he made a move. Winslow looked toward the crowd that had gathered at the foot of the bridge, and his eyes settled on several men who wore Soviet-style fedoras. Was Kruger in the crowd watching, or in one of the apartments looking down?

He took gloves from his pocket and drew the leather over his outstretched fingers, pulling it tight onto his hand. And then he did the same with the other glove. Every corpse that wasn't Kruger's was evidence that he might be alive, but proving the negative wasn't satisfying, and didn't accomplish what he needed to accomplish.

'We're treating Kruger as a fugitive,' he said, adding, 'We're not hoping to find a dead man, but if he is dead, I don't want to waste our time looking for him.'

Anne pointed at the canal, where a sturdy little tug plodded through the water, revealing detritus from the storm in its wake. 'You won't find him floating in the water. He's too clever for that.' She pointed at the corpse. 'He knows the dead can't betray him. He probably had her killed or killed her. She knew his face. And there are others. I'm not the only one who knows what he looks like.'

'You're the only one working with us,' Winslow said.

'There were broadcast cameras everywhere.'

'Miss Simpson,' Praeger said. 'We found the NBC footage from the Brandenburg Gate. There was a panel truck and a limousine, but it was dark and the distance great. Images of Kruger in the car are blurred and his face was hidden by his hat. We still need you.'

Praeger pondered Carlota's body, which was being lifted from the canal. 'If you are right, this woman's death will be added to Rudolf Kruger's crimes. He will be caught. He will be brought to trial.'

'How?' Her voice was indignant. 'You have nothing. You're looking at corpses.'

Winslow wound his cashmere scarf around his neck, tucking

the ends into his wool coat and when he was done, he turned to Anne. 'We have you.'

Winslow agreed with Anne on one point. Kruger was clever. Kruger had seen through Stefan's effort to hide his disappearance and he remembered Kruger's mastery of history and the little tricks he had played.

Winslow looked at the faces in the crowd again, studying the older men, pausing on one man. For a moment, he thought it might be his old friend, but the man stared back, irritated at being observed, and Winslow knew he wasn't Kruger. How could he safeguard himself from the consequences of not finding Kruger? Winslow wasn't prepared to give up, but he knew that the odds against success had risen. He had met the immovable object. Failure would follow from too much caution. He raised his collar against the deepening winter chill and waited for Cooper, who had taken Anne to his car.

The two Americans were side by side on the bridge under the pale sun, watching as the shrouded corpse was carried to an ambulance. Winslow had never seen Cooper more uncertain or unsteady, and the little hints of fealty he expected were replaced by doubt.

'Whatever she's thinking, Jim, you are not to let her stray. You hear her concerns, you take note, you call me. You are not to let her drift away. If she needs to weep on your shoulder, let her cry her eyes out. She's vulnerable and she is angry – at me, at Kruger, at the world. We need to use her anger.'

Anne saw Cooper talking to Winslow and she knew she must be the subject of the conversation. He got behind the wheel and she waited for him to speak, but when he said nothing, she looked out the window and pondered his silence.

Too fed up to press him, too suspicious to believe what he would say, she sank into a sullen, irritated mood. They had driven for several minutes when they arrived at the East German side of Checkpoint Charlie.

'You've done enough,' Cooper said. 'You don't have to continue.'

Anne took her eyes off the East German Grenztruppen who raised the candy-striped barrier. In the weeks following the collapse of the Wall, East Germany's discipline dissolved. It was obvious everywhere, but especially at the border, where guards were lackadaisical and indifferently waved cars through security.

Anne glanced behind at Winslow's car, and then Cooper was driving through the security zone, handing his documents to the American MP who stepped from the command hut. He turned to Anne.

'You're quiet. You're not usually this quiet. Did you hear what I said?'

'I have nothing to say.'

'Oh, come on.'

'I don't need to justify myself.' She glanced out the window at the clear winter sky that seemed to mock her mood. Hope was everywhere in Berlin, except in her little world.

Cooper pulled away from the hut and entered the American zone. 'Leave Berlin if that's what you want to do. You did what we asked. No one will keep you here against your will.'

She looked at Cooper fiercely. 'And go where? Berlin is my home. I want Kruger to suffer for what he's done.' Vengeful anger deepened her voice.

'I understand.'

'Do you?'

A long silence settled between them. Her chestnut bob was tied into a ponytail and she wore large white-framed sunglasses that masked her face. 'If you don't find him, I will.'

'You're mistaken if you think you can do this alone.'

She shot a glance at him.

'You have no idea the forces that are at work here.'

Anne had heard his vague threats before. Men in her life

had always presumed a superiority of judgment and a shocking expectation of submission. 'What does that mean?'

'I am on your side. But there is a limit to what I can do inside the agency. Winslow is calling the shots.' Cooper pointed behind to Winslow's chauffeured car. 'He *is* Langley. Good at what he does with no need to compromise. He will be the first to agree that his job requires him to put duty above decency. You're a pawn here. Praeger doesn't like you. Winslow puts up with you. Don't underestimate him.'

Cooper hesitated. 'He ran covert operations in Saigon, Mexico City, and La Paz, where he tracked down Che Guevara. They wanted him to send back fingerprints to verify Che's body and instead he sent back Che's fingers.' Cooper clenched the steering wheel. 'You don't want to cross him. You will be charged. You'll need a lawyer. You'll get an administrative hearing in front of military officers skeptical you knew nothing about Stefan. Be careful.'

She laughed.

'What's so funny?'

The idea that she needed to be cautioned after all that had happened struck her as ludicrous. 'I don't need to be more frightened. Or more threatened.'

She knew they had come to a moment in the conversation when the things that went unsaid were more telling than their words. Clues that came from a sideways look, or the length of a pause, or sudden exasperation, were telling bits that said more than any carefully constructed thought. She felt such a moment in the car. She was fully aware that Cooper didn't seem to know what to make of her reaction and her silence. While it didn't bother her at first that she had confused him, she knew it was not productive.

'When do you stop acting as his lackey?' she asked.

'I'm here to help.'

'I don't need that type of help.' She wanted to say something funny, but nothing came to mind. Driver, cook, chaperone, confidant, a man who always seemed to be at her side. 'You won't find Kruger by having me look at every corpse that turns up.'

'Leave Berlin, if that's what you want.'

'I don't want to leave,' Anne said. She felt cold. 'What's next for him? A dacha outside Moscow writing his memoir, justifying his crimes?'

'Kruger knows too much,' Cooper said. 'The KGB will silence him before they let him fall into our hands. He may try a ratline to South America, but he'll need money. Half a million West marks. It was enough for Stefan. It's enough for Kruger.'

22

WALKING HOME
A FEW WEEKS LATER

ANNE EMERGED FROM THE Turkish shop across the street carrying a string bag with food for dinner. It was not yet dark; the winter sun was a pale orange ball dying on the horizon. She gazed, enchanted by the natural beauty. For a moment she daydreamed, letting a pleasant thought carry her to a calm place. When she saw the galleon cloud drift across the pale, winter sky, she imagined riding it like a magic carpet to some imaginary kingdom.

A mother's cry from a window broke her reverie and her eyes searched for the truant child. She felt something ineffable – the urge to look back overcame her and she glanced over her shoulder, spotting a woman across the street who was watching her. She was a petite, narrow-shouldered woman with short, black hair and an intense stare that was fixed on Anne. Primitive terror went down Anne's spine. She turned suddenly and crossed the street to her lobby. She fumbled with the keys as the woman approached.

'What it was like to be one of Rudolf Kruger's victims?'

Anne flinched when she heard the word – *Geschädigte*. Her keys slipped from her fingers and she stooped to pick them up, glancing at the woman. She remembered her face and her aggressive, confrontational demeanor. She was the ARD television reporter who'd shouted questions at Praeger on the steps of police headquarters, and the one who'd reported Stefan's drowning. Anne hesitated, reluctant to speak, but also curious what brought the reporter back to the story.

In the first minute of conversation, it came out that the reporter had a few facts, remembered the bizarre circumstances of Stefan's first death, and she was trying to make sense of how a man could die twice. She smelled a story. 'I'm using my free time to research a human-interest piece for my editor.'

Anne listened skeptically. The reporter had no story, but she had a reporter's instinct, persistence, and dubious charm. Kruger's notoriety and his reclusiveness, she said, had excited wide interest among West Germans who were getting their first view inside closed East German society. Unlikely stories about life in the East were becoming contemporary legends that filled newspapers and magazines. The reporter repeated the rumor she'd heard – Stefan had been one of Kruger's Romeos planted in Berlin.

'Is it true?'

'I don't know,' Anne said, cutting off conversation. She waved off the reporter.

'Where is Kruger? Do you know? Has he gone to Moscow? Lisbon? What do the Americans want with him?'

'Excuse me,' Anne said, 'I don't know anything. I really don't.'

Anne didn't know what to make of the reporter's interest, but it was also something that she couldn't ignore, so when the reporter presented her business card, she took it to be polite, and not because she had any intention of speaking with the woman again.

Anne double-locked her apartment door and set down her string bag. She poured herself a whiskey. She glanced at the wall clock and was relieved that the time hadn't been changed and pictures on the wall hadn't been switched. Sipping her drink, she moved to the closed venetian blinds, lifting one corner, and peeked out. She stood back so as not to be seen, and looked across the street. An apartment light was on but there was no one in the window.

The phone rang.

Anne turned and stared. It was a rebellious act against the world that kept her from answering the phone. It rang a third time and then a fourth time. She hesitated, steeling herself against the thought that this was another harassing call from a former Stasi who'd gotten her number. There had been several. The first one came without warning. The man threatened her if she cooperated with the BND and identified Kruger. She'd hung up and she happened to see a figure standing in the window across the street. The man was silhouetted holding a telephone.

She knew what to expect if she answered, but she also knew that if she didn't answer the calls would continue. It was always the same man speaking crude German.

'Hallo.'

'Anne? Is that you?'

A woman's voice. 'Who is this?'

'It's me, Petra.'

Anne hesitated. 'I've been meaning to call you.'

'I have been thinking of you. I want to thank you for the money you sent. It was kind of you. Can we meet before you leave Berlin?'

'I'm not leaving.'

'Oh, I heard…'

'What?'

'You identified a body in the canal. You were leaving.'

'Who said that?'

'Dr Knappe. In exchange for *fleischkuechle* he gives me news.'

Nothing was funny to Anne anymore, not even the thought of a bespectacled man in an obvious hairpiece peddling rumors

181

for dinner. This was the old Berlin from after the War and now it was the new Berlin after the collapse. Rumors everywhere and shortages – a better cut of meat bartered for information on a missing relative. She had met this kind of black marketeer among the refugees processed through JAROC – Poles, Hungarians, and Latvians who claimed that the Mossad or MI6 would pay dearly for their information if the Americans weren't willing to meet a price. Everything for sale, for the right price. The worst of the refugees with the most outrageous demands would boast they could deliver a lock of Hitler's hair.

'Good of you to feed him.'

'He lost his job. Everyone is out of work. Everyone is poor. Things were terrible before. Now they're terrible in a different way. How are you?'

They avoided the obvious topic, but Petra was happy to explain how life in East Berlin had changed. It was different. Confusing.

'I walk outside and I have to remind myself not to look behind. I know there is no one following, but it's a habit. It's time to make new habits.'

Anne walked as she talked, the telephone cord trailing behind. She asked questions, but mostly she listened. Part of her wanted to be friends with Petra and talk openly about Stefan, and part of her was jealous that Petra had borne his son. Lover, mother, first wife. Anne was still uncomfortable thinking of herself as the other woman. The full text of her relationship with Stefan was written and whatever could be said had already been said. She tried to remember everything he confessed that night in the car, but now the words flew from her mind. She had thought she knew him as well as anyone could know another person, but now she thought she hadn't known him at all. They had shared intimate moments, but even those were contaminated by surveillance.

'Carlota disappeared,' Petra said.

Anne hadn't been listening. 'Who?'

'My neighbor. She informed on you.'

'She's dead. They pulled her from the canal. Her hair was cut off.'

Petra came to the point of her call. 'Come with me to Stasi Headquarters. It was ransacked. Everyone is going there to read their files. I want to go, but I won't go alone. Will you come with me next Tuesday? Your file will also be there.'

*

Anne found it difficult to sleep in her bedroom those days. She lay in bed at night calculating her future and trying to bury the past. She had removed his clothing and shoes from the apartment, but she couldn't expunge him from her dreams. She would wake and think he was beside her in bed, watching her, whispering something that she couldn't understand. No matter how many pillows she put on her head, his voice was in her ears and his face in her mind. Sometimes, she wondered which pillow he would have used to suffocate her.

One night, Anne dragged the mattress into the living room. She told Chrystal that she was cold and needed to be closer to the portable electric heater. Chrystal pointed out that it would be easier to move the heater into the bedroom than the mattress into the living room, and having made that remark, and sensing some disturbance in Anne, Chrystal added, 'But that wouldn't solve the problem, would it?'

Unable to sleep even in the living room, Anne meditated. Disturbing thoughts kept entering her mind. She came to Berlin reluctantly with her then-husband, and now she didn't have the strength to leave.

Watching television helped. She sat cross-legged and watched terrible late-night German television. A program called 'PEEP' was the sort of mindless programming that numbed her.

Housewives were interviewed about their sex fantasies by a handsome male moderator who asked embarrassing questions. *What if your husband brought home a male friend and wanted to watch you with him?* There were props too that the moderator presented and asked how the housewife would use them to give her husband pleasure.

Late-night horror-erotic television programs kept Anne's mind off her life and it kept her from thinking about the man across the street.

*

Months later, when she thought about those first weeks after Stefan's death, she realized how disturbed she had been. The idea that she should move the mattress to the living room seemed normal at the time. But after everything from that dark period ended and she was able to look back with a clear head, she realized her actions had been those of a woman barely able to hold onto her sanity.

23

STASI HEADQUARTERS

ANNE FOLLOWED PETRA INTO Stasi headquarters' courtyard just off Normannenstrasse. Smoke from bonfires the night before rose from piles of smoldering rubble and hung in the crisp morning air. With dawn had come an end to the vandalism. The mob had fled through the iron gates that were thrown open to the courtyard. Mist passed slowly from the place and the lifting darkness revealed a vast ruin in front of the gray brutalist building. Windows were smashed and furniture had been thrown out to feed the bonfires. As morning light swept away dawn's shadows, stragglers of the evening's army of rioters began to awaken. Anne saw how they looked around, surprised by what they had accomplished, but satisfied, too. They assembled in groups trembling with eagerness to recount the night of rampage. One man rushed past Anne, breathless with a story he wanted to share.

'I don't believe this,' Anne said. Filing cabinets had cracked open when they landed on the stone pavement, disgorging their contents like split watermelons. Two women gathered typed pages from the broken cabinets and stuffed them in plastic bags.

Petra lifted one partially burned memo that she'd recovered from a heap of ashes. 'An informer's file,' she said. She dropped the paper and it lofted into the air on the heat of warm embers.

'Inside,' she said. 'Come with me.'

The door at the top of the step was wide open. The marble lobby was littered with office equipment, which they stepped around, and they made their way to an adjacent block of offices and supply rooms in the Stasi complex. They passed an East German policeman who sat on the floor against a wall, head in his hands. His uniform was torn, but he had no obvious wounds, but nevertheless, he was in a state of shock. When he looked up, his eyes were hollow and he had the pallor of a defeated man.

'It's a lie,' he said. 'It's a lie.'

Anne stopped to listen, but Petra nudged her forward, shaking her head judgmentally. 'The ones who believed the Socialist nonsense will have the most trouble. For him,' she shrugged, 'there is nothing. He's lost his job and his country.'

The two women moved down a long corridor that was strewn with the contents of offices. Door after door they passed, they saw the excesses of rioting citizens moving through the halls of the loathed and feared institution. Mirrors were smashed, telephones ripped from the wall, and uniforms torn. Desks were plundered and broken, chairs were smashed, and food from the privileged pantry that made hard-to-get delicacies available to the Stasi elite, had been opened and savored. What hadn't been hauled off was spilled on the floor. Scottish smoked salmon, Greek olives, Italian prosciutto, and vintage French burgundy. Petra grabbed two tins of mackerel that she put in her purse. She saw Anne's surprise. 'East marks are worthless.'

Turning one corner, they came upon a middle-aged woman in a starched white uniform and bouffant hairdo. She wore white cotton gloves. She was carefully sorting paper and putting files back into manila folders, a cleaning woman's preposterous effort to reclaim lost order. At the sound of footsteps, she looked up.

'Outrageous,' the woman said, speaking to herself in a voice loud enough that she knew she was heard.

Anne and Petra moved through a heavy metal door that had been forced open. They entered a long corridor that was dark until their movement set off motion-activated fluorescent lights. Cell doors on either side were open, in one they saw a raised wooden platform with a noose and trapdoor. Anne paused and stared. At the end of the corridor they climbed steps that led to an adjoining building. Rumors had alerted citizens to the location of the Stasi's vast repository of personal files. They pushed through the door and came into a large windowless room crowded with people.

Citizens closest to the door looked up when the two women entered, but then returned to the papers they were reading. The vast room was a warehouse of well-organized documents. Long hallways passed tall rows of steel storage shelving filled with cardboard boxes and standing folders. Row after row of storage stood in front of her – a vast repository of secrets that had been compiled on the lives of two million people. Fluorescent ceiling lights washed everything in cold, sterile light. The main aisle vanished at the far end of the room and side aisles cut in at right angles. As they passed one aisle and then another, they saw people – some crying, others livid – digging through boxes, throwing what they'd found onto the floor. Reels of microfilm were unspooled. Chest-high locked cabinets lined one wall and numbered cardboard boxes were stacked three high. Nothing indicated what was inside. Aisles were marked with undecipherable labels, alphanumeric identifiers, a slash, and what appeared to be dates: 890C6/86 – 640H8/85 – 110Q1/84.

Anne turned to Petra. 'Where do we start? This will take forever.' They moved down one aisle trying to discern packing slips on the boxes. It was an unsolvable maze created by clever bureaucrats.

One man saw their confusion and directed them to a large cabinet of index cards. He instructed them on the cataloguing system – index cards connected storage boxes to neighborhoods, neighborhoods to codes names, codes names to real names. They were two among many. Everywhere in the room – at tables, at the index files, at microfilm readers, in the aisles of storage – citizens were eager to know what had been written and who had informed. Surnames were being written down; judgments were being made.

'An informant,' Petra said, pointing to a woman in headscarf and dark glasses. Her effort to disguise herself only drew attention. Petra added disdainfully, 'She wants to find what she said about others – and destroy it.' Petra shook her head. 'People talk about forgiveness, but scores will be settled before there is mercy.'

Exhausted after two hours of fruitless searching, Anne sat at a table and rested her head on folded arms.

Petra dropped a stack of files on the table. 'You weren't the only one the Matchmaker used. Here are others. I'll look for your file, but read these first.'

Anne hesitated, not sure she wanted to know about other women. But curiosity triumphed, and she read the files of several West Germans who had been drawn into marriage with Stasi agents. The accounts were written in the dry language of a dedicated bureaucrat, but the stories themselves read like pulp fiction – at turns ludicrous, funny, and frightening. Dozens of women. The names meant nothing to Anne, but she was drawn to the insidious details of their entrapment, feeling a terrible bond. She took comfort in knowing that she was not the only one. Each woman had her problem that made her vulnerable. A woman with money problems; another with a drinking problem; a third with love problems. And for each problem, the Matchmaker had a solution. A kind word from a stranger in a bar; unprovoked generosity from a new colleague; an unexpected intimacy from a handsome acquaintance. Their problems became opportunities for the Matchmaker's Romeos.

The hurt in the women's lives was a mirror to her own

pain. She stared at the field reports and the intimate details. She thought: all these women's lives wrecked for scraps of information methodically reported back to East Berlin to become part of a surveillance record that was filed away. Petty details of insignificant meetings and overheard conversations feeding the bureaucracy's quota for information. Cold War surveillance victories measured by word count.

Everything was reported. Quotidian lapses described in the sterile language of memos, which were used to justify atrocious acts. A secretary in the Ministry of Education whose throat was cut by her husband when she discovered who he really was. Her murder made to look like a robbery. A clerk in the Ministry of Defense who described the details of a classified arms production report to satisfy her husband's interest in weapons, and then threw herself out a window when confronted by the BND. And there was the woman with a deep grudge against her boss who, upon her discovery of her husband's Communist allegiance, became his active collaborator. Reports, transcripts of secretly recorded conversations, and video surveillance produced a determined record of the women's lives.

Anne stopped. She had read enough. The cumulative effect was numbing, sickening. She saw the vast sweep of a callous surveillance enterprise.

Anne happened to be sitting next to a German woman who just finished reading her file. She tossed it on the floor. 'I don't want to be German,' she said. 'We are terrible.'

She was smartly dressed, middle-aged, indignant, and bitter. 'And what will happen to them.' Her hand swept a wall of photographs of smiling Stasi in uniform who'd earned an award for Employee of the Month.

'A slap on the wrist,' the woman said. She laughed bitterly. 'They say there will be trials, but I doubt that. I hear people say the past is behind us and it is time for reconciliation.' She wagged her finger. 'There is no justice. They should be hung.

And these men,' she said, holding up a Romeo file. 'Cut off their little Stasi pricks.'

The long day became night. Anne's head was on the table when Petra placed a cardboard box in front of her. 'This one is Stefan's. You should know who he was, not because it's interesting, but if you don't look your curiosity will be a poison.'

Anne removed a large envelope of photographs. She saw Stefan in his other life, the life she knew little about. A family album. In one older photograph, he wore shoulder length hair, flared trousers, aviator glasses, and muttonchop sideburns from an earlier time. There was Stefan, Petra, and their son on a nudist beach. Anne never allowed herself to be photographed topless, and she had never been to a nudist beach. Her eyes were drawn to the family's comfortable pose.

In each photograph, Anne saw a man who bit by bit was becoming more of a stranger. None of the photographs provoked her own memories, but they did for Petra, who provided a commentary – where taken, when, and why the photograph might have been of interest to the Stasi.

'They kept track of us. This one,' Petra said, pointing to a boy seated at a piano. 'Stefan's father was a playwright in the Writers Union, who the Nazis sent to a labor camp. His mother was a music instructor. A nice, jolly woman who gave him piano lessons.'

'What was his real name?'

Petra said it. A common German surname from the North. The name seemed foreign to Anne and it took her a moment to associate his face with the new name, like putting on an old dress that no longer fit. She repeated it, saying the name to remember it. She looked at the photograph repeating the name. A look-alike, she thought. A double. A character in a novel with two names. Anne regretted asking. He would always be Stefan Koehler. That was enough. She didn't need his real name.

'There is a joke,' Petra said. 'How can you tell if the Stasi bugged your apartment?' She paused. 'There is a new television in your living room.' Petra shrugged. 'I thought it was a stupid joke until I looked inside our new television and found a bug. After that, we didn't talk freely at home. He was planning our escape so everything we said at home was stupid stuff – the weather, news, food. We took long walks so we could discuss our plans. We agreed on the details of our escape that way. He knew the risks. If you steal from the State and you are caught, you are executed. It took him longer than he hoped to accumulate enough money from inflated expense accounts and diverted funds to buy a London flat. In the end, he filed inflated expense reports for imaginary Stasi agents he'd "recruited." Some of his best secrets came from these figments of his imagination. He knew they suspected him when he was called back to East Berlin for consultations. That was September twenty-third.'

Petra paused. 'He didn't go to Vienna that week. He visited me. He knew they had discovered his theft so he arranged to make it appear that he had drowned. We were going to use his sudden disappearance, and their effort looking for his body, to slip out of East Berlin. Dr Knappe found the tunnel.'

She closed Stefan's file. 'We were victims, too. Different, yes, but our suffering was the same.' Petra's face hardened. 'And the men who did this to us? Will they be punished?' Petra laughed bitterly and pointed at the Employee of the Month gallery.

'There is no justice. Only excuses. People want to forget and the ones pleading loudest are guilty of the most crimes.'

Petra's voice softened and her eyes lowered. She continued in a matter-of-fact tone. 'I go to the trials to listen. Only the stupid ones – the obvious ones – are the prosecutor's easy targets. I sit and listen. It's dull, but I listen. There is one Stasi officer accused of killing a ten-year-old boy who tried to cross the wall in a hot air balloon that he'd stolen from a circus. The boy's mother sits in the front row every day and knits. The officer is accused of firing the shot that brought down the balloon. He was her only child – a good boy, near Peter's age – whose only crime was his stupidity. The idea that you could float to freedom. The mother is there every day knitting. Sometimes she weeps.'

Petra paused. 'The man was convicted. The next one wasn't. Justice is a lottery.' She stood. 'And where is the Matchmaker? Disappeared like Stefan. Dead like Stefan.' He voice was thick with sarcasm.

'You never saw him?'

'There was no reason. You're the privileged one.'

'The Americans want him.'

'Everyone wants him. The BND. The Soviets. These people.' Her hand passed over the crowded room. 'One of them may get lucky. Maybe he'll go on trial. Maybe he'll be convicted. Maybe a cow will jump over the moon.'

Petra sighed. 'It's late. I need to be home with my son.' She placed another file in front of Anne. 'You wanted to see your file. Here it is. Be careful what you wish for.'

Anne stayed after Petra left. She wasn't certain she should read the file. No good would come from looking, but who has the strength to resist reading about oneself? She stared at the file, balancing curiosity against the evil of knowledge. What could be worse than what she already knew? She believed she was strong enough to relegate unwanted knowledge to the dark place in her mind that held the willfully forgotten. She convinced herself that it was better to know, and be hurt, than to forever suffer unquenched curiosity.

There were photos of her first husband, and several of them drinking in a biergarten – the Stasi's first efforts to qualify her. *Qualify.* The word was in the written report. It annoyed her to think she had been watched and not known it.

There was another folder of her first husband with another woman – his affair? She'd never met the woman her husband chose as the replacement wife. The report gave her name: Betsy. *A Betsy*, Anne thought. Pleasant enough in the photographs.

Dimpled with a pageboy haircut, and average looking. *A good fuck?* She wondered. Her husband always wanted a woman whose opinions wouldn't threaten him, whose affection made him secure in his masculinity. Looking at Betsy, she thought, smugly, that he got what he deserved.

A cardboard box held a trove of official memos. The first one, dated December 23, read: *'Mrs Simpson is on holiday in The Netherlands. We believe it is a good time for our Romeo to introduce himself.'*

This was how it began, she thought. The account of the incident was there on the page, and as she read, her recollections surfaced and grew into a picture that was vivid in her memory. The Scheveningen Boardwalk. The idled Ferris wheel at the end of the pier. The gray winter North Sea. Her purse taken and his intervention.

She read on to see if the official version matched what Stefan told her that night in the car. She wanted to know if Stefan's version was the whole truth or a scrubbed version. There was nothing in the flat, officious language that hinted at his unique syntax, and she began to think there had been another person there, watching Stefan watch her, who wrote the memo.

'Our man' the memo said, and she saw references to 'our thief,' 'our target,' and 'our plan.'

'Our man returned the purse. He introduced himself and shared that he was knowledgeable about the town. He refused her offer of a reward, but as instructed, he continued the conversation in a lighthearted way to earn her trust, and when he saw that he had, he invited her to his performance in a pub.'

Anne never really believed that Stefan's appearance had been entirely accidental, but she had assumed that his charade had been a game to introduce himself because he found her sexually attractive.

She looked up from the page and tried to remember what he'd said in the car that night. He'd paid the kid twenty guilders to steal her purse, but then Stefan had switched his story, saying he'd misspoke, saying he'd offered him a twenty-guilder reward. 'You think I was capable of pulling off that sort of trick? He was one of us. I didn't need to pay him.'

One memory triggered another. The basement venue had a small stage where he sipped beer between songs. His tenor voice was well matched to the zither's alto sound. She had been happy to be there with the few other patrons listening to him sing. Stefan joined her at the small round table between sets. She said that no one played the zither anymore. 'I have the field to myself,' he'd replied. She thought it a cheeky answer, and now she read that his response had been scripted. The report described others in the tiny audience and she learned that the English couple, and the gregarious Frenchman were Stasi recruits. The whole thing had been contrived.

It was disabling and surreal to discover that she'd been the object of a carefully staged entrapment. The layers of deception weighed on her. Her memory was at odds with Stefan's confession, which was cast in yet another light by the observer's account. It was hard to know what was true. She kept thinking of what he said in the car, 'I don't believe in anything.'

It didn't surprise Anne that there was another memo that described their wedding. The private ceremony took place six months later in a small Dutch village church. He'd said that it was easier for Germans to marry foreigners in the Netherlands. The priest, she read, was a Stasi agent who'd borrowed vestments from a nearby parish and the witnesses were from the East German embassy, role-playing as old Dutch friends. The Matchmaker himself had been there. And then it struck her. The face of the man in the photograph she'd found in Stefan's drawer had been familiar, but she couldn't place it – until now. He'd been there, smiling.

The Matchmaker had written the wedding's case report. 'A perfect performance.' He had arranged for the wedding rings –

two gold threads braided together – which had been inscribed: *Omnia vincit amor.* Love conquers all.

'*I believe she is the sort of person who will remain uncurious,*' he had written. Further down the page, Anne read the Matchmaker's summary. '*She reads a lot. We were right to pick a man who knows how to give her pleasure with books.*'

Near the bottom of the box, she found a memo from September written by Kruger. '*She suspects our Romeo. She has become a risk. She will be eliminated in a way that appears she succumbed in the course of a robbery.*'

Anne dropped the report, face ashen. Her hands trembled. She felt sick to her stomach. She stood abruptly and rushed to a nearby trash can, vomiting.

*

It was dawn when Anne left Stasi Headquarters. She hadn't meant to stay, but the quantity of material and her own physical reaction conspired to exhaust her. She had put her head on the table, thinking she would rest her eyes for a moment. At one point, she stirred and moved to the floor, where she used her jacket as a pillow. There were no windows in the room and no sense of day or night. When she woke, it was morning.

She stepped into the courtyard as a crowning sun washed the sky in a rosy blush, and all around there were the first stirrings of a new day. Delivery vans spewed exhaust; winter birds chirped; and several people like herself walked out of the building.

Anne crossed the littered courtyard and through the open iron gates, and then she continued at a slow pace. Nothing was the same, she thought. She felt a deep sense of disorientation. Not depression. Not joy. Not fear. Nothing. The numbing emptiness of having discovered things about herself that she didn't yet know how to understand. It was only much later, when the dark episode was over, that she understood how the pieces of the puzzle were laid together that night.

Anne moved through the light dusting of snow that had fallen overnight. An early morning jogger in ski cap and gloves passed, and she was reminded that she had not jogged in weeks.

She walked slowly, aimlessly, without having anywhere to go that day, still on leave from work. The exhaustion, the cold, the breaking dawn, all contributed to a clarity. She began to see the extent to which her life had been violated. She knew it, and had felt it, but the photographs and the banal way she'd been described, made her *see* it.

When the insight came, she felt like she was looking at another Anne Simpson to whom this terrible thing had happened. She felt outside herself. She was aware of the gentle drifting snow, and her thoughts also drifted. Who was she? Revulsion and shame welled up in her. Had she really loved him? Was it possible? Did it matter? She began to question her own memories.

Anne found herself along the Spree. The narrow path was bordered with trees' winter skeletons. The river was gray and opaque and a pair of seagulls cawed.

Her right hand went to her wedding ring, touching it, rotating it. She had forgotten about it, but now she removed it. She threw the ring over the water and watched it hit with a tiny splash.

Anne's considered her choices, but one choice already began to loom large. She would leave Berlin and move to an exotic city that excited her imagination. Her hand felt the Krugerrands in her pocket, and she thought of the stamina required to start over again. She pondered her life, considered where she would go, and how she would live. Her father once advised her: if you have to make a big decision, do the thing that costs you the most.

Anne headed back to Stasi Headquarters.

24

THE MATCHMAKER'S OFFICE

Rudolf Kruger's name was not on the office door and the number written on the plaque gave no indication that it belonged to him. It was one door in a long corridor of similar doors, and if Anne had not been directed by a New Forum monitor, whose job was to prevent wanton records destruction, she would have wandered lost in the maze of hallways.

She looked in the office. Her first thought was that it was unremarkable. Nothing in the room suggested the evil that had been hatched there. There was a modern couch of blond wood and patterned fabric that might be seen in a lawyer's office, or the office of a bank vice president. Upholstered chairs were placed around a glass coffee table. There were no pretensions of power and no hint of the terror that had been plotted at the mahogany desk. Two telephone consoles with rows of preset buttons were the only indication of the importance of the man who sat there – private lines to Party leadership. The room was rich with the type of contradictions that make a man interesting. Bland impersonal taste was apparent in the furnishing, but a stand beside the desk held an acoustic guitar. On opposing walls, the stern photograph of Lenin faced off against a lithograph of Mozart.

The room had not been ransacked. It was clean and orderly,

except for a shredder by the desk. It had broken down from overuse. Shredded paper overflowed from the bin onto the rug. The mechanical failure spared a stack of files that someone tore by hand, but then that effort too had been abandoned, as if, suddenly surprised, the person had fled.

Anne stood behind the desk where Kruger would have stood, and then she sat in his chair. She placed her elbows on the chair's arms, settling in as he might have. She stared at the telephone console and the remaining files, thinking that by putting herself in his place she'd feel something – power, disgust, depravity, but she felt nothing. Evil didn't leave an odor or taste. It had no physical presence.

Inside a credenza behind the desk, she found his liquor cabinet. There was an unopened bottle of Russian vodka, but she saw his taste ran to whiskey and scotch. She knew the brand names in the cabinet.

What was she looking for? An address? A telephone number? She had the vague idea that she might find a clue to his whereabouts, or at least something personal that would hint at an idiosyncratic pattern. Where would he hide it? The refrain came back to her. Half a million West marks. Authorization codes. She tried to put herself in the mind of a man who knew the importance of secrets.

Her hand went into a desk drawer. Paper clips were arranged by size in separate containers and there were sheathed scissors. Embossed letterhead was neatly stacked and held down by a geode paperweight. Dictaphone cartridges were side by side. Everything was arranged by the mind of a meticulous man who ordered the tiniest details. In the rear of the drawer, she found a loaded 9mm magazine, but after a determined search, she didn't find the gun.

Her careful search yielded nothing useful. File names interested her, but when she looked inside, the contents were missing – taken. Handwritten file names had the sterile quality of random codenames. There were no computer discs, no magnetic tapes. Cards in one card file referenced cards in another file that was missing. She knew she was in the office of a man who had built a secret world that required multiple keys to gain access to his repository of agents' coded aliases. He had created a triple cross-referenced system, which meant that to identify an agent, the person looking would need to have access to three separate pieces of information in three sets of interconnected documents. There was no central registry of his secrets – no hackable front door. Aliases connected to other aliases that pointed to a final key.

Anne had found nothing of use when she put her hand in the canister of shredded paper and removed several limp strips, feeling the unheated room's humidity in the paper stock. She wondered what secrets they held. One page had not been shredded, but was torn in half. The tear was in the middle of the page. The top half had a name she didn't recognize, a few confusing instructions, and below that, a bank's address: Mirabaud Group, Claridenstrasse 26, 8002 Zurich. The tear occurred just below the address and she couldn't find the bottom half of the page. The public address of a Swiss bank could be found in any telephone book. The only reason to tear the page was to disassociate the name of the bank from information on the missing half. Stefan had mentioned a Swiss bank, but not its name. A thought struck. She dismissed it at first, but once it entered her mind, she was stubbornly drawn back to the possibility. It was simple, audacious, and in the climate of retribution in the new Germany, quite reasonable. The missing torn half had bank details extracted from Stefan. Anne had always been a methodical person, painstakingly slow, but just sometimes she had a flash of inspiration that turned her from a cautious woman to a good investigator. The tear was clean, the paper crisp and stiff, and it lacked the humid limpness of the shredded strips. It was a fresh tear, a recent act. She looked toward the office door, where a man stood.

'Did you find him?'

The man who spoke was the young New Forum monitor who had directed her to Kruger's office, and he stood in the doorway holding a clipboard.

She was startled. 'Who?'

'The man you asked for. He was here twenty minutes ago.'

'Here? Here!'

'Right there. Next to the shredder. All the old Stasi have come back, walking around, pretending they're part of the Citizens Committee, taking what they can to protect themselves. I thought you came to meet him.'

'Where did he go?'

'Downstairs? Outside?'

She stuffed the torn page into the pocket of her handbag, took one last look around the room, but left everything else. She felt remiss, but she doubted that a man of Kruger's determined caution would leave behind anything potentially incriminating.

Anne didn't notice the man at first. She had walked out the shattered front doors of the main building and into the crowded courtyard, where East Berliners had come to see for themselves how the offices of the hated State Security had been reduced to a gutted ruin. Wonder and awe were on their faces.

It was the man's lack of interest that first got Anne's attention. He seemed oddly indifferent and preoccupied. His quick movement to mount his bicycle caught her eye – a quiet, older man in a crowd of boisterous young people, and he was the only one wearing a fedora. He lifted his foot and pedaled with the awkwardness of an older man not accustomed to biking. He'd thrown a stuffed leather satchel over his shoulder and he needed to adjust it for balance. It was the way his foot slipped off the pedal. Eager to get away. And the way his hat was pulled down on his forehead.

'Rudolf Kruger!'

He glanced back to see who called his name. Then he was through the iron gate, awkwardly pedaling along Normannenstrasse. He joined morning workers on bicycles who pulled forward when the traffic light changed. She could make him out among the similarly dressed workers in dark coats, satchels over their shoulder, wearing hats.

'Stop!' Anne yelled. She ran through the gate and looked around for help, but not one person took interest. She stared at the gaggle of bicyclists pedaling away in the growing morning traffic. He was gone.

Anne refused to be put off by the conscientious secretary who claimed that Jim Cooper was unavailable, insisting that she would wait until he was available, and then in frustration, she added, 'I'm sure he will want to speak to me. Tell him it's urgent.' She had called Cooper first. He was the one that she trusted, but she knew he was the errand boy. She would let him deliver the news. She wanted to avoid Praeger and Winslow, who she had grown to dislike and who she thought of as overconfident clowns caught up in impractical schemes. She had seen how Winslow and Praeger erred in their judgments and always seemed to be playing catch-up with her discoveries.

'He's in Berlin,' she said, when Cooper got on the line. 'I saw him leave Stasi headquarters. Hiding in plain sight. Is it really so hard for the exalted BND and CIA to find one former Stasi?'

25

CLAY HEADQUARTERS
EARLY FEBRUARY

COOPER ARRIVED AT CLAY Headquarters alone. He came twenty minutes early and paced the hallway outside Winslow's office until the brusque orderly opened the massive oak doors.

'They're ready for you.'

Cooper pushed through the door impatiently, feeling his displeasure, and marched toward the long mahogany conference table. Cooper expected to see Inspector Praeger and Winslow – that's who had summoned him – but he also saw Praeger's BKA colleague, Detective Keller. They all looked up when he barged in, but Cooper particularly noticed Keller. Dark rings under his eyes and a nervous disposition gave him the appearance of a man who hadn't slept.

'Good, good,' Winslow said. 'Just in time.'

Cooper took a seat opposite the other three. A Meissen serving dish held the crumbs of a pastry breakfast and their coffee cups were in different stages of having been drunk. Cooper had a taste for coffee, but there was no cup for him. He nodded at Winslow and the two Germans. They had the same drawn expressions, the same awkward reticence. He looked from one to the next.

'We believe we know where he is,' Winslow announced.

The corners of an East Berlin map were held down by saucers

liberated from their orphaned cups. Winslow laid the tip of a telescoping pointer on a white area on the map. The empty zone had no streets. It was blank, as if someone had erased one whole section of the city.

'She saw him here,' Winslow said. 'He was traveling in this direction.' Winslow moved the pointer a few inches to the area that was an irregularly shaped jigsaw puzzle piece missing from the mapped grid. 'Honecker lives here, so do other senior members of the Party. It's a good bet Kruger rode his bike from Stasi Headquarters to his home in this zone.'

Winslow looked around the table and saw that he had everyone's attention. 'I believe he is going to escape to the West. If he lives there…' Winslow pointed to the blank space. 'I expect he will try to cross to West Berlin here.' Winslow used the pointer to trace a path from the blank zone to Bornholm Bridge.

Winslow looked directly at Cooper. 'Does she trust you?'

'Anne?'

'Yes.'

'What's this about? Does she trust me?' He looked at the three men. 'Yes, she trusts me. About this much.' He opened a two-inch gap between thumb and index finger.

Winslow nodded. 'That's enough.'

Cooper laughed. He raised his hand, questioning Winslow's ambiguous answer. 'What's this about?'

'We have intelligence,' Praeger said. 'The Soviets are worried that Kruger wants to escape to the West. We know from a source inside the KGB that they think Kruger is a risk. We know of Kruger's long acquaintance with a senior KGB officer – a man by the name of Dmitri Kondrashev. Kondrashev was seen boarding a military flight in Moscow for East Berlin.'

Winslow moved to the huge stone fireplace where dying embers gave off meager heat. Suddenly he turned. 'If Kruger wanted to reach Moscow he would have already left. But he hasn't. Anne saw him. We have to assume he was collecting files from his office. For what? Blackmail the Soviets? Bargain with us? Pay bribes?'

Winslow lowered his head and resumed pacing, hands behind his back. His stride was steady and he moved with the concentration of a man struggling with a stubborn problem.

'We can assume he is frightened. A hunted man. Hiding. He knows there are no friends in this business. What are his choices? Arrested by us? Silenced by them? Flee?'

Winslow stopped and looked at the others. 'He has a son in Lisbon. He will look to disappear. It's not a hard choice.' Winslow again placed the pointer on Bornholm Bridge.

'This is where he will cross. It isn't the closest spot, but it is the easiest. The most open with the most traffic.'

'You're speculating,' Detective Keller said. He had been quiet throughout, but leaned forward, skeptical. 'How can you be certain?'

'We monitored the son's call with Kruger,' Winslow said. 'They had a short conversation. Kruger made fun of Helmut Kohl and he asked his son to get in touch with a lawyer whose name is Vogel. Vogel happens to be the man who represented Rudolf Abel in the exchange for Gary Powers at Glienicke Bridge in 1962. So, he would be a logical choice to represent Kruger.' Winslow looked at the others.

'However, Vogel is close to the Stasi and the KGB,' Winslow said, 'and Kruger wouldn't trust him. The call was a signal Kruger planned to escape to the West over a bridge. He won't try Glienicke Bridge because it's under Soviet control. Bornholm Bridge makes the most sense.'

Suddenly, the door opened and the orderly entered. He spoke to Winslow. 'George Mueller is on the line for you.'

'I need one minute,' Winslow said to the orderly.

*

The meeting concluded. Winslow thanked his German colleagues and promised to coordinate the next steps. Having seen them out, Winslow turned to Cooper.

'They resent us. They don't like that we're calling the shots on this.'

'Do you believe Praeger?'

'I confirmed his information with someone we have inside the BND. The KGB doesn't want Kruger to get to the West.' Winslow paused. 'I also confirmed that Vogel is in East Berlin. Kruger will cross on Bornholm Bridge. Kruger is a student of history and he would know that Abel crossed the Glienicke Bridge on February 10, 1962. It will give him some satisfaction to escape East Berlin on the anniversary of Abel's exchange.' Winslow looked at Cooper. 'He studied Thucydides while the rest of us read Hemingway.'

*

Cooper was opposite Winslow's desk when he took the telephone call from Langley. Cooper listened to one side of the conversation. A call from the deputy director of Central Intelligence was always an important event that provoked curiosity. There were two telephones on the desk. Winslow had picked up the red one.

Cooper couldn't help eavesdropping on the conversation, even as his eyes wandered across the room and the desk. An amethyst geode paperweight held down Winslow's call list for the day. The desk's meticulous order reflected the mind of a controlling man – a glass sat on a coaster beside an elegant silver water pitcher and a Montblanc pen lay straight on a blank notepad. Cooper was finishing an elaborate doodle when he heard a voice squawk from the telephone. Winslow held the handset away from his ear waiting for the deputy director to finish his agitated speech. Cooper couldn't understand what the deputy director said, but his harsh tone was clear.

'Of course,' Winslow said. 'Everything by the book. No embarrassments. Keep the Germans happy.' Winslow kept his eyes on Cooper as he spoke. 'Yes, Cooper. A good man. I'll fill him in. Everything by the book.'

Winslow put down the telephone, ending the conversation, and looked at Cooper with skeptical eyes. 'Somewhere along the line you must have impressed George Mueller. What I'm going to tell you doesn't leave this room, understand?'

Winslow folded his veined hands on his desk and spoke with the reluctance of a man conditioned to say only what was needed to get what he wanted. 'We have a Soviet defector – Yuri Nosenko. You may have heard his name.'

'He approached me in Vienna in 1962. His defection was a coup. In his debriefing we learned that he was the KGB officer responsible for handling Lee Harvey Oswald when he showed up in Moscow offering his services. He claimed that Oswald was a nutcase and unsuitable for intelligence work. I saw signs from the beginning that Nosenko might be a plant. There were contradictions in his story and unlikely circumstances that he couldn't explain. He admitted to lying about his reasons for defecting, but he refused to confess that the KGB sent him as an agent of disinformation. I was the skeptic on the team. I knew that his clumsy performance and self-contradictions made him a plant. Others argued that the contradictions were evidence he couldn't be a plant. A plant would have a better story. I argued that the best plant was the one who was least likely to act as a plant.'

Winslow nodded at the telephone. 'Mueller believed him. So did others. The dispute was settled when I was removed from the case.'

Winslow paused a long moment. 'We've always feared there is a Soviet mole high up in the agency. I now believe it was a mole who engineered my removal. I was getting too close.' He looked at the telephone again. 'Mueller was Nosenko's advocate. Mueller pushed me off the team.' Winslow let the implications of his comment amplify in the silence that followed.

Afternoon light streamed into the office and cast a deep shadow on Winslow's grim face.

'That is what this is about?' Cooper said.

'This stays between us. Kruger will know the truth about Nosenko, and with luck, he'll lead us to the mole. Kruger is important to us. He's important to *me*.'

Winslow unfolded his hands and became quiet. His eyes came off the telephone and he looked at Cooper. 'They force us out at a certain age. It's always better to leave on your own terms. I haven't stayed in the game for a pension, or a pat on the back, or a flattering roast at a restaurant. I know the risk of success here.'

Winslow rose. The meeting was over. He walked beside Cooper and they stopped at the door. 'I don't believe in ghosts, but sometimes when I'm alone in this office I think about what it must have been like for Goering sitting at that desk in the final months of the war. Germany was defeated, the city was in ruins, and people were dying from bombs and hunger. What was on his mind in those final weeks?'

He put his hand on Cooper's shoulder. 'We need to bring Kruger in. We need to find him before Krondashev gets to him. The stakes are high. A failure here won't be good for my career – or yours.'

The two men faced each other.

'It's up to both of us, but you're the one she trusts.'

26

KEMPINSKI HOTEL
THAT NIGHT

Anne was upset with herself. Rain hadn't turned to snow and it hadn't let up and she regretted her choice to leave home without her umbrella. By the time she rushed through the hotel's revolving door she was soaked. The humid warmth in the lobby fogged her glasses, and she removed them to wipe the mist, but in doing so her eyesight blurred, and she accidentally tripped a tall, elegant Russian woman, who stumbled into the arms of the doorman. She turned to Anne, insulted, and demanded an apology. The doorman intervened against the aggressive posture of the Russian woman's companion, a Soviet officer, and in that moment, the civility of the German and his indignant Red Army opposite recalled the terrible first days of the Soviet occupation of Berlin at the end of the war. Anne apologized to the woman and thanked the doorman, which brought peace to the moment.

Anne found Cooper in a booth at the far end of the bar. She was agitated and her wet hair hung straight down. 'Don't ask,' she said, cutting off the question that she saw forming on his surprised face. She cleaned her eyeglasses on a bar napkin.

'Why did you want me to come?' she asked.

'We think he's going to cross at Bornholm Bridge.'

Cooper looked up at the smiling waitress who approached. 'Another Fruh Kölsch,' he said.

'The same,' Anne said. She looked at Cooper skeptically. 'How do you know?'

'He has a son. We intercepted their conversation. Kruger would expect us to think he'll cross into Austria or Hungary, but because that's what he expects us to think, we believe he is planning to slip into West Berlin and wait for his son to arrange onward passage.'

'You're certain'

'Nothing is certain. It's what we believe.'

Anne sipped her beer when it arrived, and watched Cooper finish a third of his. 'Why are you telling me this?'

'Oh, come on, Anne!'

She sat back, startled. She had an urge to stand and leave, but she didn't. She centered her beer on its coaster, turning it around, looking at the amber liquid.

'I'm sorry,' Cooper said. 'There is a lot riding on this. How are you sleeping?'

Sleeping? She lifted her eyes and stared at him.

'I don't mean to be sharp. This whole thing has become complicated and urgent.' Cooper drank more of his beer and met her eyes. 'Winslow is a complicated man with his own ideas, his own agenda. Right and wrong change places.' He finished his beer. 'I'm rambling.'

'How much have you had to drink?'

'Not enough.'

Anne blocked Cooper's hand when he went to signal the waitress. 'Which Jim Cooper am I with? Jim Cooper, friend? Jim Cooper, handler? Or, Jim Cooper who has drunk too much?'

'All three.' He placed something wrapped in tissue paper on the table and pushed it toward Anne. 'For you.'

Anne found a single yellow tulip inside. 'What's this for?'

'A token. An all-purpose apology.'

'For something you did or something you'll do?'

'Both.'

Anne raised the tulip to her nose. 'Good to look at, but no fragrance.' *Like him*, she thought. She tried to look inside his mind to understand his intentions. 'You're either too honest to be in the CIA, or you're cleverer than I think.'

'I'm not honest.'

'You put on a good act.'

'I have been asked to bring you to Bornholm Bridge to identify Kruger when he crosses. There you have it. I've done my duty.'

Anne knew his capacity for guile, so it didn't surprise her when she thought his eyes betrayed a lie. She sipped her beer and laughed. 'I don't know why I'm laughing. I should throw my beer in your face. I never know which Jim Cooper I'm speaking with. This Jim Cooper,' she said putting her hand on her heart, 'Or this one.' She finger-pointed a pistol at her temple. 'It's never dull to contend with the two of you.'

'You're the only person who can identify him.'

She leaned forward. 'What happens to him?'

'If he's not shot trying to escape?'

'Yes.'

'He'll be brought to justice.'

'Whose justice?' She met his eyes and saw the answer in his expression. The false pretense, the flower, the dissembling honesty, and his polite appearance – all in the service of persuading her to cooperate. She drank the rest of the beer and wanted another.

'Whose justice?' she demanded.

'Maybe there will be a trial. The world isn't always fair. The important thing is that he doesn't end up in Moscow.'

*

Outside, the freezing rain drew a veil over the city. They stood under the hotel's canopy beside a doorman in top hat and white gloves, who had just summoned a taxi for the tall Russian woman and her Soviet army companion. The couple laughed brightly with the carelessness of happy drunks until the woman saw Anne, then she assumed an air of haughty superiority.

'I'll get us a taxi,' Cooper said. 'I'll drop you at home.'

He'd put his jacket over her shoulders to shield her from the rain. Anne accepted his gesture and felt a sudden comforting distrust. He was close to her, speaking in the practical way of a man who knew what he needed to accomplish.

She was lightheaded from the beer and, without knowing it, drawn to Cooper. He had lied terribly, but she knew it, and now his arm was around her shoulder. She felt a dangerous attraction. He drew near her and she allowed him to place his hand on her neck. His fingers brushed her auburn hair, drawing it away from her forehead, tucking it behind her ears. Her hair had dried and had fluffed. It was thick in his hand. She sensed that he wanted to kiss her. She put her palm on his cheek and met his eyes. And then, when the taxi with the Russian couple pulled away, standing alone under the canopy, there was an invitation to embrace.

Anne pulled away. 'This isn't right.'

'What's not right?'

'I'm not ready for this.' She looked at him, eyes searching. 'I'll make my own way home. I'll see you tomorrow at the bridge.'

27

BORNHOLM BRIDGE

WINSLOW RAISED HIS BINOCULARS and looked through the open apartment window toward Bornholm Bridge two hundred yards away. Flood lights illuminated the humped steel structure and it glowed pleasantly in the gently falling snow. The storm had begun early and continued throughout the day, casting a false peace on the border crossing.

East German Grenztruppen stood idly by the raised candy-striped stanchion, ignoring the occasional passing car. They stood in pairs smoking. The novelty of an open border had drawn thousands to the bridge in November, but three months later the crossing was a quiet place guarded by men ambivalently loyal to a crumbling government. From time to time a humble pedestrian walked across the bridge, enduring the storm.

Winslow focused his binoculars on a Trabant that slid as its tires spun on the bridge's slight incline until it reached the anti-tank hedgehogs in the middle of the road, weaving through and proceeding to the control hut on the West Berlin side.

'It's been too long. He won't show.' Praeger stood at the open window next to Winslow.

'He'll show.'

'He has no reason to take the risk.'

'There is more risk if he stays in the East.'

'It won't work,' Praeger scoffed. 'The idea he would cross here. There are a dozen border crossings.'

'He'll come.'

'What makes you certain?'

'Glienicke Bridge. Vogel. The call with his son.' Winslow looked at Praeger. 'He'll come because he knows it's the obvious choice and he assumes we'll dismiss the obvious choice. For you this is a job. For him, it's his life. He is playing a mind game.' Winslow raised his binoculars and looked toward the East German guard tower. An armored personnel carrier parked beside the tower was joined by a Chaika limousine. The officer who stepped from the rear door wore a peaked cap with black visor and a long slate-gray overcoat.

'That's a Soviet uniform,' Winslow said. He handed Praeger the binoculars. He had come to know that Praeger was a rigid thinker easily made impatient by the uncertainties of an improvised plan.

'If this fails, someone will be held accountable,' Praeger said.

Winslow had requested that all border crossings be closed to funnel Kruger to Bornholm Bridge, but Praeger had rejected the idea. Winslow had argued vehemently with Praeger, but he had come to the moment when power shifted against him. He explained that urgent problems required expedited solutions, but his plea failed, and he had settled for a poor substitute.

Winslow scanned the scene at the East German crossing. The Soviet officer was now in the guard tower. His peaked cap had the single red star of a lieutenant general and he peered through binoculars across the bridge. Winslow couldn't see the officer's face, but then a nearby floodlight illuminated the tower, and Winslow recognized the man. For a moment, Winslow was surprised, but the officer's presence confirmed his suspicion.

'Krondashev,' Winslow whispered. He handed the binoculars to Praeger again. 'He wouldn't be here unless he thought Kruger was crossing tonight.'

'How would he know?' Praeger's breath fogged in the cold air from the open window. 'A student of history,' he scoffed. 'We'll see what happens to the CIA's great reputation tonight.'

Winslow looked toward the guard tower and the man he knew was Krondashev. The KGB would already have Kruger in custody if they knew where he lived or where he was hiding. Friendly collaboration between the KGB and the Stasi didn't protect men who were seen as a threat. No amount of gnomic thinking and careful planning could prevent the catastrophic intelligence loss that came with a high-level defection. Krondashev's presence confirmed how important Kruger was to the Soviets and how dangerous his secrets were. There were no friends in this business. Everything about the past weeks and the long night, culminating in Krondashev's arrival, confirmed what Winslow believed – Kruger knew enough to jeopardize the Soviet mole. Kruger was a cautious man and no cautious man would cross the bridge that night unless he was a fox flushed from his burrow and desperate to reach safety.

A ringing telephone broke the silence in the room. The BND command post officer presented the handset to Winslow.

'For you.'

Winslow announced himself and recognized Cooper's voice. 'The Soviets have closed all the border crossings.'

'How do you know?'

'An East German. He came off the bus. He said more buses are coming. The Soviets are funneling everyone to Bornholm Bridge.'

Winslow gave the phone to Praeger. 'Listen to this.' He scrutinized the East German side of the crossing, looking for clues to explain the unexpected. 'This isn't right.'

'It's what you wanted,' Praeger snapped.

'Something is wrong.' Then to himself, *Shit*.

*

'Anne.' Cooper whispered in her ear, touching her shoulder. 'Wake up.'

Her eyes opened and she sat bolt upright. She looked around, remembering where she was, and again looked out the hut's window at a slumped-over man who was coming across the bridge. She forced herself awake, stretching her arms and turning her head side to side to shake off fatigue. She had succumbed involuntarily to sleep brought on by hours of faces moving past West German control. Eyes closing, giving into the sweet narcotic of sleep.

'There,' Cooper said.

She looked at the hunched man. 'No.'

'Coffee?'

She shook her head. 'You're exhausted.'

'Aren't you?'

'Another bus pulled up. There will be more people coming. I'll get coffee.'

An East Berlin city bus was stopped on the far side of Bornholm Bridge and passengers disembarked. After twelve hours, it was hard for Anne to distinguish men's faces. She compensated for her fatigue by matching what she saw against patterns in her mind. She found a way to triage the people crossing – too short, too tall, the wrong nose, or jawline that didn't match her memory. When a woman of Kruger's height passed the window, she looked for an Adam's apple.

Anne held the hot cup, sipping. A dozen passengers stepped off the bus and made their way past the indifferent surveillance of the East Germans, walking in the falling snow. She gazed through the hut's large plate glass window at each face as the group approached, and she looked again as men stepped up to the West German police, handing documents. They seemed to know they were being observed behind the window's silvered smokiness. Her eyes moved from one face to the next, dismissing the nose, the jawline, the narrowness of the face.

215

'None of them?' Cooper asked.

She shook her head.

'Are you sure?' He looked at his watch. 'We have another hour before the border closes.'

'He knows we're here,' she shot back.

'He'll come. He is close to his son.' A pause. 'Listen.'

Mechanical rumbling disturbed the night and shook the hut's windows. The bridge was obscured by falling snow – the picture of winter serenity at odds with the approach of a deep-throated diesel engine.

*

Winslow watched the Soviet T-62 tank across Bornholm Bridge as it maneuvered to face the span. Its treads ground through a turn and when in position, the lumbering behemoth shuddered and stopped. Soviet soldiers dismounted from the rear of a troop carrier that came up behind the tank, and they took up positions on either side of the bridge.

Already a line of cars was backed up at Bornholm Strasse: Trabants, Volkswagens, and Mercedes were in a queue waiting their turn to be waved through. The brief relaxation of border control was suddenly gone and passengers were asked to step out while guards took up positions. Several drivers yelled indignantly at the delay and acted with new bravado. A border guard, his MPi-K assault rifle slung over his shoulder, demanded documents from the driver in the first car, tapping on the closed window. His flashlight lit the driver's face and the backseat. He waved the car through and repeated his search with the next car.

'What did you think would happen?' Praeger asked, disdain visible. 'They want him more than you do.'

Winslow turned. 'Go to hell.' He felt the urgent consequences of failure closing in on him.

Another city bus arrived on the other side of the bridge. Rumors of an invigorated Soviet interest in sealing off East Berlin had brought anxious East Berliners to the bridge. Citizens confused by the unannounced border closings spread a wildfire of fear. One rumor fed another, and those people awake at that hour looked out their windows, watching for Soviet troops moving through the streets.

The first cars in the queue were joined by others, and soon drivers stood outside their cars asking other drivers why there was a wait.

Men traveled on foot making their way onto the bridge, showing identification, and after being waved through, they hurried along the pedestrian path to the West German side, where their documents were again requested. Border police matched identification photos to the faces. They stood in front of the silvered glass window long enough for Anne to make her judgment. One face followed another. Each face different with its unique features, some similar to Kruger. Same dark eyes, similar thin lips, the same haughty expression of a vain older man unhappy to be subjected to arbitrary authority. Anne hesitated several times, numbing exhaustion playing tricks on her eyes, seeing a likeness that she matched to her memory.

'How about him?' Detective Keller asked, pointing to a man of ambiguous age wearing a long coat, librarian's wire glasses, and a Soviet-style fedora pulled down on his forehead. A scarf wound around his neck leaving lips and nose to comprise his identity. Anne considered the glasses, the forehead, his height, his nervous lips. *Stefan?* She stared.

'Take his hat off,' Keller shouted through the glass.

Suddenly, the man turned and stepped out of the queue. It happened in a split second. His face had turned away for an instant and he stepped back from view.

'Stop him,' she shouted.

Somewhere outside, a melee. 'Halt! Halt!'

The man in his bulky overcoat was walking away, collar raised against the possibility of being recognized. He ignored the shouted commands and had started back toward the bridge with the long stride of a hurrying man not wanting to draw attention to himself. An alert Polizei left his position at the bridge and apprehended him, hustling him to a police van by the control hut. Exhaust plumed in the cold air and the rotating roof lights cast a sickly yellow glow into the night.

Anne burst out of the hut without her coat, running. When she arrived at the van's open rear door she trembled. 'Move,' she shouted. 'I want to see him.'

She hit a policeman's shoulder when he didn't move fast enough, and when he stepped aside, she pushed past. Inside, two policemen had pushed him to his knees. A scuffle. Curses, fists punching. Resistance. The drama of an arrest. One policeman restrained the prisoner and another searched the bulky overcoat, pulling papers from pockets, but he found the prize sewn in the coat's lining. He displayed the contents of a cloth bag: East German military ribbons and service medals. The contraband of a defeated army.

Keller knocked off his hat and pulled him by the hair, presenting the frightened face to Anne.

She gave a cry of fright. She looked and then looked away. The eyes, the mouth, the deceiving similarities that she'd seen in her brief glimpse through the window. For a moment she thought a dead man had come to life.

'No,' she said, turning away. 'It's not him.'

Keller tossed the bag of contraband at the man. 'Send him back. Let them judge him.'

She was out of the van by the time Cooper arrived. She felt his arm on her shoulder and she shook her head, accepting that the day's exhaustion and the parade of faces had tricked her. She said nothing. Had nothing to say. Startled by her mistake, she realized that deep inside a part of her wanted it to be Stefan. 'The eyes,' she lied. 'Like Kruger's.'

*

Winslow arrived at the van out of breath, having left the command post when he saw the altercation. Winslow objected to the man's release, but then he saw the error and relented. He glanced at his watch and confirmed his fear. Time was running out. Time had always carried him along like a raft on a river, but the mystery of time deepened with age and further deepened in moments of crisis. Ordinary time, everyday time with its clocks and wristwatches weren't reliable reminders when stress changed time into something elastic. Time was running out and with its end would come a terrible reckoning.

'He's not coming,' Cooper said.

'He knows the risks,' Winslow said. 'He'll wait until the last minute.'

'He's got an hour. You were wrong about her, you're wrong about this.'

'He is on the run. He's here. They found an abandoned car two blocks away.'

Cooper stared. 'How do you know?'

'How?' Winslow grunted. The two men were side by side, but adversaries in the moment. Winslow nodded at Anne, who had returned to the hut and was a vague presence behind the plate glass window. 'You think I'm only relying on her?'

Cooper was surprised, but said nothing.

'She has a part to play,' Winslow said. 'But Kruger is smarter than her, smarter than all of us.' Winslow turned to the bridge where snow drifted in the flood lamp's gauzy light. Snowflakes melted on his face. He spoke with grim conviction. 'She is exhausted and unreliable. Look for a man my age. If you look at him, he'll look back. He will be just another man hoping to get out of the storm. He'll be dressed like an ordinary man, speaking German like an ordinary German, and he'll move like a man uncomfortable with his age.'

The two men faced each other.

'If you don't trust her, this night will be a waste.'

'What have you told her?'

'Nothing.'

'When we've caught him, tell her as much as you want,' Winslow said.

Cooper stared. 'She has her own views of him.'

'Don't we all.'

Winslow rejected the steaming coffee handed to him by Detective Keller, who had joined the conversation. Winslow stood rigidly with the stern expression of a thwarted man. Praeger, too, joined the group, having emerged from the storm. The four men stood together silently, tired from the long day and holding back an urge to assign blame.

*

Winslow knew it might be a bust. His irritation raged, provoked by the prospect of failure. He had seen it happen to other senior officers – men who'd let a personal grudge overwhelm their professional judgment, with terrible consequences. Plans put together quickly with too many wrong assumptions and too little good intelligence. Sometimes they got lucky and Winslow knew that he, too, had counted on luck. Winslow had vowed not to become one of those men, but here he was. A new error compounding an old error. *There will be an inquiry,* he thought.

Winslow looked at the bridge. East German guards stood on the other side like toy soldiers in the falling snow, illuminated by the arc lamps. Everyone waited for the night to be over. Snowflakes drifting in the still air gave the iron bridge the illusion of peace. They were only ordinary soldiers oblivious to the night's drama, and they waited for the end of their shift to go home and get in bed. Two men and a woman trudged across the bridge carrying suitcases, wheels of a car trying to make the slight incline spun, and a man walked his bicycle. Winslow looked at his watch.

'He's already gone through,' Cooper said. 'While we were searching the smuggler.'

'He's still coming,' Winslow said, unwilling to concede failure. 'He's waiting.'

'You give him too much credit.'

'Don't underestimate him.'

'He's played you. You've lost your judgment.'

Winslow considered the remark, but didn't answer. He wasn't ready to concede that arrogant stubbornness might have let the blinders of what he wanted to believe keep him from seeing the obvious blunder. Had Kruger crossed over? Was he hiding?

'Don't take it out on her,' Cooper said. 'She's done her part.' He looked at her through the plate glass window. 'She's been at this all day.'

Winslow glanced at his watch. The border would close in ten minutes. Another border crossing, he thought. Another failure. Nothing ever happened the way it was intended. Faulty intelligence and impetuous choices came up against the resourcefulness of a frightened man on the run. Winslow clenched his fist.

A cry of alarm.

'There, there.' Anne rushed from the hut. 'It's him.'

She pointed to a man pedaling his bicycle in the snow, pulling away from the West German barrier. He wore a puffy down coat and a fox *shapka* and he was hunched over his handlebars showing no concern for the excited cries. He moved deliberately through the blanketing snow and made his way along the dark road moving beyond the checkpoint's perimeter of light.

Anne stood outside the hut. She stared at the man awkwardly pedaling, making his way along the slippery road. He leaned over the handlebars, trying to be small in the empty street and he pedaled hard toward the sheltering darkness.

'That's him,' she shouted. She turned to Cooper, alarmed and excited. She looked around to confirm she'd been heard.

All at once, the whole world erupted in sound. From everywhere whistles joined the pulsing police sirens and an urgent chorus of voices rose. Two police cars in pursuit spun wildly in the snow.

Winslow saw Detective Keller aim his service pistol and he ran to the German policeman's side, knocking his arm. 'We want him alive.'

A police car skidded to a stop, blocking Kruger's path, and a second car pulled up behind. Kruger dismounted and dropped his bicycle. He raised his arms in the air, surrendering.

'Don't shoot.' Winslow waved off the three nervous Polizei who had drawn their guns and advanced, pointing their weapons. Cooper and Winslow ran the short distance to join the group and Winslow moved toward Kruger, brightly lit in the police cars' converging headlights.

'Put your hands down,' Winslow said. 'Walk toward me.'

Winslow commanded the West German police to recover the fallen bicycle and ordered them to stand down now that victory was in hand. The day's fatigue and the endless waiting were gone and exuberant excitement punctuated the moment.

Anne joined the group. She saw a gentlemanly figure with an uncertain expression, a man who'd lost his bluster. He tolerated the growing armed presence, and he seemed to adapt to the changed circumstance, as if he knew that he might be caught. Anne was appalled by his calm – a man so sure of himself that even in the moment of his capture, he wore his dignity smugly.

'It's him,' she said. Her voice had the sting of a verdict. She stood beyond the perimeter of light, but close enough to be certain. She turned to Cooper. 'Am I done here?'

Kruger was surrounded, but he kept his confident composure in spite of being caught. Winslow stepped forward and looked at the East German, studying his face, which was older, like his own, with vaguely recognizable features laid down in the blush of youth.

'So, it is you,' Kruger said.

Winslow and Kruger faced each other, taking each other in, two men with a distant history and the knowledge of what the other had done over the years.

'Better you than the Soviets,' Kruger said.

A gunshot rang out. Startled yells filled the night and Cooper knocked Anne to the ground, protecting her with his body as he looked for the gunman. Stunned silence filled the small patch of earth in the confusing moments that followed. Celebration of the night's success vanished and wary police looked toward the bridge for a Soviet sniper. Everyone waited for a second bullet.

Praeger stepped forward, gun drawn. He stood over Detective Keller's fallen body. The BKA officer was crumpled in the snow, shot in the back of the head, execution style. Crimson blood from the mortal wound stained the snow. His face had a dead man's vacant expression; eyes fixed, gazing at nothing. In death, his grip had loosened on his service pistol and it lay by his open hand.

'KGB,' Praeger said, holstering his pistol. 'He asked questions that he had no reason to ask. We knew we'd been penetrated by a Soviet agent, but we didn't know the full scope until we found evidence in the Stasi files.'

Praeger looked at Winslow. 'His code name is Petrov.' Praeger looked at the dead man. 'The Soviets closed other border crossings knowing their assassin was here.' He turned to Kruger. 'Another moment and you'd be dead.'

Kruger looked up from the dead man. He spat his words without a trace of irony. 'My old friends.'

Kruger turned to Winslow. His expression was that of a man reaching back in his mind to connect an old memory to the face of the man before him. He was unmoved, but when he spoke he was philosophical. 'Now, maybe it is time for new friends.'

Winslow led Kruger to his embassy car. Before stepping inside, Kruger turned to Anne, who stood by herself with a weary expression.

'He was sorry for what he did,' Kruger said. 'He wanted you to know.'

28

METAMORPHOSIS

A THAW SET IN THAT week and all over Berlin piled snow became dangerous slush. The cold of February became the ambiguous rain of March. It was in those days that Anne began dreaming in German. And from dreaming, she found herself in quiet moments thinking in German. Thinking and dreaming in a different language gave her distance from her old self. English contained her and preserved habits and behaviors that held her back. German freed her from unwanted fearfulness and it allowed her to embrace the possibilities that came from living through the words of a new language.

Anne remembered her compact umbrella this time, but the storm came suddenly, and as she pulled it from her bag and popped it open the downpour was upon her. Sheeting rain passed quickly and then was a remnant drizzle.

She rushed under the cover of the Kempinski Hotel's canopy, shaking water from her umbrella. *It's over*, she thought. Her part was done. But even as she willed herself to believe her part was over, she knew in the way that unsettled questions are their own answers, that her life was not put back together. Stefan dead. Kruger alive. Trials of former Stasi languished in political limbo. Right and wrong changing places.

Anne slipped into the booth opposite Cooper. The call to join him had come that morning. She had returned to her job at Clay Headquarters and taken up jogging again. She found comfort in little routines. The tediousness of her job kept her mind from thinking too much. She had convinced herself that her work was important and that she was good at it.

'I got the message.' she said. 'And?'

He lowered his head, avoiding the question. She turned and looked across the haze of cigarette smoke that hung above laughing patrons and tried to catch the waiter's eye. The place was filled with a mix of uniformed American GIs with arms around German girls who tolerated the Americans' big swaggering smiles, and a few male couples who'd come for the evening's cabaret act. Anne waved at the waitress and turned to Chrystal on the well-lit stage holding a microphone in one hand and a phosphorescent drink in the other.

'Hello, darling,' Chrystal called out, spotting Anne.

Anne answered Chrystal's air kiss with a reluctant wave.

'Not you, sweetie. The handsome man next to you. A politic worm.' Laughter filled the room.

Cooper whispered to Anne, 'I have been called worse.'

Anne looked at Cooper. 'I'm sure.' She took in his gray worsted wool suit, crisply starched shirt, and tightly knotted necktie. She reset a rebellious corner of his canary yellow pocket square, admiring the unusual formality of his ensemble.

'Interview,' he said, noticing her interest.

'Leaving the CIA?'

'New position in another station.'

Anne nodded at his empty beer glass. 'Am I late?'

'I came early. The booths fill up when there's a show.' Cooper nodded at the stage. 'He's funny when he wants to be.'

'Chrystal is a she.' Anne thought Cooper a victim of some incurable illiteracy. 'Yes, she's funny, clever, helpful, and a friend, confidante, hairdresser, and a singer.' Anne stared at Cooper, waiting for his response.

He raised his hand to get the waitress's attention. 'Beer?'

'Whiskey.' She saw his surprise. 'I'm not a fan of beer. When are you leaving?'

Drinks were placed on the table by a waitress. Pleasant laughter came from eager drinkers at the bar, entertained by insults Chrystal directed at her German audience. Cigarettes went to their lips, clapping enthusiastically.

Anne picked up her whiskey, but put it down again, centering it on the coaster, studying the amber liquid. The bar was loud, but her mind was quiet – the flat endless hush of uncertainty. She felt his comforting arm on her shoulder and she let the moment linger. She looked up from her glass. 'You didn't invite me here to tell me you're leaving.'

'No.'

She threw back her whiskey. 'What then?' She motioned to the waitress for another.

Anne was surprised when Winslow suddenly appeared, slipping into the banquette as if he'd been close by, waiting for his cue. He smiled, without giving the impression that he had anything on his mind, and nodded grimly. His eyes were tired, he had the pallor of a man who had not slept well, and he folded his hands, interweaving knobby fingers. She saw him looking at his hands, strong hands with manicured nails, and she thought he had the hands of a desk man, a thinker, but a man who could pull a trigger as well as any assassin.

'My job makes difficult demands of me,' Winslow said. He waved off the drink menu offered by the waitress and asked for a glass of ice water. 'Sometimes I think the KGB and CIA are drunk fighters stumbling around the ring in the ninth round, throwing wild punches. And then we fall on our faces.'

Anne centered her drink on its coaster. 'What do you want?'

Winslow extended his legs, wearing his age like a reluctant concession to vanity. 'There is talk of reunification and forgiveness and it will happen in due course. They've lost, but they haven't surrendered. West Germans are paralyzed by the

227

speed of the collapse, but there are those in Bonn who want to move more quickly. They are the ones who wanted to forget the Third Reich and now they want to forget the GDR. There is no appetite for trials. Maybe Honecker will be put in the dock to make an example out of him and appease the critics, but the men who did the dirty work won't stand trial.'

'And Kruger?' she asked.

Winslow's expression revealed nothing of his thoughts. He turned his glass of water on its coaster, gazing at the ice. 'We don't think so.'

Anne turned to Cooper, startled.

Winslow added, 'There are people who want to protect him and others who want to punish him. He may stand trial.'

Even then, early in the conversation, Anne felt a startling shift in Winslow's casual admission.

'He had Stefan executed,' she said. Her voice rose. 'He ordered Stefan to kill me.'

'These are not normal times.'

She was aghast. 'Set free?' she asked. 'Is that what you're saying?'

'We don't condone what he did,' Winslow said, 'but he can be useful to us. He is debating our offer.'

There was a beat of silence. 'What offer?'

'He has information that will help us piece together an answer to an important national security problem. That's all I can say. It's all you need to know. I have helped him see that it's in his interests to cooperate.'

Anne's hand trembled. She muttered something inaudible.

'We know Praeger has questioned you to build a case against Kruger. I can't tell you not to pursue the case, but I think you'll find that the BND's hands are tied. Politicians are uncertain. Kruger's at home, weighing his choices, waiting to see if he'll be tried before accepting our offer. Kruger's playing a waiting game. I would do the same if I were him.'

Stunned, Anne looked at Cooper. 'This wasn't our bargain. That's not what I was told.'

Winslow added, 'He can face a trial here and see if he is convicted, and if convicted, whether he spends time in jail, hoping to stay alive. Or, he'll be flown to Washington to work for us.'

She turned to Cooper.

'Their case is built around you,' he said. He hesitated. 'No one else is speaking up. You shouldn't, either. It will come out better for you.'

Anne felt like she'd been punched in the gut. Her voice was thick with sarcasm. 'How decent of you to instruct me.' She looked from one to the other. 'Decent men who must put duty above decency and how it must weigh heavily on your conscience. You come to enlist me, not impeach me, for which I am grateful. Justice is a small sacrifice to keep official secrets.' She glared. 'Decent, honorable men doing their duty.'

Winslow set down his glass of water and slowly centered it on the coaster. 'Langley is calling the shots.'

She spoke with contempt. 'You are Langley. There is a God with a ledger of right and wrong. This is wrong.'

Winslow drew the shallow breath of a patient man. 'You may be right, but in this case, at this moment, we know what we must do. You don't have to like it. You don't have to pretend to understand.' Winslow was expressionless. 'Nothing in this world is certain, but intelligence from men like Kruger helps. And it comes at a cost. To protect our values, sometimes we must violate them.'

Anne's glass dropped from her hand, shattering on the floor. She picked up the pieces, cutting her finger on a sharp edge. She waved off Cooper's concern and made an effort to smile. 'I need to use the bathroom.'

Anne stood and felt a sudden weakness in her knees, and a disabling dizziness. She steadied herself and focused on a way through the crowded bar, passing laughing drinkers who glanced at her, seeing her distress. Anne felt the world around her was a frightening hallucination.

She entered the stall closest to the bathroom's door, locking it. Her mind was a jumble of fevered thoughts and unspeakable contempt. She wrapped toilet paper on her cut, but she hadn't come to the bathroom for first aid. She needed time to think. An unreality came over her. Then she felt a kind of blasphemous guilt for having listened to Winslow calmly lay out his case.

Anger flushed her face. She wished it was a different day, a future day, and that the calendar pages had magically flipped forward to transport her to the other side of this terrible moment. But that was not how time worked. She was prisoner of the moment, as she was of the past, and the moment had a claim on her.

Anne stared at the stall door. Her thoughts drifted to all the incidents and decisions that had brought her to this precipice. In her mind's eye, she saw her choices, each a different type of hell. She rested her head in her hands. Humiliation overcame her, and depression. She came to see that her failure as a child, as a woman, as a person, was her willingness to tolerate the ways others used her. In marriage, in friendship, in love. In return, she had gotten disappointment and betrayal. Her clenched knuckles whitened. She was cold. It was warm in the stall, but she was shivering.

Metamorphosis is a painful process. She felt the excruciating agony of the caterpillar turning into the butterfly, closing up inside its hard chrysalis. Deep inside her, in a process she was only dimly conscious of, she left behind the part of her that greeted each day by enjoying birds chirping outside her window.

The idea came to her slowly. It emerged first as a vague thought. Then it took form, assumed a shape, its elements fit together, and it became a plan. When the consequence of her action settled in, she felt nothing. She saw the arc of the moral world bending away from justice. In that moment, she regretted that it had taken her so long to understand that there would be no trial. A hard shell of vengeance wrapped around her. To endure pain, she would inflict it.

*

Cooper began to measure her absence by the number of sips it took to finish his beer. He swigged the dregs and set the glass down impatiently.

'What's taking her so long?'

'Patience, Jim. She has no cards to play.'

'You don't know her.'

'I don't have to know her. I know what hand I'm playing.'

Cooper aligned pieces of his napkin that he'd torn into halves, quarters, and eighths. He looked up when Anne sat down.

'Everything okay?' Cooper asked. He nodded at the toilet paper wound around her finger. 'You were gone a while.'

She nodded.

'You don't look well.'

'I'm fine. Kruger called me earlier today.'

Winslow had been cleaning his eyeglasses with his necktie's silk lining when she spoke. He replaced his glasses and looked right at her. 'When?'

'This morning. When I returned from jogging.'

'Why didn't you tell us?'

'I'm telling you now.'

'How did he know how to reach you?'

She stared at Winslow a moment and then laughed dismissively. 'He picked me. Placed me. He knows who I am. He knows more about me than either of you.'

Winslow nodded, forgetting. 'What did he want?'

'To talk. He has doubts.'

'Doubts about what?'

'Everything. He is confined to his apartment. He lost his wife last year. He can't see his son. His world has collapsed and he's been vilified. You think it's easy for him?'

'What did he say?'

'He wants to apologize. I told him to fuck off. That didn't make him feel good.'

'That wasn't helpful.'

'I don't need to be helpful.'

'You should want to be helpful,' Winslow said. Calm. Threatening. 'You haven't been cleared and you can still be charged. Think about it before you act hastily.'

'You want him to apologize?' Anne said. 'You want me to give him the satisfaction of an apology?'

'If that's what he wants, yes. Contrition. Remorse. Apology. Whatever is on his mind. If he wants to apologize and it helps him agree to cooperate, then let him have his moment of contrition. What else?'

'He wants to meet me.'

'When?'

'I didn't agree to meet him.'

'Call him back. Take the meeting. The sooner the better.'

'I don't have his number. He called me.'

Winslow took out his Montblanc and wrote a telephone number on the cocktail napkin. 'Here.' He handed it to her. 'Tell him you'll listen and you'll meet him. Tell him whatever is needed to make him comfortable. Call him tonight.'

'It's too late. Tomorrow. This is wrong,' she said.

'Wrong? Right? There is no justice in what we do.'

Anne folded the napkin and placed it in her purse. She glared at Cooper.

Winslow put his hand on Cooper's arm as he went to respond.

He looked at Anne. 'He's not to blame. If you need an enemy, make me the enemy. The world is a dangerous place. Ordinary people experience horrible things. Prosecuting Kruger won't change what happened, or bring back those who suffered, or return dignity to his victims. But Kruger's cooperation will help us solve a national security problem and it will make the world safer.'

'Bullshit.' She added sarcastically, 'Safer for who?'

Winslow arched his eyebrow. He went to respond, but thought better of it. 'Your view of the world isn't the world I live in. Deploring the morality of spies is like deploring violence in boxers.' He leaned forward and spoke softly. 'You misjudge what's at stake here, and you misjudge me. I don't mind if you think I'm without scruples, but if you're going to hold that opinion, and it's your right to hold it, then you should know what's at stake. I'm not lecturing you – but you need to know – in defense of freedom we sometimes do things that we don't like to talk about. Kruger is important to us.'

'You put your trust in a traitor.'

'A traitor to a lost cause. The GDR has collapsed. The Soviet Union will fall next.'

Anne and Winslow stared at each other. She thought him dangerously cynical and she knew that he viewed her as hopelessly naïve. She listened to him put forward opinions full of dubious claims and she knew he was trying to shape her thoughts with pleasant fictions. He used words like a magician used hands – offering a diversion while the real action was in what he wasn't saying. Anne threw back her whiskey.

'We've offered Kruger asylum.' Winslow lifted the glass and sipped his ice water. 'He'll tell us what he knows and in exchange he will live out a quiet retirement in rural Virginia, or if he prefers, Santa Barbara. He'll get a new name and a pension. Maybe he'll write his memoir.'

She heard him trying to sound reasonable, as if he were a

butcher upselling a reluctant shopper to a better cut of meat – a simple transaction part of routine work.

'Through Kruger, we will establish the truth about a problem we have. Nothing in this world is certain or secure, but intelligence helps. Intelligence won't prevent war, but it will keep us from losing a war.'

Winslow looked at Anne, hoping that some of what he'd said convinced her, but seeing her skeptical expression, he said, 'For Christ's sake. Kruger's not Mengele. We're not talking Nazi science or concentration camps.'

Anne was quiet. *Unbelievable*, she thought. She turned to Cooper, seeking an ally against Winslow's expedient arguments, but she saw only complicit reluctance.

Anne stood abruptly. She shoved one arm in her coat sleeve and then the other. She had gone a few steps toward the bar's exit, when she turned.

'You're as bad as he is. You're all the same.'

*

When Anne left the Kempinski Hotel she was numb with disgust and alive with terror, and later, when the scandal in Berlin was far enough in the past for Anne to have perspective, she understood that when she walked out of the bar, she was already the person she would become. That revelation came to her much later when she read transcripts of the CIA Inspector General's inquiry, which revealed the full extent of their deception, and it helped ease the pure horror of what she did when she left the Kempinski Hotel.

29

POINT OF NO RETURN

ANNE SAT BEFORE HER vanity mirror and adjusted her wig. Lush blond Medusa curls came over her ears and fell to her neck. Her straight auburn hair was gone and she could recognize herself but also saw a completely different woman. She let herself become comfortable with her new persona.

The frantic barking of a dog had woken her the night before, and she'd been kept awake by going over and over the same difficult choices and troubling concerns. By the time dawn came, she knew she had arrived at the point from which there was no return. She was deadened to the consequences of her appalling choice, but also comfortable with the unavoidable act.

'Gorgeous,' Chrystal said. She stood back a few steps, evaluating her contribution to Anne's makeover. 'When you let go of your stress, you are a knockout. Who wants to be close to stress? Look at you now. If you weren't a woman, I'd do you.'

Chrystal completed her work, taking fastidious care with each step of Anne's transformation. She thinned Anne's eyebrows with a pair of tweezers; added eyelashes for a darker mood, massaged her favorite aloe cream into Anne's check. She completed the makeover with ruby-red lipstick and a paste-on beauty mark.

Chrystal stood back. 'Magnifique. Berlin's weather forecast is dismal but you'll brighten someone's gloom.'

Anne looked in the mirror, trying to imagine the impression that she would make on a stranger. She wasn't disguised, but she wasn't herself, either. She had never made a calculated effort to look sexually alluring, but Chrystal knew how to create the look, and she thought Chrystal had succeeded. Anne wore long petal earrings her first husband had given her, saying they made her look sexy. It was for that reason she had never worn them, but now they filled a need.

'Are we done?' Chrystal asked.

'Yes.'

'Perfect. The lips. The rouge. The eye shadow. Perfect, except for one thing. You're sad. You look like you're going to a wake.'

Anne forced a smile.

Chrystal kissed Anne on both cheeks. 'You'll tell me all about it.'

'I don't think so.'

*

It was time. An hour had passed and with it her doubts. Her mind went to a numb place that banished second thoughts. She felt the tyranny of time.

On her way out, she stopped at the living room's credenza and studied the phone number she'd taken from Kruger's office. She compared it to the number Winslow had written on the cocktail napkin. They were different. She evaluated both and called the latter.

'Hello. Who is this?'

'Anne Simpson.'

She didn't hear him respond, so she repeated her name.

'Why are you calling? What do you want?'

'I have some material I'd like to discuss regarding the offer the Americans made.'

'How did you get this number?'

She answered the uncertainty she heard in his voice. 'The CIA. It's important.' Her voice lowered. 'I was rude at the bridge. Forgive me. What you said surprised me.' Anne complimented Kruger's work and shared a heartfelt lament about the madness of the changes. 'Can I come by? I have a better proposal.'

'What?'

'It's better if we speak in person. The telephone… you know.' Anne knew that the man who'd led the Stasi's ubiquitous surveillance apparatus would understand her caution.

'This is nonsense. I've already rejected their offer.'

'We respect your time. A few thoughts. An improvement. It won't take long.'

A beat of silence. 'An improvement? Fine. Come at 8:00 p.m. Don't be late.' Kruger gave an address.

Before stepping out, she put on dark glasses. Anne left her apartment with her tan raincoat covering her miniskirt and low-cut blouse. She cinched the coat tightly at the waist, and pulled on leather gloves. Inside a cloth shoulder bag, she carried flats to exchange for her stiletto heels and a rhinestone purse she'd borrowed from Chrystal.

Slipping into the night, she was confident in her appearance. She trained her mind to play the role of a beautiful film actress who, ill-tempered in life, was a sullen romantic on screen.

*

Anne chose a charmless hotel a few blocks from Alexanderplatz that she knew attracted Soviet businessmen and Red Army officers of the U.S.S.R. occupation force billeted overnight before flying back to Moscow. The popularity of the hotel had been easy to ascertain from her interviews with defecting

Soviet soldiers who harbored grudges against the privileges of their officers.

Impatience was her companion on her way to the hotel. She wanted to get on with the evening so idle doubts wouldn't undermine her resolve. She felt a special relief when she entered the lobby and confirmed it was unremarkable, except for loud Russian being spoken in the bar.

Anne took a stool at the end of the bar and ordered a whiskey. The alcohol settled her nerves, but it also deadened her to the consequences of the night. She watched a girl in a booth – a darker, younger professional who was there taking advantage of the GDR's newly unenforced prohibition on prostitution. Anne saw how it was done. Disinterest followed by shy interest, an offer of a drink and a bit of efficient flirtation to make the man comfortable, and to read his potential for being an undercover policeman. The girl's talent gave Anne the lesson she sought. She watched another girl – the clothes, her coy cheerfulness, and her artful control over the man.

Anne put herself in the girl's place, rehearsing how to ignore the man's breath, his stupidity, and the inevitable clumsy groping. In her mind, she practiced the role she would perform.

She chose a Soviet officer who sat at the other end of the bar, silent over his drink. A coarse man with a balding crown, and a pockmarked face who was obviously drinking too much. She found him repellent, which made it easy for her to go forward. Her revulsion helped her assume the role that he would expect, and in her disgust, she found her confidence. She knew there would be no tenderness to mitigate the horror.

On his third glance, Anne stood and joined him. She recognized his battalion service badge and confirmed his rank. They talked briefly in a short businesslike exchange without any gloss of pretense. She made a point of asking how long he would be in East Berlin and she was satisfied to hear he'd been there a week and would return to Moscow early the next morning. A price was agreed.

At her insistence, they entered the elevator together arm in arm, denying the vigilant concierge a pretense to stop her. Quiet filled the car on the slow ascent to the fifth floor. He'd had a great deal to drink and seemed incapable of small talk even in Russian, and she was silenced by the sensation of living outside of time.

Their coupling was quick and mechanical, without any affection. She endured what was required, and when it was over, she didn't object when he said he'd have to pay in rubles because he only had enough East marks to pay for his taxi to the airport. He offered to pay her double if they did it again and she accepted on the condition that he shower first.

While he was under the streaming water, singing happily to himself, she removed his 9mm Makarov service pistol, closing the leather holster so its disappearance wouldn't be noticed. It was the first thing she had looked for when she spotted him in the bar. She confirmed the pistol had bullets and slipped it into her raincoat. She quietly left the hotel room.

In the lobby, Anne entered the woman's bathroom and transformed back to herself. She kicked off the stiletto heels, removed her miniskirt and put on a baggy turtleneck sweater and jeans. She stuffed the wig in her cloth bag and vigorously removed all traces of makeup. One quick glance in the mirror, and she was satisfied there was no sign of who she'd been minutes before.

Outside, she dropped her cloth bag in a trash bin at the corner, and coming upon one of the city's newly impoverished elderly women, she dropped the rubles in her outstretched hand, accepting the woman's surprised appreciation.

30

OMNIA VINCIT AMOR

ANNE SAW THE OLDER man enter the East Berlin apartment block and walk with a determined step, avoiding the streetlamp's pooling light. She knew it was Kruger. His tan raincoat reached his knees, he moved cautiously, and his Soviet-style fedora was pulled down on his forehead. Before entering the dark building's front door, he glanced over his shoulder, and then disappeared inside. When she saw a light go on, she counted the four floors to his apartment, and confirmed that windows in the neighboring apartments were dark. She quickly crossed the street.

Inside the vestibule, vandals had spay-painted DEATH TO STASI on one wall and graffiti defaced the apartment directory. Several names were listed, but a few residents' names were missing, including those on his floor.

Anne pressed the bell of a lower floor.

'Who is this?'

'I'm from the fifth floor.' Anne spoke into the staticky intercom and gave a name from the directory. 'I left my keys upstairs.'

Anne opened the buzzing door and entered the lobby. She passed the elevator and climbed the stairs, knowing she was less likely to encounter a resident who might later be questioned by the VoPo. The staircase entered the fourth-floor hall through a heavy fire door. She dismissed the apartment with children's toys outside and debated which of the remaining two was his, and settled on the door with twined newspapers outside.

Anne knocked twice, softly. 'Hallo.'

Kruger opened the door a crack and peered across the chain. 'How did you get in?'

'A woman in the lobby.'

He looked at her for a moment. 'You're early.'

She begged an apology. 'The bus came sooner than I expected. I have information for you. As I said on the telephone, there are a few questions. A proposal.'

'More questions? I told him what I need.'

'It will only take a few minutes. Winslow sent me.'

'What proposal? Speak up.'

'Asylum.'

He hesitated. 'Come in.'

The chain was undone, the door opened, and Anne found a slight man wearing a cardigan sweater over a shirt and tie and house slippers. His suspicious expression relaxed when he saw that no one accompanied her. He double-locked the door.

'East Berlin is safe,' he said. 'Not as safe as it was, but safer than West Berlin. Hooligans spray-paint obscenities and call it free speech.'

He led her through a spacious living room with dull modern furniture, a glass dining table, and an abundance of floor-to-ceiling bookshelves. Hardcover and paperback books in Russian and German were arranged by author and she saw the names of respected writers whose works were officially out of favor. She followed him to a study with two windows that looked down onto the street. There was a carved wooden desk, a divan, two facing chairs, more bookshelves, and on one side of the desk, a Spanish guitar in its upright stand.

Kruger turned off the speaker and it was only in the resulting silence that she realized that Baroque guitar music had been playing. She sat forward on a chair, knees together, and watched him sit opposite. Her mouth had gone dry. In Kruger's presence, she felt the urgency of what she had come to do. Seated, she was visibly nervous.

'What's wrong?'

'Nothing.' She forced a smile and avoided his eyes. She saw that the study was in the process of being packed up. Cardboard boxes were filled with files and memorabilia that would accompany him on a journey, and by the door, standing alone, one suitcase ready for immediate flight.

'I met with Winslow,' Kruger said. 'He didn't mention you. We talked about things from long ago. He had a lot on his mind. Are you cold?' He pointed at Anne's leather gloves and raincoat, which she had not removed.

'This won't take long.'

He shrugged. 'It was two days ago. He wore a nice suit, as if a good tailor and a starched shirt would impress me. He brought a bouquet of flowers and an expensive wristwatch.' Kruger laughed. 'I told him that I didn't have a price, but if I did a Cartier watch was a pathetic gesture for what I know.'

His eyes came back to her. 'I wanted to show him I could be hospitable, so I offered him a Cuban cigar, and then I discovered he is one of those maniacal American anti-smokers. He asked me not to smoke in his presence. I said if he didn't like my habit, he was free to leave.'

Kruger smiled. 'I enjoyed watching him suffer.' Kruger hit a pack of cigarettes on his forearm and offered one to Anne. 'Do you mind?'

Anne shook her head.

'The doctor tells me to stop, but old habits are hard to break, even when I know the dangers, so I indulge myself and this gives me a little pleasure when big pleasures are hard to come by.'

Anne knew that his garrulousness was the gloss of a

242

calculating mind, and she knew not to be seduced by his false candor.

Kruger held the lit cigarette high and to one side of his head, smoke curling, and he studied her for a moment. 'He said that Virginia was pleasant but that Santa Barbara had better year-round weather. I joked that Siberia too could be agreeable during certain times of the year.' Kruger drew on his cigarette and exhaled slowly. 'This is what you've come to discuss?'

'Yes.'

'He invited me to visit Langley. He offered to pay for a facelift to make me feel safe from the KGB's assassins.' Kruger dismissed the thought with a careless wave of his hand. 'I'm not afraid. Let them find me. In the early days of the GDR, there were still many Nazis among us. I lived with the enemy then, and I do so again. So, this is not the first time I'm going through this. We succeeded in spite of the weak among us. Under Socialism, we had nothing to fear, no crime, no prostitution, no unemployment.'

'Only people looking for work,' Anne said softly.

'Ah, ha!' he blurted out, indignant. 'What do you know? You don't remember what it was like before. How could you? But now it's irrelevant.' Kruger nodded at the boxes. 'I will be traveling soon. The border with Poland is still open. I had a friend in Moscow, but now I hear he no longer trusts me. I could give you a whole lecture on trust.' Kruger leaned forward and stared. 'Well, speak up. You're nervous. Take your coat off.'

'I'd like to talk about the Romeo project.'

'That? It was inconsequential. If you want me to cooperate, let's talk about how I built the institution of state security after the War. We started with nothing.'

Anne listened to the egotistical bragging spewing from his mouth and she felt that things were not happening as she expected. Her mind tried to shut out his grandiose ideas of his accomplishments and she willed herself to repeat the steps she had rehearsed.

'Fine,' he finally said, 'we can talk about that. The CIA, MI6, and the BND had nothing to match our success. We used psychology and an understanding of the human psyche. All they had were crude traps with prostitutes and queers.' Kruger scoffed at the countermeasures of his Cold War adversaries.

'I read my file.'

Kruger raised an eyebrow. 'Everyone had a file. There is nothing special in having a file.'

It was Kruger's arrogance more than his coldness that angered Anne. She saw in him a pattern of predictable bullying followed by smug reasoning that she had come to despise in a certain type of German.

'You're wrong,' she snapped.

Kruger looked at her curiously, recognizing a shift in her tone. 'You make a mistake in thinking your file is about you. There is nothing personal in the choices we made. There is nothing special in a file – or in one life.'

'I want you to talk about that.'

Kruger narrowed his eyes. 'I am happy to talk, but I don't have a lot of time. What does this have to do with asylum?'

Anne's hands trembled and she made an excuse for her nervousness. She repeated to herself the words that she had rehearsed. 'Your crime,' she whispered.

'My crime?' He dismissed her claim with a wave of his hand. 'The GDR was an eloquent expression of Socialism. Now our methods of keeping order are ridiculed. Souvenir hunters gleefully buy up uniforms and medals that we proudly wore until a few months ago.'

'Water, please.'

'Speak up.'

'Do you have a glass of water? My mouth is parched.'

'Water, yes. There is tap water. Sit. I'll get water.'

Kruger had reached the study's door when he turned suddenly. 'You know what Brecht said? A good Communist has many dents in his helmet and few of them are from his enemies. I should have been more careful with Stefan Koehler.'

When Kruger was gone, Anne stood. She took the 9mm Makarov pistol from her raincoat and undid the safety. She confirmed there was a bullet in the chamber. The pistol was heavy in her gloved hands and she concentrated her mind on what she came to do.

'What's that?'

Anne swung around and faced Kruger in the study's door, holding a glass of water. She aimed the pistol at his chest, hands trembling.

Kruger's eyes were wide. 'Who sent you?'

'You used me. You murdered him,' she said, repeating the accusations she had rehearsed.

Kruger became visibly irritated. 'He brought dishonor to us. He betrayed his country. He paid the price a traitor pays.'

'And me? A pillow over my head. Kill me for what? To protect your failed ideology and a sick, defeated country.' The drumbeat of revenge beat in her chest. A small voice cried in her fevered mind. *Shoot him! Shoot him!*

'I can see you're a smart girl. This won't go well for you. Give me the gun.'

Anne's arms were outstretched pointing the pistol. She felt the hypnotic force of his calm eyes and his lucid reasoning slowly weaken her resolve.

'Come. Let's talk.' His voice was sympathetic.

Anne felt a sudden paralysis in her hands and the pistol began to drop. *Shoot him! Shoot him!*

'Who put you up to this?'

'No one,' she mumbled.

'I don't believe you. The Soviets? The West Germans? Mossad?' Kruger took a step forward and offered the glass of water that he held in his hand. 'Sit. Let's talk. Have a drink of water. No one needs to know about this. It is easy to allow yourself to be used, but I can see that you bear no ill will toward me. I know what you are made of. Killing a man goes against your faith.'

'Stop talking!' she screamed. Her hands trembled.

'You can explain that I wasn't home. They'll believe you. Give me the gun and you'll be free to go. Ah, look! You're trembling.'

Anne watched him take another step forward. She saw his calm eyes become intimidating and grow bold as he took another step, reaching for her weapon. Suddenly he lunged forward to wrench the pistol from her hand, cursing.

Anne fired once. The bullet entered Kruger's open mouth and it exited the rear of his skull. The sound of the deafening gunshot knocked out her hearing, but then the silence ended and she was aware of the tyrannical ticking of the cuckoo clock on the wall. She stood over Kruger, who lay crumpled on the Persian rug, a crimson stain widening under his head. The water glass had fallen from his hand and was shattered on the floor. His eyes were wide and vacant, already his face had the pallor of death. She had planned to shoot him a second time in the nape of the neck, a signature of Soviet assassins, but she didn't have the stamina to fire again.

Anne felt nothing. No anger. No contempt. She felt only the grim satisfaction of having done what she came to do. New blood wiped clean the stains of old blood. She looked at his face and, in that moment, she whispered, '*Omnia vincit amor.*' She hadn't planned to say it, but contempt fell from her mouth like a judgment. Love conquers all.

A plaintive *coo-coo* from the clock's mechanical bird marked the hour and reminded Anne what she must do. She placed the Soviet service pistol near the front door where it would have been dropped by a fleeing assassin. From his attaché case she took one file, examined it, and then took another, quickly leafing through the typed pages. She didn't find what she was looking for and she laid the files on his desk in deliberate disarray to give the impression the intruder had searched for something of importance. She contemplated the body on the floor and then slipped his wallet from his jacket pocket. The folded, torn page with bank instructions was inside. She wasn't surprised. Fugitives hold secrets close but a means of escape closer. She found a hidden microphone behind the speaker. Out of an abundance of caution, she removed the cassette tape and tore out the microphone. There would be no record.

Anne picked up the desk telephone and called Cooper. She said what she would repeat in those words and others several times that night, and then the next day at police headquarters.

'When I arrived, I startled a man, who fled. Inside, I found Kruger's body. He had been shot once in the head. I ran after the gunman, but he was already gone. He dropped his pistol when he left.'

31

FRIEDRICHSFELDE CENTRAL CEMETERY

ANNE STOOD BY THE freshly dug grave holding a black umbrella against the early April rain. She was beside Petra and a few others who stood quietly sharing the melancholy of the moment. Grievous injustice had touched each of their lives and Stefan's interment was a feeble effort to honor the incomprehensible. Yellow daffodils dotted the lawn, lightening the mourners' mood.

Anne had stuck to her version of events in the days that followed Kruger's murder, even in the face of skeptical questioning. Her account convinced the BDN because it was believable. Soviet intentions provided a credible motive and the Makarov pistol provided the means. Anne was the only witness. Her surprise was real, her horror real. Only her innocence was false.

Later, she would come to see how each incident that led up to the killing had been inevitable. She wondered if things might have turned out differently, but when she questioned each turning point, she understood she had done the only thing that was possible to get justice. The violent end was the fated outcome of a series of seemingly inconsequential choices. And yet, she wished she could do it all over again. Her life felt like a bad rehearsal for the life she wanted.

The coffin with Stefan's urn of ashes was lowered into the

wet earth. Workmen let out the taut straps, guiding the box into the ground. Anne thought it a waste of a good plot, but Petra told her that Stefan had picked out his grave next to his parents, and she wanted to use the plot he'd already paid for. Anne thought Petra was still living in a world that judged the value of life by the scarcity of its goods.

Dr Knappe was there, standing behind the two women and next to him stood Chrystal, who honored the event's gravity with a wide-brim, floral hat, dark glasses, and an ankle-length dress. Further back, alone under a tree, stood Praeger. He had respectfully removed his hat and stared at Anne until she sensed that he was there, and stared back. Winslow had planned to attend, but he'd been unexpectedly summoned to Langley by the CIA's Office of Inspector General.

Petra and Anne wore matching black veils so that a visitor who happened upon the group would not know one from the other. Two women with a boy between them.

Petra still wore her wedding ring. Anne touched the finger where her ring had been. She thought Petra's ring was less expensive, but more honest in its simplicity. Anne had never known as much about anyone as she knew about Stefan – his opinions, his habits, his secrets, his fears, but still, knowing all that, she realized that she hardly knew him at all. He had been remote in life and now he was gone. He was a puzzle locked inside the ashes that lay in the coffin.

The brief ceremony ended when the coffin hit the bottom with an audible thud. The five people who stood graveside each threw a handful of earth into the grave, completing a funeral ritual that the Socialist state had stripped of its religious meaning. No one spoke. How quickly one becomes aware of silence even in so silent a place as a cemetery. Only the light tapping of rain punctuated the quiet.

Anne was the first to break the silence when she said, 'Amen,' and then the small party stirred. Anne hugged Peter and turned to Petra, who lifted her veil, and the two women gazed at each other. Petra wiped away a tear. They held each other in a long embrace and when Anne pulled away, she put Kruger's torn document in Petra's hand. 'This belongs to you.'

Petra recognized bank details and returned the paper to Anne's palm, closing her fingers over Anne's hand. 'It's blood money.'

The two women looked at each other, two widows considering what the other had done, gazing into each other's eyes, thinking about the offer, the rejection, and what would come next. Anne withdrew her hand, accepting Petra's judgment. Their eyes met for one moment and then they nodded tearfully in shared grief. Anne had nothing more to say. She lacked the will to assert herself, and even then, she tasted the bitter root of everything that she'd lost.

'You must,' she insisted, taking Petra's hand, closing her fingers over the document. She nodded at Peter. 'Call it what you like, but don't be foolish. It's for your son's future.' Anne closed Petra's hands tightly over the paper and then she turned to Peter, pulling him close in a loving embrace.

'Where will you go?' asked Petra.

'I don't know. You'll come and visit.'

'I would like that.'

Mature trees, mossy with the green of spring, lined the narrow path back to the parking area. Anne contemplated the chirping sparrows on the lush green lawn. Her eye caught a butterfly fluttering in the rain looking for shelter. As she walked along the stone path, she found herself moving past the cemetery's Socialist Memorial, where an inscription was cut into the stone: THE DEAD REMIND US.

Anne considered the admonition, but continued on. *Who needs reminding?* she thought.

Cooper stood just beyond the cemetery's wrought iron gate. He leaned against his car, arms crossed over his chest, and he waited for Anne to approach. He was alone in the cobblestone roundabout and watched her walk with quiet purpose. When Anne reached his car, he expected her to stop, but she walked past without acknowledging him, and she continued to make her way toward the exit – a tall, auburn-haired woman in black, looking straight ahead.

Cooper came off his car. 'Anne!'

He waited for her to respond, but she did not, and he watched her continue on without looking back. He went to call out again, but her name died in his throat.

ACKNOWLEDGMENTS

The Matchmaker was inspired by Markus Wolf, who served as chief of foreign intelligence of the Ministry of State Security of the German Democratic Republic for thirty-four years. Even his staunchest foes admit that he was one of the most effective Communist spies on the European continent during the Cold War. He didn't create the link between romance and espionage, but his development of Romeos advanced the tradecraft.

My agent, Will Roberts, contributed to the manuscript with many patient readings of early drafts, and he improved the book with his keen editorial eye. I am indebted to the entire team at No Exit Press, particularly my editor Ion Mills, and to my US publisher, Pegasus Books, its publisher Claiborne Hancock, my editor, Victoria Wenzel, and the marketing team under Jessica Chase. Among the book's early readers were my fellow writers in the Neumann Leathers Writers Group – Mauro Altamura, Amy Kiger-Williams, Aimee Rinehart, Dawn Ryan, and Brett Duquette. Joshua Vidich and Gwendolyn Bellmann graciously provided insights into Berlin. Rae Edelson, Bruce Dow, Stephen Schiff, Fred Wistow, Dwyer Murphy, Joseph Kanon, Andrew Feinstein, Lauren Cerand, Kevin Larimer, John Copenhaver, Jayne Anne Phillips, Milena Deleva, Elizabeth Kostova, Polly Flonder, Mark Knox, Mark Sitley, Anne MacDonald, John Clark, Paul Burke, and Nahid Rachlin have been generous with their support and encouragement over the years.

Several books were indispensable sources of information about the West Berlin and the collapse of the GDR. They are: *Stasiland: Stories from Behind the Berlin Wall* by Anna Funder

(Harper Perennial, 2002); *The Collapse: The Accidental Opening of the Berlin Wall* by Mary Elise Sarotte (Basic Books, 2015); *Man Without A Face* by Markus Wolf with Anne McElvoy (Public Affairs, 1997); *Born in the GDR: Living in the Shadow of the Wall* by Hester Vaizey (Oxford University Press, 2014).

I owe particular thanks to my sons – Arturo for his keen editorial suggestions which helped polish important scenes, and Joe, for his loving support. And to my wife, Linda – partner, editor, and astute reader, who touched each of the novel's pages.

BECOME A
NO EXIT PRESS
MEMBER

BECOME A NO EXIT PRESS MEMBER and you will be joining a club of like-minded literary crime fiction lovers – and supporting an independent publisher and their authors!

AS A MEMBER YOU WILL RECEIVE

- Six books of your choice from No Exit's future publications at a discount off the retail price
- Free UK carriage
- A free eBook copy of each title
- Early pre-publication dispatch of the new books
- First access to No Exit Press Limited Editions
- Exclusive special offers only for our members
- A discount code that can be used on all backlist titles
- The choice of a free book when you first sign up

Gift Membership available too – the perfect present!

FOR MORE INFORMATION AND TO SIGN UP VISIT
noexit.co.uk/members